To save the nation, he must confront his past...

Fifteen seconds.

Ferrar stared at the alphanumeric keypad. Images of his life passed rapidly through his mind, not the thoughts of a dying man, but of someone trying to unscramble the unrelated tidbits of his life in search of a clue.

Ten seconds.

Then an image of Bonnie floated to the fore. She was young again, college-aged. She was leaning toward him, offering a mug of foaming beer.

Five seconds.

Also by Fritz Galt

FRITZ GALT

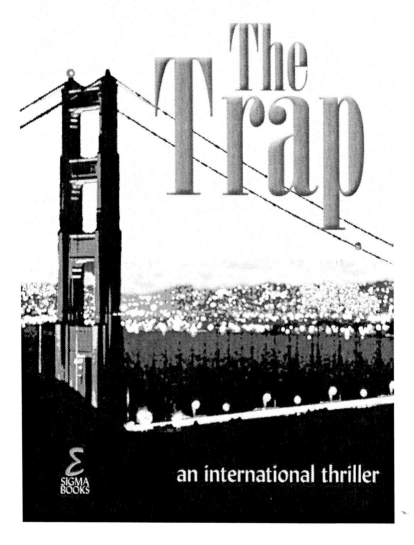

The Trap

an international thriller

SIGMA
BOOKS

The Trap
An International Thriller
Copyright © 2003 by Fritz Galt
All rights reserved.

ISBN 1-58961-048-2

Published by PageFree Publishing, Inc.
733 Howard Street
Otsego, Michigan 49078
616-692-3386
www.pagefreepublishing.com
Printed in the United States of America

I know what's happening here. This country is about to kill the only man that can save it.

Congressman Ralph W. Connors (Oklahoma)

One

AN ICY December wind howled from the Hindu Kush down over the White Mountains of eastern Afghanistan. George Ferrar tried to shrug away the cold that seeped through his Pathan waistcoat and vest. He pulled the woolen shawl up over his mouth to conceal his breath in the frosty air.

The nighttime was crawling with armed and desperate men, and the commando in charge of his undercover unit was an unstable jerk.

But it was a good time to be in Afghanistan.

Sure, Ferrar trudged along plagued by uncertainty, and reeling from the effects of September 11. But he was trying to restore order to the world.

America had come under attack. World markets were faltering. Terror had begun its incipient reign. And for the moment, Afghanistan was where he belonged.

Ahead of him, five other veterans of undercover warfare picked their way up a steep trail toward the mouth of Tora Bora's main cave.

He couldn't keep his eyes off the evidence of previous mortar attacks. Huge craters pitted the cliff. Corpses of fighters affiliated with al-Qaeda and the Taliban lay headless, limbless, and stiff. Unexploded ordinance littered the crags of the slope.

Now he would finish the job.

He hefted the assault rifle to his shoulder. A gun was a normal accoutrement for local tribesmen, and he needed to fit in. It would serve him well, as would the entire arsenal beneath his waistcoat.

He hadn't started out his career in the Army as a walking battle platform, but technological improvements and the aggressive Green Berets had turned him into one.

In addition to all the gadgetry, he still clung to the know-how he had acquired through long experience of undercover warfare. And he still had his Maine farm boy instincts.

1

Under the myriad stars that illuminated the mountainside, he looked hard at Alpha, the jerk in the lead.

Operation Jawbreaker used code names like Alpha, Bravo, Charlie, etc. But *jerk* fit the guy much better.

Alpha was signaling them with a cautionary motion of the hand. The group stopped and waited.

From his position at the end of the line, Ferrar swept the surrounding hillsides for signs of the enemy. Anyone else in that desolate valley would be unfriendly, because the rest of the Allied troops were nowhere near. In fact, they were busy creating a predawn diversion down at the airport that morning.

As usual, his eyes came to rest on the large, strong frame of Alpha. The guy lowered his assault rifle and casually rested it on the frozen corpse of a terrorist fighter.

Ferrar knew Alpha well enough. As a soldier, Alpha was as ruthless and dominant as any alpha bull. As a man, he was Tray Bolton, the foster son of the Director of the CIA. As a former friend, he was the muscle-bound, backslapping jock that Ferrar had competed against in classrooms and gridirons from high school through college.

Only desperate times could throw the two of them into the same unit. And desperate times had indeed arrived. Quite simply, with her freedom at stake, America needed her best.

Bolton was pulling a night-vision spotting scope out from under his waistcoat.

Ferrar winced. Bad move, Tray.

Above the team of men, a boot scraped against loose scree near the entrance to the cave. A shot rang out.

A second later, the commando designated as Bravo somersaulted down the steep slope, a bullet hole drilled through his forehead.

Retreating footsteps echoed above them.

The unit scattered behind several outcroppings of rock. Ferrar edged closer to a sharp overhang that had snagged his fallen comrade. No breath escaped from Gopher O'Brien's lips. That's okay, he tried to communicate telepathically with the still body. You don't have to hold your breath anymore.

Except Gopher wasn't holding his breath.

Ferrar bent over and cursed silently, trying to clear his throat. "Bravo is down," he finally rasped into his voice-activated headset.

Ferrar had engaged in many nighttime operations before joining the CIA's handpicked Special Operations Group, and he had never used a night-vision scope in close combat situations before. Its objective lens could easily reflect light and tip off the enemy.

Instead, he would sniff the air for a trace of sweat or gun oil. He rolled the brim of his Pathan hat off his ears to listen.

Alpha had played it far too casual.

Sure, in the preceding weeks the war had come to a swift conclusion in Afghanistan, and Taliban and al-Qaeda scumbags were on the run. American and allied ground troops had moved in trying to smoke the terrorists out of their mountain strongholds. And the last pockets of resistance held out in God-forsaken places like that Tora Bora region.

But the unit of combat-hardened special ops veterans couldn't afford to let their guard down yet.

If they were lucky, they might flush out leaders of the Islamic terrorist group, maybe even snare bin Laden or Mullah Omar. Perhaps they might come across a cache of al-Qaeda weapons, ammunition, equipment, documents, videotapes, maps, or false passports. If al-Qaeda left nothing behind, at least the mission could establish that the terrorist organization had slipped out of the region.

The only thing that they couldn't do was to get killed, like Gopher O'Brien.

With the entire might of the U.S. Air Force, Navy, Army, and Marine Corps behind them, they would not fail to take the cave.

He looked out from under his heavy black eyebrows. The only way they could fail was if someone had tipped off the enemy in advance.

Above him came the sound of resistance fighters waking and scattering, their feet pounding deep into the cave complex.

Well, the enemy was certainly tipped off now. The covert operation had turned overt.

He yanked off his fabric hat, ripped open a pack of greasepaint, and smeared it across his broad face. Then he pounded a dull green helmet onto his head, and stared at Bolton's back. Tray Bolton had already lost one man and given up the element of surprise. Now he was letting valuable seconds tick by. Was Bolton waiting for an invitation to tea?

Tray Bolton finally motioned for the unit to advance and pursue the retreating foe. Ferrar scrambled up the remainder of the trail and flattened himself against the lip of a neatly carved, squared-off entrance to the cave.

He pressed both shoulders against the cold stone and held his rifle barrel close to one ear.

Kneeling beside him, Charlie tossed a CS tear gas grenade into the cave. It bounced and popped, coming to a hissing skid some fifteen feet away.

Ferrar and the rest of the men threw off the last of their tribal gear and pulled gas masks over their faces. Listening through the sucking noise of the ventilator in his mask, he heard no choking inside the cave and no more footsteps. The al-Qaeda fighters had retreated sufficiently far into their lair.

Charlie and Delta darted past Ferrar and took up positions inside the entrance. Over his shoulder, he noticed that the sky was turning a faint indigo up the valley where Pakistan lay. Unfortunately, the unit would be silhouetted against the dawn.

Slipping past him, Tray Bolton and Echo hugged the walls of the cave and advanced until they reached the cave's next aperture.

Another tear gas grenade bounced deeper into the complex. In the deadened space, the released tear gas hissed down further chambers inside.

With the four other operatives safely inside the cave, Ferrar was the last to enter. He kneeled on the stone floor beside Bolton and aimed an ultrasonic radarscope straight ahead. The faint LCD screen displayed an orange image of the room. There were three openings in the next chamber.

Bolton hand-signaled for the men to fan out. Charlie and Delta, who were the ex-Army Rangers Pug Wilson and Al Moxley, would take the right. Meanwhile Echo and Foxtrot, the former Green Berets Colt Sealock and Ferrar, would advance down the center.

Presumably, Bolton, the former Navy Seal would take the left.

Without a sound, the men separated and began the time-honored tradition of covering and advancing down the rough-hewn sandstone corridors.

With tear gas still lingering in the air, Ferrar had to keep his mask on and couldn't use his night vision scope. Instead, he and his partner wordlessly switched to the radarscope. Colt attached it to the floor and aimed it like a black flashlight into the gloom.

The readout showed the subterranean complex expanding into still more openings. It was essentially a labyrinth. Their unit would never be able to investigate the entire excavation. Moreover, they would most certainly encounter hidden nooks, trapdoors, concealed rooms, and...

A sudden shockwave from his right nearly knocked him out of his boots. He grabbed his ears as an explosion thundered through the cave.

"Landmines," he whispered fiercely into his headset transmitter. The place was booby-trapped.

The explosion deafened him momentarily, but not enough to mask the anguished cries of Pug Wilson and Al Moxley.

Colt whipped out a metal detector the size of a long-barreled pistol, and jabbed the earpiece in an ear.

While Colt scanned the floor for buried mines, Ferrar whispered into his transmitter, "Charlie and Delta are hit."

He stared hard into the silent, acrid-smelling blackness.

They were losing men fast, and they weren't finding a thing. Of course al-Qaeda wouldn't give up without a fight. And the cave, built eons ago to fend off invasion attempts and reinforced to withstand Soviet bombardment, was not about to give up all her secrets at once.

For the unit to continue would be sheer folly. Half the men were down. With only Bolton, Colt, and himself left, Ferrar saw the odds stacking up rapidly in the enemy's favor.

He yanked Colt by the collar.

"We're falling back."

That same night, across the parched, flat landscape of central Afghanistan, CIA Operations Officer Paul Stevens and several hundred Marines were on the move in a very different kind of operation.

Humvees laden with ammunition raced through the still, morning streets of Kandahar on a mission to take the civilian airport. Soon they had passed the two-story buildings and neighborhood mosques and were heading south across the scrubland.

"Secure the perimeter," a voice crackled over the open radio channel.

Paul Stevens watched with approval as the Humvees spread out and raced toward the desert landing strip.

Careful to avoid landmines, they remained on paved access roads. Two groups converged on the ends of the dual runway and a third group approached the International Terminal.

As he neared the building, Stevens could tell from the chinks in the concrete and the dilapidated window frames that the structure had seen better days.

The radio channel came alive with reports of "all clear" from the field.

"Turn down the volume," he told the Marine escort who was driving the vehicle.

Stevens' handheld radio was tuned to a different frequency. While he wanted to follow the progress of the airport operation, his thoughts were burdened with the deteriorating condition of the small special ops force for which he was responsible high in the mountains.

In the pre-morning chill, he was listening to the heat of battle.

Ferrar had already reported that Bravo was down.

Ominous silence followed in which he was prepared for any kind of news. With their secrecy blown, the entire covert unit could have been taken out by a single bazooka blast. They might never have had time to report to him by radio. What man had the presence of mind or inclination to radio his commanding officer once he realized that in the next instant he would be in heaven, or hell?

He felt his vehicle come to a jarring halt, and righted himself in his seat. All the soldiers piled out except for Joe Capella, Steven's logistics man.

"No resistance, sir," the Marine driver reported to him as he stared out at the black airport that the Americans were attempting to take.

Just then, a burst of orange flames licked the bushes at one end of the runway. That flash was followed a moment later by the sound of small arms fire.

The Marines had encountered their first resistance of the war.

"A Marine is down," a voice shouted excitedly over the airwaves.

"Jesus," the driver said.

"But he's not the first American casualty," Stevens muttered.

"Huh?"

There was a beep on his handheld radio, nearly drowned out by the static on the driver's radio.

"Turn that thing off," he roared at the driver, and pressed his ear to his receiver.

"Charlie and Delta are hit," Ferrar's voice whispered fiercely over the airwaves.

"Oh shit," Stevens said. "That leaves three men, and one of them is Tray Bolton."

"Bolton," the driver repeated over his shoulder. "Isn't he the—"

"—son of my boss, Lester Friedman, Director of the CIA. This will not go down well in Washington."

He watched as more orange bursts erupted, this time at the other end of the runway.

Al-Qaeda was striking back on several fronts.

Ferrar scrambled toward the blue rays that seeped into the cave. Then suddenly he heard a whisper from just behind him.

It could have been Bolton, but he wasn't sure.

Colt froze, and Ferrar knelt quietly with his rifle poised by his side, ready to fire into the darkness.

In the reflected blue light of dawn, he glimpsed a shadow running yet deeper into the cave.

"After him," Ferrar ordered.

Colt crouched low, and began to pursue the shadow.

They had to come up with something. They wouldn't lose Gopher,

Pug, and Mox for nothing.

Curse the operation.

"Aaaieee!"

Colt's frame stiffened, rose upward, and staggered back, a knife hanging out of his neck. Warm blood spurted onto Ferrar's combat uniform. He eased Colt to the cave floor and dove headfirst into a shadowy form that had emerged from the walls.

He butted into the man's abdomen and met firm resistance. God, these guys were tough.

He regrouped for a second attack and charged forward, propelling the man into the wall.

He didn't stop there. He came up with his knife drawn and sliced into the fighter's gut. The flesh turned taut, then quivered. Ferrar jabbed deeper, seeking the heart. Face to face, Ferrar smelled the man, held the man off his feet, and wished to kill every man like him.

The man's hand tightened its grip on Ferrar's gas mask, pushing his face away. Then the hand suddenly relaxed, ripping off Ferrar's mask as the man slumped to the ground.

Ferrar dumped the hulk against the wall. Behind him, Colt lay still, his gas mask askew and his eyes open wide. His face bore no expression, even the slightest emotion, as the first sharp rays of sunlight pierced the cave.

Ferrar whipped his mask fully off his face and inhaled the peppery air. Then he gathered up his assault rifle, clenched his teeth, and sprayed the depths of the cave with a prolonged burst of automatic fire.

At the Kandahar airport, Paul Stevens crouched to avoid stray bullets as Marines moved in and took up positions around the terminal.

Mujahideen from the Afghan Northern Alliance accompanied the Marines and were the first to storm the building. Their submachine guns shattered glass, and then blazed away inside.

Covering one ear to hear his radio, Stevens knelt beside a row of empty petrol barrels. His hands were frozen from nervous anticipation as well as the cold, and he felt the radio slipping from his grasp.

An arm slapped him across his back, and he jumped forward, rolled over one shoulder, and landed on his feet in a fighting stance.

It was Joe Capella, his subordinate.

"Shit. Don't creep up on me like that," Stevens said, wiping the dust off his face with the back of his sleeve.

"Any word from the cave?" Capella asked, unfazed.

Stevens returned to his crouched position.

"Yeah, I got word. They're picking us off one by one. Gopher, Pug, and Mox were hit. That leaves three inside. I don't know what the hell is happening up there."

"Damn these al-Qaeda bastards. They're mean suckers."

Another set of footsteps approached.

Stevens spun around. From the polished army boots, he looked up to see a dark, grease-painted face. It was the Marine Commander Colonel Richard Paxton.

"We've got the airport secured," Colonel Paxton informed him.

"Good work," he said, cautiously rising to his feet. "Except, our men are suffering casualties up in the mountains."

"Time to send in reinforcements?"

"I think so," Stevens said. "They need close air support, and fast."

Colonel Paxton raised a radio to his lips. "Scramble fighter jets and choppers from Zebra Base. We're flying in to Tora Bora."

Two

DEEP INSIDE the cave, Ferrar took his finger off the trigger of his chattering rifle and listened to the echoes. They continued to resound in three directions.

Then his radio vibrated against his thigh.

Flattening against a wall and pulling the dead al-Qaeda fighter up as a shield, he whispered into his lip microphone, "Speak."

It was Bolton's voice over the airwaves. He sounded like he was calling from miles away, and his words were barely audible.

He pressed the receiver more tightly to his ear. "Repeat that."

All he could tell was that Bolton was in dire straits. Why? There was no attack underway at the moment. Or was there? He ripped the night-vision scope, gas mask, and radio headset off and listened carefully to the dead space in the cave. He picked up a distant cry.

Every fiber in his body told him to escape while he could. Except that his lifelong rival Tray Bolton was still alive inside the cave, screaming his head off.

"Our birds are in the air, sir," Marine Commander Colonel Richard Paxton informed Stevens, his CIA counterpart.

Stevens looked up as a squadron of F-18 Hornets and a black cloud of Huey and Super Cobra attack helicopters buzzed over the Kandahar airport against a brightening blue sky.

Then crackling noises and a terrified shout came over the radio. He held it away from his ear.

Wild yelling and scuffling ensued, followed by several gunshots.

"I can't hold out," the deep voice gasped, this time more clearly.

It was Tray Bolton, whispering into his radio microphone.

Bolton's words continued more clearly. "Ferrar has led all of us into this chamber...then he started firing...we're all dead."

9

"Holy shit. Ferrar's gone postal," Capella exclaimed. "What the hell has gotten into him?"

Ferrar was no longer a dependable asset. Stevens turned to Paxton. "How soon before the air cover arrives at Tora Bora?"

"Due there in three minutes."

"Smoke Ferrar out of the cave," he ordered. "You have permission to take him dead or alive."

Ferrar going rogue. He could scarcely believe it himself.

Ferrar spun around as shouts and gunfire erupted from the depths of the cave. With grudging feet, he headed in that direction.

Fierce echoes had drowned out Bolton's precise words. But the gist was clear. He was in trouble and needed backup fast.

Picking up his speed, Ferrar ran along the walls, using his fingers to guide him in the increasing gloom. His night-vision scope, gas mask, and radio headset ripped off and hanging around his neck, he only had instinct to guide him.

The smell of gunpowder burned in his nostrils and his eyes filled with water. Suddenly, his boots slid on a wet substance, and he came to a halt. Reaching down in the darkness, he found parts of Mox's body.

He couldn't make out Mox's partner Pug anywhere, but a thin trail of warm blood led around the corner.

Feeling a cool rush of adrenaline, he stood and followed the cave wall deeper into the complex. Several dark corners later, he was at a junction. He reached down once again and felt the cold stone floor for droplets of blood.

Then he heard a metallic click.

A chattering of bullets sprayed from the muzzle of an automatic rifle.

He felt a heavy object topple against him, its surface sticky. It was Pug, his hand feebly attempting to pull his pistol from its holster. Then his helmeted head flopped lifelessly back into Ferrar's face.

He stumbled backwards and fell under the weight of Pug and the lead bullets that riddled his body.

Peering over Pug's shoulder, he made out the faint outline of their assailant against a blue ray of light. The orange glow of a cigarette briefly illuminated the man's face.

Fair-colored hair, smoke drifting from his rifle, a grim look of determination on his face—it was Bolton.

What the hell?

Bolton had just fired on his own man. Had Pug turned on them?

"Ferrar? Is that you?" came Bolton's bass voice, conveying an odd mixture of calm, curiosity, and threat.

Then Ferrar saw something in the grim lines of Bolton's face. Bolton's intentions were suddenly all too clear. The entire unit was marked for elimination.

Pug's body gave a final shudder. His last comrade had expired.

Embers of Bolton's cigarette flared once again and reflected off his raised rifle.

Ferrar furtively tried to slide his rifle from under Pug's body. It was stuck. He freed a leg and managed a judo kick that connected with Bolton's groin.

"Aargh!"

Ferrar picked himself up and made a frantic bid for the cave entrance. Behind him, Bolton unleashed the full force of his automatic weapon.

All around Ferrar, rocks chipped off the ceiling and showered him. He bounced off unyielding walls toward the light.

In the fierce early morning light of Kandahar Airport, Stevens heard an anguished scream over his radio.

"That was Bolton," he cried.

Then they heard wild, nonstop machine gun fire reverberating inside the cave.

Another scream came over the radio.

The tortured, dying wail carried out over the airfield and disappeared into the desert scrubland around him. The CIA had just lost the son of its Director to a madman, a rogue operative, and the worst of its kind—a traitor.

"Good God," Stevens said, disbelieving. "Ferrar has just killed Bolton. He's wiped out our entire unit."

Al-Qaeda seemed to be everywhere. They had even infiltrated the ranks of the clandestine Central Intelligence Agency.

"Anything I can do to help?" Colonel Paxton offered.

Stevens rose to his feet. "Decimate the cave. Blow Ferrar to oblivion."

Ferrar heard a roar emanate from the cave entrance. It buzzed like a dragonfly, a sound that was curiously out-of-place in the Afghan wilderness. Suddenly the entire complex started to shudder.

Dust and debris shot into the cave. Missiles began to thud all around the entrance.

Bunker busters. He came to an abrupt halt in the cave. The ground heaved below him with each horrific explosion. The Americans were trying to destroy the cave with earth-penetrating explosives. He'd hoped for close air support, but this was a little too close for comfort.

A second wave of missiles zeroed in with even more deadly accuracy, shaking the entire mountain like a giant earthquake.

Then he caught the black specks of helicopters rising over a distant hilltop. Fighter jets zoomed overhead, their wings glinting in the sunlight. Lines of cannon fire traced through the sky across the face of the mountain. Were al-Qaeda troops emerging from a second exit?

Who were they trying to kill, al-Qaeda or him? He resumed his sprint toward the entrance.

Bolton was just behind him, his bullets ricocheting around madly.

Ferrar's only hope of escape was out the main entrance. But with American jets dumping ordinance there, he had to choose between a bullet in the back and one in his chest.

Gathering his last reserve of strength, he rushed toward the blinding light.

Air. He needed air. Coughing, he burst through plumes of dust and explosives and lingering tear gas.

Rubble was covering the last glimmer of daylight. Below the cave, the cliff led straight down to the valley floor.

He clawed his way over the broken rubble that smoldered from exploded missiles.

The nose of an American Super Cobra helicopter rose to face straight at him.

"It's me, guys," he yelled, waving his hands above his head. He knew that he couldn't be heard, only seen, but he didn't know what orders they were under, either. "Hold your fire."

The cannons on the hovering gunship began to rotate, spitting shells that narrowly missed him. One of its wings released a TOW missile straight toward the cave. A mushroom cloud billowed just to one side.

Had the whole world gone mad?

Behind him, he heard Bolton's feet approaching around the last corner. He clawed toward freedom, and possible death.

The attack helicopter rotated toward him, adjusting its aim.

He sprang through the bright opening and rolled down the heap of rubble. Holding his breath, he vaulted out over the edge of the cliff.

In an instant, the cold air howled in his ears and stung his eyes. Through the blur, he made out upward-rushing rocks. He pulled a cord by his shoulder and looked up.

The sky spun dizzily above him, and a second, larger helicopter, a Huey, cast a long shadow over the sun. Then the canyon walls erupted in another hail of shells, rockets, and bunker-busting missiles.

Below him, he heard an avalanche crumbling. He was going to bounce off an unforgiving wall, then hit the ground hard.

Finally, over the sound of the battle, he heard a gentle, airy puff. His heart took another beat. Then the suspension lines yanked taut, knocking his helmet forward over his eyes.

His parasail had opened.

His feet swung upward, inches from rock. His canopy had snapped open just before he splattered the hills of Tora Bora.

The Cobra was descending with him, matching the speed of his fall. It had to maneuver quickly to check its descent and face him head on. Meanwhile, the Huey circled around below him. He was surrounded.

If he ever got out of this alive, he would kill Bolton. No questions asked.

On the Cobra's armed wing, a rocket launcher aimed directly at him. Wildly whipping his parasail around, he was able to avoid the first rocket pod that streaked his way.

Despite the thin atmosphere, his parasail left him hanging high like wet laundry. He was an easy target.

He would have to fight back. But how?

He reached down to his hip, and found his automatic pistol.

While tugging on his lines to avoid an aggressive machine gun assault by the Cobra, he flicked back the safety.

Terribly outmatched, he was never going to defeat a chopper that was built to withstand small arms fire. Instead, he straightened his arm upward and unloaded a round of bullets into the parasail. The fusillade shredded an enormous gap in the nylon fabric.

He began to fall like a rock.

The icy wind and engine vapors of the Huey seemed to rise quickly from below him. His sail would get caught in its blades, bringing down the chopper and sending him to an ugly, mangled death.

He yanked hard on his lines, trying to circle away from the whirling danger.

With his quick descent, he had lost most of his ability to maneuver. He jerked again and again, and finally veered slightly, his sail barely clearing the blades.

Passing before the Huey's cockpit, he noticed a stern expression on the pilot's face. He looked intent on crushing Ferrar against the rocks.

Oh, shit.

He pitched himself forward into a swan dive, trying to clear the oncoming Huey. His head and then feet cleared the bottom of the chopper. Whew. Now he faced his next challenge. Nothing but air separated him from the unforgiving valley floor a hundred feet below.

Suddenly, as the large chopper passed overhead, he found himself plucked out of the air with a violent tug. He pushed back his helmet to see what had happened. The Huey had caught him. One of the chopper's landing skids had snagged what was left of his parasail, leaving him to dangle from his tether lines.

Gingerly, he tested his neck, rotating it in both directions. Thank God it wasn't broken.

Maybe he could free himself. He pedaled his feet, trying to disengage the sail. But it wouldn't slide off the slight hook at the end of the skid. He was caught like a prisoner in a hangman's noose, dangling from the gallows.

Then he saw a rope ladder thrown down from the cargo bay of the Huey.

It was about time. They were friendly after all.

He stepped onto the end of the ladder and closed his eyes. The pressure of his weight on his own feet had never felt so good. He pocketed his pistol and shrugged out of his parasail harness. With frozen fingers, he began to haul himself upward, step by step.

The chopper swung by the al-Qaeda cave. The entrance had been completely obliterated, and was obscured by smoke. Bolton was nowhere in sight.

As a pair of strong hands pulled him into the fuselage, Ferrar found himself staring into the grim eyes of eight Marines.

Their weapons were drawn and pointed in his face.

Three

Two HANDS were helping Ferrar up the ladder into the arms of a new, undeclared enemy—the U.S. Marines.

He had only one real option. He had to fall once more to freedom.

He twisted away from one hand, yanked down on the other, and jumped off the rope ladder with the full weight of his two-hundred-and-ten-pound body.

But the hefty, sandy-haired Marine at the other end of the strong grip was built like a brick. The lad's neck muscles bulged and veins nearly popped out of his forehead as he hauled upward on Ferrar.

But, before the Marine could brace himself completely, Ferrar spun around, throwing the young man's shoulder out of joint.

With a blood-curdling cry, the Marine pitched out of the helicopter, just as it banked to ascend out of the canyon.

Falling fast, Ferrar maintained his grip on the Marine's wrist, and together the two men plummeted toward the valley floor. Ferrar flattened himself out on a cushion of air and swooped down cleanly to guide himself underneath the tumbling Marine.

The Marine's body slammed into him from above. Ferrar caught hold of the lad's ammo belt and held on for dear life. With his other hand, he clawed at the Marine's shoulder for a parachute ripcord.

There wasn't any. He groped the other side for a cord, and found only the man's dislocated shoulder. The young Marine flinched and tried to push him away.

"Where's your fucking chute?" Ferrar yelled.

He looked upward into the young man's face, and was met by a mischievous grin.

Ferrar looked down. They were mere seconds away from slamming full force into a dry, rocky creek bed.

Then he heard a sudden whoosh of air, like the unfurling of a flying jib on a sailboat. The Marine had already pulled his ripcord.

Ferrar clung to the Marine with both hands and wrapped his legs around the muscular body. A second later, the high-altitude, low-opening parachute caught the breeze, and both men came to a sudden, swinging halt.

Their combined weight didn't drag the huge black HALO parachute down too rapidly, and they floated the remaining forty yards to the barren ground.

Ferrar twisted and released his grasp a second before impact. He landed hard on both feet, rolling over on his right shoulder in a cloud of dust. His helmet fell off, and he was left sitting on his butt. His jump school instructor would have called his PLF Parachute Landing Fall a disgrace.

The Marine touched ground beside him and staggered forward, trying to reel in the wind-blown chute. He finally regained his balance, only to be met in the back of the neck by the handle of Ferrar's pistol.

Ferrar bent quickly over the slumped figure. "Thanks, pal," he said. "I'll borrow these now."

He stripped away the Marine's assault rifle and slung it over the back of his combat fatigues. Then he hefted the ammunition belt onto his other shoulder. Lastly, he removed the young Marine's K-bar, his serrated and sharp-pointed knife, and slid it into his own empty sheath.

"I'll be going now," he said, and headed nimbly down the dry riverbed toward the distant Pakistani border.

An hour later, Paul Stevens and Joe Capella arrived at Tora Bora from Kandahar. Colonel Paxton, his Marine counterpart, was already standing before what was left of the cave complex.

Stevens stepped off a troop insertion helicopter onto a demolished ledge near the cave's former entrance. "You haven't left anything standing," he observed.

"I didn't intend to," Colonel Paxton confirmed with a wink.

Stevens looked around at the forbidding mountains around him. "Any indication of where Ferrar might have fled?"

"None whatsoever," Paxton said. "We're using the infrared scopes, but it's just a lot of rocks and boulders down in the ravine. Or he could be climbing up to one of these passes." He pointed to a snowy mantle high above them.

"I doubt it," Stevens said. "He's not equipped to survive long in the snow."

"He could be hunkered down in some uncharted cave."

"That doesn't sound like Ferrar."

"Or he could be making his way down that river bed."

"Where's it lead?"

"The ravine broadens into a valley. At that point, he could take one of a number of routes. But basically, there's Pakistan down that way."

"Well, are we setting up roadblocks?"

"There are no roads."

"How about manning the chokepoints?"

"I'm afraid we don't have enough troops to mount a manhunt in this kind of terrain."

"We've got to stop Ferrar. He may be the key to al-Qaeda's whereabouts. He might be the one who activates their cells. He might know where they intend to strike next."

"Then I'll alert the Pakistani border patrol," Paxton said. "But they've proven to be fairly noncommittal, if not incompetent, thus far."

"Do what you can. Now, do you have any sign of Tray Bolton?"

The Marine commander scratched his head. "We're not exactly sure what is in that cave. And I'm not itching to insert any troops in there, especially after what just happened."

"You heard what happened," Stevens said, looking to his assistant for confirmation. "Bolton didn't say anything about al-Qaeda resistance. It was Ferrar who opened fire on our men."

Capella nodded.

"Just the same," the commander said, looking dubiously at the cave. "These are extensive underground complexes, and I, for one, don't care to risk it just yet."

"Oh, for God's sake," Stevens said. "I'll do it myself." And he began to mount the hill of rubble that covered the entrance.

Stone by stone, he dug a small, man-size hole and lowered himself into the cave.

"You coming with me or not?"

Paxton stayed put, but Capella scrambled up the hill.

He lowered himself halfway down the hole, then let out a low whistle. "Kinda dark in here. Don't we have some sort of cave spelunking corps in the Army?"

"Turn on your flashlight," Stevens hollered from inside the cave. "The military will sit on its ass for weeks before they mount an operation inside here. We've got to take the initiative."

"What if we bump into someone?" Capella said, jumping down beside him.

"That's exactly what I'm hoping to do. We're after the CIA's Holy Grail. These are the men who leveled the World Trade Center. Of course it'll take some balls, so get a move on."

They switched on flashlights and flashed them around the cave. Step by step, they moved to the next room. Then the next.

The first bodies they came across were those of the team they had just sent in two hours before. Pug Wilson, Al Moxley, and Colt Sealock lay twisted in anguish, their bodies still warm, their blood sticky and creeping along the cave floor.

Capella turned pale. "Ferrar did all this?"

"It makes you sick, doesn't it?"

Beside Colt lay another body, that of an Arab fighter with the handle of a U.S. Army-issue combat knife sticking out of his abdomen.

Stevens sucked in his breath. "This might have been Bolton's last stand as he tried to defend his men."

"But where *is* Bolton?" Capella asked, heading for the next chamber.

They wandered in widening circles for another ten minutes. At various spots, the cave ceiling seemed weak, and occasionally they encountered fresh damage caused by the bombing. In some cases, entire tunnels had caved in.

No matter where they looked, however, there was no sign of Bolton.

"The only thing I can imagine," Stevens said, "is that after Bolton was shot by Ferrar, he got buried by one of our bunker buster bombs."

Capella didn't answer. Instead, he was shining his flashlight downward at something quite unusual. It was a circle of papers spread out on the floor.

Stevens could imagine a group of al-Qaeda planners crouching on the ground flat-footed, looking over the pages.

"Proof of al-Qaeda?" he asked.

Capella frowned as he kneeled down for a better look at the documents. "More than that, I'm afraid."

He pointed to a set of pages.

"If I'm not mistaken," Capella said, scanning over the diagrams, "these are instructions on how to set off a nuclear device."

Stevens squatted beside him and looked at the diagrams under his assistant's trembling flashlight.

"My God, let me look at that."

For several minutes, they dug through the treasure trove of documents. They found maps of the United States, names and telephone numbers of various cell leaders, and instructions on how to detonate several types of nuclear bombs.

At the top of each page was a date. At first Stevens ignored the date and continued reading. Slowly something about the date drew his attention. His eyes shifted to the top of the page in his hands.

"It's dated December 11," he said.

His assistant's eyes met his.

"Today is the third of December," Capella said.

Stevens calculated quickly. "We're talking about a major nuclear strike a week from tomorrow."

Capella sat down hard. "There's no way to stop it."

Stevens sucked in his breath. "The date coincides with the three-month anniversary of September 11."

"That's not good, sir."

"But where will they get the bomb?"

A beam began to creak above them.

"Pick up the evidence," Stevens said, quickly gathering up all the documents around him. "Let's scout out the adjacent rooms for Bolton, then get out of here."

Evening was falling gently along the C&O Canal in Georgetown.

On the jogging path, CIA Director Lester Friedman was putting his tall frame through its paces with a serious run.

With each stride, the pressure of official duties seemed to dissipate from his shoulders. Yes, there was life beyond the thorny quagmire of high-stakes Washington politics.

Two bodyguards from the Office of Security jogged ahead of him and two behind. Twenty-four-hour protection had become a fact of life. But it didn't destroy his enjoyment of the sunlight glinting off the still water, the fresh breeze of early winter, or the crackle of leaves underfoot.

Suddenly, a bodyguard ahead of him pulled to a stop and pressed a hand tight against an earpiece.

With a pale expression, he signaled for Lester to stop.

Lester drew up, but jogged in place, his form-fitting Lycra suit tight against his muscles.

"It's an operations officer in the field in Afghanistan," the bodyguard said, removing his earpiece and handing him the secure mobile phone.

Lester stood still for a moment and took the call. "Yeah, what is it?"

"This is Case Officer Paul Stevens here in Kandahar. We've got a problem. What do you want to hear first, the bad news, the bad news, or the bad news?"

"Whatever." He didn't have time for comedians.

"I'll start with the easy stuff. First piece of news is we've got a double agent in our ranks. He's just ambushed and murdered five of our operatives. Shot them in cold blood while they were combing through the Tora Bora Cave."

"Where is he now?"

"On the loose. Presumably on foot heading for Pakistan."

"Have my office alert Pakistani border patrols," he said, his voice only slightly out of breath. He was used to bad news, and dead officers were among the best of the bad news he could handle. He could even handle a wacko turning on his own men. It took something like the bombing of the World Trade Center and Pentagon to reach the worst end of the scale.

A young woman jogged ahead of him down the path. "I'm in a hurry. Next piece of news?"

"It's about some evidence we found in the cave, sir," came the distant, delayed voice. "There's another al-Qaeda plot afoot."

"Just as we anticipated. Any hard facts." The anti-terrorism campaign could speculate forever, but it lived and breathed on specifics.

"This one involves nuclear bombs, sir. On American soil."

"That's good news."

"Sir?"

He couldn't believe his good fortune. He would definitely offer this man a promotion. "Do you know where it will happen?"

"No, sir."

That was not good news. "Do you know when?" he asked hopefully.

"December 11."

"Jesus Christ."

His initial euphoria was shot to hell. Eight days was not enough time to track down a nuclear bomb when he had no idea *where* the terrorists would strike.

"You get through to my aide, Charles White, and tell him about the attack. We don't have a moment to lose." The young woman had disappeared in the distance. "I'll turn around and head back to the office."

"I don't think I'd do that just yet," Stevens warned.

"I don't suppose you've got worse news than that."

"I do have worse than that, sir. It appears that one of the casualties at Tora Bora was your son."

The phone suddenly felt like lead in his hand.

"'Casualties'?"

"More like missing in action."

He felt himself slowly swiveling toward the water that sparkled in his face.

"Actually, sir, we believe that he was killed in action."

The news hit him like a falling building. There was nothing to investigate. No further intelligence required. All his power as head of the world's premier spy agency was useless.

"But you said that this was the work of a mole."

"Yes, sir. An inside job. Inside the Agency, that is."

An image came to mind of his wife at their Georgetown townhouse. "Security," he said aloud.

He cupped a hand over the mouthpiece to call over a bodyguard.

"Increase security on Becky. One of our own operatives has just killed Tray. It was an inside job."

The bodyguard placed a call right away.

Lester lifted the phone once again, dreading to hear the voice of the man on the other end of the line.

"I'm sorry, sir," Stevens said. "Is there anything I can do to help?"

He was busy trying to regain control of his senses. He felt the numbness begin to disappear. His heart started thumping wildly, his breathing escalating to a pant.

"Find out whoever did this," he said between gasps. "And kill the son-of-a-bitch, whatever it takes."

"Colonel Paxton," announced a sergeant-at-arms.

Paul Stevens listened to the soldier's words booming through the hangar at Kandahar Airport.

A large group of officers scrambled up from their folding chairs. They were helicopter and fighter jet pilots, flight crewmembers, and representatives from tank, light infantry, special forces, and military intelligence divisions stationed in Afghanistan.

"Take your seats, men," Marine Commander Richard Paxton said as he passed through a side entrance.

The highest-ranking American officer in Afghanistan, he commanded all troops on the ground. Leaning over the podium, he addressed the assemblage.

"After action reports?"

Stevens stood with his assistant, Joe Capella, at the back of the dusty room full of portable computers and hastily set up tables. The hangar had become the U.S. military's latest forward deployment for operational command.

One by one, the pilots stood and gave their accounts of the attack on Tora Bora.

He heard nothing that he hadn't already known.

The bandaged Marine's account of Ferrar pulling him from the chopper and descending by parachute didn't even strike him as particularly dramatic or out of the ordinary. After all, he knew Ferrar.

Finally, the meeting turned to Joe and his discovery.

Stevens walked in front of the room and held up a stack of papers.

"Gentlemen, what we have here is a ticking time bomb. I've been on the phone with Washington and alerted them of the threat. We've uncovered a bona fide plan for a nuclear attack on the United States of America. The date of attack is December 11, and that's next week."

The officers reacted with silence. It was the same reaction he had gotten from Director Friedman of the CIA.

Only now, he had to translate it into action.

He looked at Colonel Paxton, and noticed a trace of red around his collar.

Stevens went on. "We have only one true lead on this case. It's our own man Ferrar. It appears that he's part of this intricate plot against America. So what I want to know is, where is the son-of-a-bitch?"

Colonel Paxton cleared his throat. "It appears that he survived the cave detonations, the helicopter attack, and the fall. I'd call him one lucky bastard."

Stevens glared at him with a surge of anger and pride. "Ferrar doesn't usually operate on luck. But he'll really need it this time around. I want you to track him down. Check every hill and every mountain pass, even if it means combing every goddamned bazaar in Asia. We've got to obliterate this threat no matter what the cost."

"Does that mean we can shoot on sight?" Colonel Paxton queried.

"If need be, but ideally we would extract key information from him about the impending attack."

"Intelligence has its work to do," Paxton said with a detectable smirk. "And we've got our work to do."

The roomful of officers turned back to its commander for operational guidance.

Stevens retreated to a quiet corner of the hangar, where Capella whispered to him, "What are our chances, sir?"

"We've got the worst case scenario on our hands. A turned agent who knows who we are and how we operate."

"Then we should know the same about him."

"That's the thing about Ferrar," Stevens said looking far off beyond the windows. "He's impersonated celebrities, broken out of foreign prisons with his bare hands, seduced the wives of several prime ministers, and chauffeured a drug lord for half a year. He's completely unpredictable."

Four

THE STUDENT residence cafeteria at the Université du Québec in Montreal had cleared out for the night, the doors closed and locked against a flurry of snow. Chairs sat upside down on the tables, and a cleaning crew of six young men began to swab the floor.

They muttered to each other in mingled bits of Canadian French, Pakistani Urdu, and Saudi-accented Arabic.

One man seemed to be their supervisor, as he occasionally lowered his mop handle, stood straight to survey the room, and issued orders, moving them from floor duty to kitchen cleanup.

If it wasn't a university, one could easily get the impression that the supervisor was a ringleader, and the others were his five cohorts.

With the milk and ice cream machines emptied, trays from the salad bar taken back to the refrigerator, and aprons hung along the tile walls of the kitchen, the troop headed downstairs without a word.

The décor changed radically from shiny tile and chrome kitchen to dank concrete. A single light bulb hung over the men as they filed into a square, undecorated room.

Reaching down in a corner, they grabbed their personal prayer rugs and unfurled them on the floor.

Kneeling southeast toward Mecca, they began a cycle of prayers, bowing repeatedly and lowering their foreheads to the floor.

When dusk prayer was over, they put their rugs away and sat in a circle. The supervisor stood in the center and began to speak.

His manner and speech had changed from pious invocations to the brusqueness of an angry man. He also changed languages from Arabic to Urdu, a language used in Pakistan and parts of India and partially understood by Afghans and Persians.

But one word would have been understood in any part of the world: "Osama."

Buried in the torrent of words he showered on the men was also the

23

term "ten-megaton atomic bomb."

Their eyes glowed as they looked at each other. It was as if their destiny in life would hold far more glory.

"Ten-megaton," they repeated among themselves, barely aware of its exact meaning. But the implication of "atomic bomb" was clear enough. Then the leader quieted down, and he and his men got down to discussing details.

Alone, Ferrar picked his way over a desolate, rocky mountain slope just within the Afghan border. His breath puffed into clouds like a steam engine. His combat uniform was smeared with blood, and his helmet was lost at the jump site, with no hat to cover his frostbitten ears.

Snowfields lay just above him, and a constant, howling wind ripped through his fatigues and woolen undergarments straight to his skin.

He needed warmer clothing fast.

Just below him wandered a mule train of Pathan traders heading toward the Pakistani border. They were the only humanity he had encountered, except for the occasional fighter jet screaming by overhead.

The men would have to do. He scooped up a handful of crumbled ice from a nearby patch of snow and wiped the greasepaint from his face. Then he began to slide down toward the men, his frozen toes feeling nothing in his combat boots.

"*Asalam Aleykum,*" he called ahead. It was a congenial way of saying "Hello" in Urdu.

The group stopped and sniffed the air like a herd of deer. Probably more like a pack of wolves.

Grinning amicably, Ferrar held out his M16A2 assault rifle. That got their attention.

He came to a stop and studied their stern, weather-beaten faces. He had hoped to make a fast trade for their clothes and be on his way. But their expressions told him otherwise. Things didn't work that way.

He could see them talking for half an hour, drinking hot *chai*, and squatting around a warm fire before they got anywhere.

Curious, an older Pathan reached out for the rifle.

Ferrar removed the ammunition and handed it to him. The man broke it apart with fast, expert movements.

"*Tika,*" Ferrar said, his jaw and lips nearly frozen in place. Good quality.

The man grunted.

"*Awah?*" Ferrar offered. "Yes?" He spoke some Urdu, but was far from fluent, especially when he could barely move his lips. "*Awah?* Buy the gun?"

They seemed duly impressed with the rifle, though not his Urdu.

Their guns were homemade copies of all sorts. There was a town not far from Peshawar that made nothing but guns.

The old man pointed to a huge sack on his mule's back.

"What...what is...is it?" Ferrar said through chattering teeth.

Flashing a friendly smile like a carpet salesman, the man yanked down a bundle and pulled out a plastic bag full of white powder. He hefted it to show the weight.

"Opium?"

"Pure grade," the man said in English.

The men were leading four mules packed with drugs into Pakistan. How absolutely normal. What safer cover than that?

Afghan farmers working in their poppy fields constituted the world's largest producer of illicit opium used to produce heroin. Their big rival was Burma, another case of an economy subsisting on illegal trade.

He shot them a complicit smile. That brought a toothless grin.

Buying a bag of opium was all he would need to gain their good graces. He was a customer.

He handed them his rifle and took the plastic bag of opium.

"Give me your clothes, too," he told the man with the opium.

The man gestured a trade for Ferrar's fatigues.

"It's a deal."

Ferrar took a deep breath, tore off his shirt and pants, and in return received floppy pajama trousers called a *salwar*, a tunic called a *kurta*, a coarse woolen coat, a shawl, and a *chitrali* cap, named after the near-by, mountainous region where such caps were popular.

The old man seemed to appreciate the fresh blood splattered across the front of his new uniform. He didn't seem to care whose blood it was, Afghan or otherwise.

"Boots, too," the man said.

"Give me your shoes."

The man grunted, and the exchange was made.

The shoes were small, but lined with wool, and Ferrar sighed with relief in his new, warm wraps. He clasped the salesman on the back, and mumbled in English, "Now take me to the goddamned border."

A mile from Pakistan, Ferrar began to hear shouting up ahead. It sounded like a violent scene of Pakistani border patrol fighting back Afghan refugees.

As he and the traders rounded the shoulder of the final mountain, they caught a very different sight across the barren land. It was a public rally in a refugee camp consisting of dilapidated tents.

"Afghans?" he asked.

One of the men nodded. "Taliban."

Ferrar adjusted his newly acquired local garb. He should have grown a beard as well.

As they approached the camp, he made out men in white *chitrali* hats shouting with raised fists. There were no bullhorns and no apparent leaders. Rather, the men and boys were rampaging unchecked up and down the dusty road of the camp.

Strange, there was no enforced border, no barbed wire fence, or even a check house. The only military presence was Pakistani soldiers standing around looking intimidating. They were more interested in quelling the disturbance inside their border than patrolling the frontier.

Consternation was written on his companions' faces.

"Don't you like the Taliban?"

"That's not it," a trader said. "This will slow us down today."

To the drug traffickers, the rally only brought disruption to commerce.

Ferrar slid his hood over his head. With his dark hair and wind-burnt complexion, he just might pass for a displaced tribesman.

If that didn't work, the bag of opium that he had bought with his rifle might buy him passage.

Approaching the dusty encampment, the mule train blended easily into the fray. As a goods carrier rumbled past the tents in a cloud of dust, Ferrar took the opportunity to separate from the traders and grab hold of the truck's tailgate.

His cold fingers could barely hold on as the wood-sided vehicle ground its way southward toward Peshawar.

Five

Peshawar was a crowded city, the provincial capital of Pakistan's Northwest Frontier. By the time the truck pulled into the western edge of town, Ferrar found himself choking on thick, smoky air. He could barely see a hundred feet in front of him. Winter was the wet season, and all around town, people were burning fires to warm their homes.

He was still shivering in the chilly air. He had yet to revive the warmth in his hands and feet. But despite the cold, he grew more relaxed as he entered town. Seeing more people about improved his sense of security.

Several years before on a previous assignment, he had lived farther south in Islamabad and had visited the rugged Wild West of Pakistan on several occasions. Principally, the city of Peshawar was built on an important trade route, the last camel train stop before Afghanistan's dicey Khyber Pass.

He had visited the American Consulate before, and knew exactly where to find it.

The truck passed under the lovely trees of University Town. But soon, the trees largely disappeared, cut down for firewood. They passed through the Cantonment, an old British military station and the realm of Peshawar's expatriates and wealthy citizens. Soon they entered a busy downtown area, where he jumped off.

Amidst the sizzle and pop of a man popping corn over an open fire, Ferrar launched into the tangle of back street Peshawar. Women shuffled along wrapped in *chador* scarves and warm woolen shawls. Men leaned out of their richly appointed shops selling specialty items, from beaded necklaces to old furniture. A vibrant economy was absorbing the influx of Afghan refugees with ease.

Although their guns may have been confiscated at the border, Afghan refugees still bore the marks of their native land. Nothing could hide the hollow look in the eyes of a person cowed into submission for the previous twenty years.

Still dressed in his tribal vestments, Ferrar decided to head into a *suq*, a warren of streets randomly segregated into different markets, to spruce himself up for a visit to the Consulate.

He passed through several different sections looking for new clothing. There was a section for hardware, another for electrical supplies, one for paint, and another where people sold decorative gifts with money stapled on them for weddings.

He passed through a place for fabrics and other sewing things, and began to sense that he was nearing his destination, when just as quickly he was surrounded by household goods. Everywhere, people came up to him carrying trays filled with whatever array of merchandise they were selling—candy, small toys, or threads and elastics.

At last he found a small shop selling Western clothes. He settled on a long-sleeved T-shirt and a pair of jeans, briefly haggled over the price, and took them away for a song.

He found a place named Green's Hotel along Saddar Road, one of the area's main shopping streets. It wasn't a hole in the wall, but it wasn't the Hyatt either. It was just the kind of place travelers stayed in if they didn't want to scrape bottom, but didn't want an indoor pool either.

He checked in, and was relieved to find that no name or passport were required.

He moved into a room that faced the back alley, a mere ten-foot-wide pedestrian walkway with colorful cloth hanging along the sides.

Steam was rising past his window, so he leaned over to investigate. Below were pots filled with boiling dyes. Customers walked around carrying fabric that they wanted to turn a different color.

Boy, did his clothing reek.

He shut his curtains and stripped down. Lukewarm was the best that he could get out of his shower, but it served the purpose and he scrubbed down. Soon he slid his washed body into the T-shirt and stiff new jeans.

He looked in the mirror to comb back his raven-black hair. Looking back was a tall American with a well-developed physique and wide-set blue eyes that glittered intensely. He hardly looked like a wanted man. He looked more like a man with a mission. And that mission was to expose Tray Bolton for the fraud he was, and to put a halt to whatever scheme he intended to perpetrate.

It was dusk by the time he approached the American Consulate. A local guard saw his American features and clothing and waved him through the perimeter wall and toward a metal detector.

A couple of locals in uniforms frisked him and sent him through the detector. No weapons found, he stepped up to the scuffed-up bulletproof window.

He was not surprised to see that the Consulate had added Marine Security Guards. Before the war in Afghanistan, it was a couple of local guards standing behind the glass.

Now a Marine wearing a khaki uniform and white service cap, stood there receiving visitors at Post One. He seemed young, his voice crisp and efficient.

"Good afternoon, sir. How may I help you?"

He decided to take the cautious, indirect approach. "I'm looking for a man named George Ferrar," he said as boldly as he could.

"Mr. Ferrar is a wanted man, buddy. You'd be looking for trouble," the Marine guard replied.

"What did he do?" he asked, feigning ignorance.

The young Marine bit his lip, then seemed to let his outrage get the better of him. "Rumor has it he killed some American troops, including the son of the CIA Director."

He swallowed hard. Last he saw him, Tray Bolton wasn't dead. And *he* certainly hadn't killed Bolton. If anything, Bolton had nearly gunned *him* down.

"In fact, the Director's son was kind of a role model of mine," the Marine went on, his voice choking somewhat.

Great.

Bolton had been a good operations officer, and highly decorated as a Navy Seal. But there was nothing like "death in the line of duty" to help one achieve hero status.

He had learned all he needed to know. He was a wanted man.

"One favor please," he asked. "Do you know of any good restaurants around here?"

"There's no fact sheet on restaurants," the Marine said. "Basically, there's just no place to eat. There's the American Club in University Town, but they renamed it the Khyber Club after the 1998 cruise missile attack, and you need an escort to get there anyway. Then there's the Khan Club, a former caravan stop, but you have to eat on the floor in the stable now. That's near New Rampura Gate in Old Town, which kind of gives me the creeps anyway. That leaves you with," he shrugged his shoulders, "the Pearl Continental, our five-star hotel."

Ferrar thanked the young man, and left.

He was hungry. He'd find something to eat.

Ceremonies at CIA Headquarters in Langley, Virginia, were never public events.

But damn it, they should be.

Oklahoma Congressman Ralph W. Connors shifted his enormous weight as he stood inside the entranceway listening to two ringing hammers. Before him, a pair of stone carvers solemnly etched five additional stars into the marble wall commemorating all the fallen CIA heroes who had died in the line of duty over the years.

Beside him stood CIA Director Lester Friedman with squared shoulders, a straight back, and a resolute look on his face. Lester had just lost his foster son in combat, the pride still evident in his bearing. Such sacrifice for one's country was too great not to be a matter of public record. But the only recognition Tray Bolton would ever get was a simple, anonymous star carved on a lobby wall.

Beside Lester Friedman, a slim woman wasn't taking it so well. No more than forty-five years of age, Rebecca Friedman was fighting to hold back her tears. Every few seconds, her hands darted up to her hazel eyes and cleared a tear away. Her coffee-brown hair in bouncy curls quivered occasionally, but she continued to stand erect, her eyes affixed on the speaker.

"Today we commemorate the lives of five valiant federal government employees who died in the line of duty," an Agency chaplain was saying. "Their service to this nation will be forever enshrined on this wall."

With that, the last stroke of a hammer rang out against the hard marble. Silence ensued.

"Ashes to ashes and dust to dust."

No ashes for Tray Bolton. They couldn't even find his remains in the caves of Tora Bora in Afghanistan. If Connors ever got his hands on the traitor who slaughtered these fine men, he would administer as much pain as his fifty-six-year-old, two-hundred-and-fifty-pound flab could inflict. Capital punishment wasn't good enough for such scum.

As ranking member of the House Intelligence Subcommittee, he felt it his personal obligation to protect the men and women in invisible uniform.

His eyes traveled to the other couples present. The names of their sons would never be mentioned in this or any other official context again. Their names wouldn't be etched into a wall, or even associated with the fighting in Afghanistan. They would go the same way as the elderly, the drug overdoses, and the stillborn, into the bottomless anonymity of history.

But their parents' presence in those hallowed halls on that special day would forever sanctify them and bring their souls peace.

Now where was that damned bastard who shot 'em up?

At the American Consulate, the Marine at Post One felt a tingle at the ends of his fingers. There was a slight electricity in the air where the stranger had just stood.

The entire country was on heightened alert, and, as point man for the Consulate, he was especially so.

He reached for the phone without another thought and dialed his detachment commander.

Gunny John Rojas picked up the phone in the Marine barracks at once. "Rojas here."

"Sir, this is Post One. We've just had a walk-in who seemed a bit suspicious. He was asking about Ferrar."

"What's his name?"

"Didn't get that, sir."

He heard a shuffle of papers on Gunny's end. "Give me his description."

"Tall, good-looking, white, American accent. I'd say around forty years old. Could have been a Marine once."

"I'm looking at a physical description here, and it doesn't say nothing about 'good-looking' or 'coulda been something.'"

"Sorry, sir. I'd put him at six feet three, weight around two twenty, black hair, blue eyes."

"Can you still detain him?"

"No, sir. He's left the premises. Why?"

"That was probably Ferrar."

"Jeez. I didn't have any documentation on him. I didn't expect him to walk right up to the Consulate."

"Stranger things have happened," Gunny Rojas said. "Now, you hold the fort while I put me together a unit to track him down."

Ferrar shivered in his long-sleeved T-shirt. He should have also brought along his Afghan vest to keep out the cold, damp air.

The night market in Peshawar was poorly lit. No streetlights illuminated the horn-blaring traffic that shot in fits and spurts down the middle of the street. People returning from work or foraging for dinner crowded the outer lane and paused before the fried meat stalls and vegetable stands. Individual light bulbs hung over the stores, and fluorescent lights illuminated the interiors of dry good stores, shoe stores, banks, and family dwellings.

It was a perfect place to get lost, and that's why Ferrar was there.

After leaving the Consulate, he had headed south through the organized streets of the Cantonment, then backtracked and loitered on a side street to see if he had aroused the suspicion of the Marine guard. Ten minutes after he had left the guard booth, he watched a white Consulate van loaded with Marines in full battle gear veering out of the compound and heading south, the direction that he had initially taken. That was all he needed to know.

His Most Wanted poster must have made the rounds already, and the Marine guards were after him.

He snaked his way eastward down an alley, and killed some time walking past bakeries, that were garage stall-sized enclosures with a round hole dug in the concrete floor. Each bakery seemed to employ half a dozen men squatting around the hole.

One guy had a pile of hot fresh-baked flat bread, somewhat like pita, in front of him. Another two guys were rolling out globs of dough the size of a peach, and other guys were taking the flat, oval loaves and slapping them onto the smooth clay sides of the oven. The hair on their arms was singed from the hot fire at the bottom.

Word began spreading down the street from man to man. Curious, several bakers left their posts and headed up the street into the posh part of town.

His stomach growling, Ferrar quickly bought several warm pieces of bread and stuffed them in his mouth as he followed the crowd. They were heading in the general direction of the Consulate, but stopped at a stone wall. It was the Pakistan Army's main base in Peshawar.

He shielded his eyes in the glare of halogen lights that bathed the main gate to the base. Troops were milling around with great excitement.

Then from within the wall, engines were rumbling closer.

He heard the crunch of large tires rolling forward, and hurried up to the floodlit area to watch.

Two olive-green trucks flying the green and white Pakistani flag pulled out of the base. Standing atop a container on the first truck, a sturdy figure barked out orders in clear and distinct Urdu.

Then Ferrar caught a flash of blond hair.

He tried to get a better look at the man confidently directing the convoy.

As the trucks lurched toward him, several military police pushed him back, until he was pressed up against a house. Several unmarked cars accompanied the trucks, the beefy men inside bearing all the hallmarks of Pakistan's dreaded intelligence service, the Taliban-friendly ISI.

Just as he passed Ferrar's position, the man on the truck bent down to the driver on the right-hand side and issued an order in English: "Take these bombs to Karachi with all deliberate speed."

Ferrar tried to free himself from the crowd to get a better look.

As the truck headed away, the man swiveled back his way and pointed a cautionary finger toward the throng.

He was in clear view now. It was Bolton.

More guards swarmed against the bystanders, and Ferrar felt himself backpedaling once again.

"So you're not as dead as people think," Ferrar muttered. What the hell was Bolton up to?

He examined the trucks as they passed from view. Both carried one steel container, the kind of standard-sized shipping box used to transport goods by air, ship, and rail.

The hubbub at the base entrance settled into a mildly excited buzz, and then quieted down altogether within minutes, as if nothing had happened.

But Ferrar knew differently. Something big had just gone down.

Six

MORNING BROKE slowly over the bleak, wintry streets of Georgetown. Students walked briskly up Lester Friedman's cobblestone lane toward class at Georgetown University. Lester's foster son never had the privilege of attending the university as Lester had so dearly hoped. Nor had his foster son ever gotten to compete with the graduates for the great job opportunities in the workplace.

Instead Tray Bolton had chosen a far nobler path, working abroad to defend a country he would never live to enjoy. The lack of justice in life was infuriating.

And it seemed to be eating away at Becky, too.

Rebecca Friedman also had made many sacrifices in her life, as she had made abundantly clear to him on many occasions. Intentionally kept in the dark as a submarine captain's wife, then kept out of closed-door sessions as the spouse of a Washington insider, she had suffered through her share of tensions and fears. But government service had been his life's calling, and, recognizing that, she had done everything in her power to advance his career.

But her inconsolable weeping in the darkened living room stemmed from her ultimate frustration—her inability to control her own life.

Lester wiped his sweating palms against his freshly pressed business suit. "My car will pick me up any minute now. Will you be able to manage alone today?"

"I'm having some of the wives over to help me out," she whimpered, drying her tears.

"That's smart."

"I just can't stop thinking about that boy," she admitted.

"What boy? Tray?"

"No. Not him. You know who I'm talking about. I hope you track him down and give him the death sentence. You know it's a federal offense to kill a federal employee."

"Who've you been listening to?"

"I think about these things."

He rolled his eyes and looked impatiently out the window.

"You remember how he took that girl away from Tray?" she resumed.

"I do, dear."

"She was a good soul. Straight as an arrow. She even joined the Coast Guard after college. He proposed to her and everything."

"Who? Tray?"

She nodded solemnly.

"When?"

"Senior year of college on the Golden Gate Bridge at sunset. He even had a ring for her."

"You're kidding. He never told me that."

"That's because of what she told him," she said sourly.

"Well, what did she say?"

"Something like, 'I can't respect you.'"

There was silence for a long time while Lester absorbed the new information about his own son.

At last he said, "And that's when the phone calls resumed. We started hearing from his old drug connections."

"And he started borrowing from us again," she added.

"Stealing."

"Enough of this. I don't want to think about it. It's always been a battle for Tray. We could only be there for him. We couldn't give him his self-respect. He had to earn it for himself. But when that George fellow stole her, it sent Tray over the edge."

"But he finally straightened himself out," he countered. "He went to fight for our country."

He began to view his son's courage with renewed admiration.

"George Ferrar took away our son's girl," she said. "He stole Tray's pride. And now he took our son's life." Once again, she dissolved into tears.

"Our *foster* son," he reminded her.

"Nevertheless, he was our only child," she shot back defensively.

"For only three years," he said.

He had to be more patient. They had had that conversation many times before.

"Stop it. We got him from that dreadful foster family," she said reflectively.

"He was already fourteen years old. He was a fully formed man. He was practically living in a juvenile detention center."

"We managed to turn him around," she said with pride. "He's been highly decorated."

"We haven't seen hide nor hair of him for years now."

She hesitated, breaking the cadence of their timeworn argument. When she spoke again, she was once again on the offensive. "Lester. He was *our* son, and you won't let that boy get away with this."

"You know I won't, dear," he conceded.

His cell phone rang. It was one of his bodyguards calling to say that they were just approaching the house. The call was a precursor to a carefully orchestrated sequence of events in which a bodyguard would escort him from his private residence into the official, bulletproof limousine.

"Today they want me on Capitol Hill," he said.

Still in her bathrobe, she approached him out of the shadows with long, slow strides. Draping both arms around his neck, she stared soberly into his eyes.

"I know I can count on you to do the right thing," she said.

"There he is. Ferrar!"

The gruff shout carried through the heavily scented night air of Peshawar.

Ferrar glanced over his shoulder. Two Marines were racing toward him down the alley from which he had just emerged after having watched the Pakistani Army trucks.

Young kids. The youngsters who guarded his nation's Embassies were strong and fast, but still wet behind the ears.

Sure they had found him, which was worthy detective work, but they needn't have shouted out his name and alerted him.

He lowered his head and scrambled briskly into the nearest cluster of pedestrians, where he scooted among the *chapal* sandals.

Unfortunately, he was back in the Cantonment, where the wide streets and walled enclosures provided little cover. Nighttime and the crowd of people were his only friends for the moment.

He sprinted ahead of the crowd and came to a major crossroad.

Ahead, he saw two pairs of military boots passing quickly before the headlights of oncoming traffic. More Marines were converging from in front.

Okay, so they thought they had him cornered.

He dodged sideways down the cross street, but the cover was meager—a lone burro pulling a cart, a small truck, a horse-drawn, two-wheeled *tonga* bearing a pair of lovers.

Pounding footfalls kept pace behind him.

A shot rang out.

Was it a warning, or was it aimed at him? He didn't have time to find out.

A straight-backed young man in a white skullcap was leading an ill-treated, malnourished nag with open sores on her legs in his direction. That would have to do.

Rushing up to the poor creature, he grabbed the reins, turned the beast in the opposite direction, and jumped on her bare back. The young man protested and reached for the reins.

Ferrar kicked the horse in the flanks, and before the young man could grab her back, the mount accelerated quickly, even eagerly, leaving her owner immobile in the middle of the street.

More shots rang out. The mare bucked under Ferrar, and he jabbed her even harder with his heels, bending low to keep his balance. In the end, the shots helped him. The poor pony's stride was that of a veritable quarter horse and her hooves pounded down a good quarter mile of narrow city streets before she came limping to a halt.

By then, Ferrar was exhausted and bruised and sore from the lack of a saddle. He was far enough away from his pursuers and the Cantonment area that he could jump down.

He slapped the horse on her rear flank.

"Good girl," he said. "Now find yourself a new master."

He headed off in another direction. He was but a half block from his hotel.

By the time he entered his room, locked the door behind him, and strode over to the open window that was illuminated by storefronts and vendors below, he could see a handful of exhausted Marines giving up the chase.

He lowered himself into the thick Afghan rug and closed his eyes.

While the Marines were busy tracking him down, Tray Bolton was transporting bombs to the port city of Karachi.

As soon as he could, Ferrar would also head south. But first, he had to visit a very special place.

Joint hearings of the House and Senate Intelligence Committees were rare, and as a rule were held *in camera*, behind closed doors. That day was no exception.

Briefing Congress had become a bi-weekly exercise for CIA Director Lester Friedman. And Congress was due another briefing after the hiatus in which he attended his foster son's memorial service and burial *in absentia* with honors at Arlington National Cemetery.

Typically, the hearings were comprised of Lester keeping Capitol Hill up-to-date on events in Afghanistan and other terrorist battlegrounds around the world.

Congressman Ralph W. Connors of Oklahoma, the committee chairman who was late for everything, still had not arrived. So his Senatorial counterpart reached for the gavel and pounded it to open the hearing. "The committee will now come to order. The chair will now call Mr. Friedman."

As the doors clicked shut in the Dirksen Senate Office Building and Capitol Hill police assumed their positions just outside, Lester felt a tide of warmth coming his way. The Senators and Congressmen began to individually express their sympathy to him across the two-tiered dais.

He nodded in gratitude, but said nothing. He was beyond the initial shock, then the bewilderment, and finally grief. He was well on his way toward seeking retribution.

Finally, the room turned to a junior Congressman from New Jersey. "I can only barely contain my outrage at the events that led to your son's death," the young Congressman said. "It was more than a major breach of national security to fail at such a valuable mission and to lose so many of our own Federal officers. I see this as nothing short of a crime against humanity."

Lester had to smile. Okay, but there was no need to overstate the case.

"I assure you," he finally said, switching on his microphone. "This occurrence will not have long-term consequences. We will find bin Laden and his crones. And as far as the loss of my son's life, I can only say that I am proud that it was my own family's blood that was spilled on the frontlines of this war against terrorism."

Suddenly, shouting erupted from the corridor and the elected officials turned their backs on him as everyone listened to the jostling behind the door.

The legislators looked wildly at each other. Was this another terrorist attack?

At last the tension was broken when the door opened wide and an unkempt Congressman Connors stumbled into the room. As chairman of the joint hearing, he immediately took his place behind the central microphone.

Composing himself, he turned on the mike and addressed Lester and the rest of the CIA staff seated beside him.

"I apologize for my late arrival," he said. "Now on to the business at hand. I understand that you are prepared to reveal to us the culprit behind this atrocity at Tora Bora."

Lester gathered his papers and cleared his throat. Then without referring to his notes, he proceeded to recount the entire failed assault on the Tora Bora Cave.

"And who was this sixth member of the unit that apparently killed his countrymen and sabotaged the mission?" Connors demanded.

"His name is George Ferrar, sir."

"Ferrar?" Connors said, incredulous. "I know him. Hell, I've had him over for dinner on numerous occasions."

"Well," Lester said, somewhat taken aback with the revelation. "Then you've been taken in by a con artist."

"In no way, shape, or form," Connors retorted. "He saved my family's lives."

Again, Lester had to pause to absorb the information. "If you'll pardon my putting it this way, Mr. Congressman. At this very moment, Ferrar is out to destroy life as we know it."

Connors thumped his desk. "I'm here to tell you, he's a patriot through and through. If you only knew some of the things he did for me."

Lester frowned. He was unprepared for this broadside attack. He turned off his microphone, leaned toward his chief aide, a young egghead named Charles White, and whispered, "Get me the poop on Ferrar's relations with Connors and his family."

"Right away, sir," the aide said, and stood to leave the room.

He switched his microphone back on. "My good friend, we'll let our differences of opinion rest for now. I'll just let the evidence speak for itself." He reached for the reel-to-reel audio tape player sitting on the table in front of him, and switched it on.

As the tape slithered through the machine, the room held still with mystified anticipation.

They heard the voices of Bolton and Stevens shouting over the radio. Bolton then whispered distinctly, "Ferrar has led all of us into this chamber…then he started firing…we're all dead." This was followed by gunshots and Bolton's anguished scream. It was not only the scream of a man in agony, but of a soul facing his end. Ultimately, it was a cry of rage.

By the time he clicked the tape off, the chamber was filled with irate voices and cries of condemnation toward the traitor, Ferrar.

The uproar was finally broken by Congressman Connors confiscating the gavel and pounding it against his desk.

"We will take a short, fifteen-minute recess," he announced, his face pale.

Seven

THE CIA listening post in Peshawar, Pakistan, was treated by the Agency no differently than any other listening post around the world.

As George Ferrar stood in early morning shadows across the street from the small, vine-covered bungalow on Artillery Road, the lights turn off inside. Moments later, two Pakistani men emerged, locking the door behind them.

Listening posts were inconspicuous by nature, and didn't draw attention to themselves. Consequently, they were often very poorly guarded.

He had been to that particular listening post on one previous occasion. He was familiar with the entry procedure, and remembered the general layout without having to turn on lights.

Since he had waited up watching the building since midnight, he was sure that no other people were still inside. He moved swiftly and with precision. He could enter through a side window by jimmying the frame open.

Indeed, a crowbar that he had borrowed from a mechanic's shop worked nicely. Within seconds, he was standing inside, with the window shut and locked behind him.

Since so many different people entered and left the house, the alarm key should still be in the alarm box. If not, he was in trouble.

With sixty seconds to act, he made his way swiftly through the dark toward the entrance hall. He found the door to the coat closet, slid it back, and saw the alarm box in the glow of its own green and red indicators. The green light signaled that the security system was turned on. The blinking red light meant that his surreptitious entry had set off the alarm.

With one deft movement, he reached up and found the key vibrating in the warm alarm box. He turned it at once. There was an electronic click, then both indicators turned off.

He was safe until the next shift arrived.

From his previous visit to the listening post, he knew that it was used for eavesdropping purposes rather than clandestine meetings. Deep in the interior of the house, he found a bathroom. He turned on the light, stepped inside, and quickly closed the door. He stared at the flat, porcelain Turkish toilet. A hidden room lay behind it and was accessible through a single painted piece of plywood.

He stepped onto the toilet's two sculpted footprints, and pressed his knuckles against the board until one side gave way. It swung into the opening, and he entered the small room.

There, he found a desk lamp and switched it on, revealing two desks weighed down by bulky electronic surveillance equipment. A second room seemed to be for storage. In it, he found what he was looking for. A large cardboard box held a jumble of field surveillance equipment.

He reached in and pulled out an efficient little pack consisting of a bugging device and its matching receiver and earpiece. The bug was no more than a simple disk the size of a point-and-shoot camera battery. He squeezed the raised "On" button, thus activating it, and slid it under the carpet between the two rooms. He slipped the receiver and earpiece in his jeans pocket.

He might not have access to professional surveillance equipment for quite some time, so he checked the box for what else he might take with him.

He dug out a signal transponder and its accompanying tracking device. They could come in handy tracking people or vehicles. He reached around some more and pulled out what looked like a roll of Lifesavers, the Tropical Fruit variety. It was the perfect spy camera, complete with photoelectric microchip and USB connection.

He discovered a waterproof pouch elsewhere in the room, and attached it to his waist. Then he put all the items he had selected into it. Finally he pulled the receiver's earpiece out of his pocket, jammed it into an ear, and turned on the receiver.

"Testing one, two, three," he said aloud, directing his voice into the part of the room where the bug lay under the carpet. A microsecond later, he heard his own voice transmitted into his earpiece.

"Gotta go," he said.

"Gotta go."

He smiled at hearing his voice repeated through the earpiece.

Swiftly, he turned off the light, left the room, and made sure to close the panel behind him. He reset the alarm, which gave him a minute to exit the listening post before the alarm armed itself.

Then he slipped out of the house through the back door.

Congressman Connors pounded the gavel once more, and called the hearing to order.

"Mr. Friedman," he began. "That was a rather impressive and moving recording of the final moments of your officers' lives, especially that of your son. We all owe a tremendous debt of gratitude to them and pay tribute to their valor. I only wish that the exact identity of the perpetrator of the crime could be as evident and clear."

He eyed Lester Friedman across the carpet from him. Lester bore a smile that he would rather see beamed at terrorists than at him.

"But be that as it may," he continued, "I'd like to turn to even more pressing business. I understand that you have disturbing news of another al-Qaeda target."

"That's right, Mr. Congressman," Friedman said. He leaned forward and spoke with a conspiratorial whisper into the microphone. "I am prepared to testify that the Central Intelligence Agency has learned of a pending terrorist attack on a massive scale against a singular target in the United States."

His words lingered in the air.

"How credible is this evidence?" a Senator from Florida finally asked.

"This intelligence is based on documented evidence found in the Tora Bora Cave complex."

The Senator cleared his throat. "And just exactly how big is this intended strike?"

"Let's use the words of the document itself in translation from the original Arabic," Friedman said with emphasis, and held up a page to read. "Quote: 'This plan is designed to exceed the scope of the airplane attacks of September 11.' End quote."

The Senator from Florida was energetically pursuing Friedman now. "And what specifically is this *singular target?*"

"That we do not know," Friedman admitted. "But you can bet that we're looking into it, both from a raw intelligence standpoint and by analyzing what can be accomplished in the short amount of time remaining."

"And what's the timeframe we're looking at?"

Friedman held up the page once again and read, "'December 11.' The three-month anniversary of September 11. That's eight days from today, gentlemen."

Connors felt beads of perspiration forming on his brow. He felt like he was standing on a volcano that was about to explode. "And exactly how do you intend to come by this *raw intelligence?*"

Friedman looked him squarely in the eye. "Through George Ferrar."

"Do you have him in custody?"

"We have made a positive identification of him in Peshawar, Pakistan. As you know, Pakistan is not an easy place for a foreigner to hide. I think I can safely predict that we'll have him rounded up within twenty-four hours."

Lying back on his bed in the one-star Green's Hotel in Peshawar, Ferrar turned on the eavesdropping receiver and listened through the earpiece. At the moment, nobody had entered the listening post.

It was early dawn, and people outside his window were stomping their feet to keep warm. He heard the scraping noise of shop owners opening their very tiny stores that sold notions for sewing. Women began stoking fires beneath the pots of dye.

A *muezzin* used an electronic speaker mounted on one of the mosque's minarets to call out the dawn prayer, and for several minutes the city came to a standstill. What were the vast majority of Pakistanis praying for—the Saudi-funded *madressah* religious schools that taught Pakistani youths how to fire rifles and build bombs, or the forces of modernization that could ultimately lift Pakistan out of its near zero growth rate?

Ten percent of the country would pray for the orthodox hardliners, and fifteen percent, the elite of the country, would pray for a modern state. The remaining three quarters, made up of one hundred million Pakistanis, was the big question mark. Maybe their industrious, can-do spirit would turn toward the almighty rupee.

The silence was broken by sounds transmitted directly into his ear. The surveillance team, known as transcribers, had just entered the hidden room at the listening post.

There were two voices, both speaking in Urdu.

That made sense. The CIA hired native speakers of Urdu to monitor the various bugs placed around Peshawar in its several major hotels and in the boardrooms, as well as headboards, of the big Islamic players.

His understanding of Urdu was limited, but developed enough to catch the gist of a conversation, and certainly sophisticated enough to understand the emotional content.

The transcribers hired by the Americans didn't sound agitated in the least. Their talk of tea and sweet cakes relieved him. Neither had noticed his prior intrusion.

A donkey-pulled cart creaked by in the alley below, and children began calling out to their schoolmates. He rolled out of bed and closed the window.

He fit the receiver back into his ear. The two transcribers were discussing key terms to listen for in their various bugged transmissions. In the course of their conversation, one mentioned a recent treasure trove of al-Qaeda documents that the Agency had uncovered at Tora Bora. So there *was* valuable evidence in the cave. Perhaps that's what Bolton was trying to protect.

Then the men discussed a date, December 11, for a "big strike" against America. He froze as he lay there. It had to be Bolton and the bombs.

A big strike next week meant he had eight days to track down Bolton and derail his plans.

Out of the dizzying volume of information the men were inadvertently imparting to him, a term hit him like a cold splash of reality. As they began discussing smuggling, the name "Beaver Tail" came up.

Beaver Tail Island was a tiny, wooded islet little known even to locals, and unmarked on any maps. It lay off the larger Mt. Desert Island which itself lay off the central coast of Maine. Beaver Tail Island was in fact where he and Tray Bolton had spent their youth.

Bolton was definitely heading for Maine. And it made sense, from a terrorist's point of view. Maine had a rugged coastline perfect for smuggling weapons and outlaws from Canada into the United States.

With one smooth motion, he rolled out of bed.

The train would take a good twenty-four hours or longer to reach Karachi. Pakistani or American security forces might be watching for him at the airport. A long taxi ride across the country would be too conspicuous. He took a deep breath. He had only one choice.

Fifteen minutes later, he found himself in the middle of a big bus "depot" area next to the old Grand Trunk road, the old main road from Islamabad to Kabul. In truth, the depot was part parking lot, part access road.

Amidst the mishmash of donkey cart taxis and two-stroke auto-rickshaws were overloaded, brightly painted buses all waiting to depart for who-knows-where, black smoke pouring out of their exhaust pipes.

Somewhere in that confusion was a bus for Karachi.

Outside the Dirksen Senate Office Building, Lester Friedman found Charles White, his prematurely balding aide, waiting for him in the limousine. The two men left at once for Langley.

"Give me the history between Connors and Ferrar," Lester snapped.

"It turns out Ferrar rescued Connors's daughter from the Abu Sayyaf terrorist organization in the Philippines," Charles began.

"Really? But Connors made it sound more like Ferrar saved his entire family."

"Yes, technically the Congressman is correct, sir. It turns out that the group holding her hostage was demanding a ransom, and Congressman Connors had to deliver the money in person deep in the jungles of the Philippines. Ferrar was there to arrange the transfer of money, and personally negotiate for the release of Connors' daughter."

"So we're talking about a fucking hero here."

"Maybe. Maybe not, sir," Charles said with a shrewd grin. "As you know, elements in Abu Sayyaf were trained by al-Qaeda, and the organization is even linked to bin Laden through marriage."

"Go ahead," Lester said, allowing himself a smile. "I think I see where you're going with this."

"I'm only suggesting that the fact that Mr. Ferrar was so closely connected with Abu Sayyaf during Mr. Connors' ordeal, and the fact that he successfully negotiated Mr. Connors' daughter's release when so many have failed in other such negotiations, might indicate possible collusion…"

"Between Ferrar and Abu Sayyaf," Lester completed his thought. "And therefore between Ferrar and al-Qaeda in Afghanistan."

"Unfortunately, I have no direct evidence to support this."

"In this case, I think no more evidence is needed."

As the Peshawar-Karachi bus jostled him against fellow standing passengers, Ferrar grabbed more tightly onto a handrail above him. It was his only support in the swaying forest of sweating locals for the next ten hours.

He peered out an open window at the fallow fields of the Punjab. Farmers were out there with hoes, clearing old growth from between the mounds where they would plant next season's crops. The hardscrabble life brought back memories of his own rural upbringing in Maine.

He had been raised on a farm on the mainland, but passed his summers in the wilds of Acadia National Park on Mt. Desert Island and trawling for shrimp off the shores of Bar Harbor. He often pulled oars in a race against his high school pal Tray Bolton as their rivalry spilled over into every aspect of life.

They had even lusted after the same girl, and Bonnie Taylor was worth it. A fully formed woman at fifteen, she radiated vitality and a sunny smile. Bolton had claimed her first, boldly stating his intentions to Ferrar on numerous occasions. Football stars, the two young men had their choice of cheerleaders and fans, but Bonnie was the only one they cared enough to compete for.

In a quiet manner, the youthful Ferrar had accepted his fate. Bonnie was Bolton's girl whether he or Bonnie liked it or not.

Sure, he and Bonnie had traded intimate smiles, walks on warm summer evenings down Main Street in Bar Harbor, passing glances in hot rods roaring side-by-side while waiting for the light to turn green.

Somehow competition had driven the two men closer to each other, rather than apart. For Bolton, the whole thing was the competition. For Ferrar, the whole thing was Bonnie.

Bonnie had joined them on their rollicking cross-country drive to California. She had checked into the International House at Berkeley, and the two men were forced to settle for bachelor living for four years.

Bolton had boasted about his conquests whenever they happened, which was often. Ferrar chalked up Bonnie's willingness to the licentious Seventies, forgiving her for being a victim of the times.

Conversely, on the rare occasion when he stole a kiss from her, he celebrated the openness of the times—she could give herself to more than one man.

In retrospect, Bonnie was neither of theirs, no matter how much they claimed her heart or her body. In the end, she had departed the left-leaning institution for the Coast Guard Academy. Armed with her mathematics degree, she had graduated from Officer Candidate School on the Thames River near New London, Connecticut, and two weeks later Ensign Bonnie Taylor was underway on a sea tour aboard a U.S. Coast Guard cutter.

And where were Tray and he? Their testosterone levels soaring to new heights to meet the challenge, they both enlisted in the military.

Tray's foster father was an officer at the submarine base across the bay from Bar Harbor, and Tray opted for a career in the Navy. Eventually the Seals asked Tray to join their elite ranks and he disappeared into the murky waters of special operations.

Ferrar looked up at his hand, severely creased by the handhold he was using to keep his balance. He was a farm boy since birth, and the Army was his destiny. It wasn't so much the allure of military service as a desire to emulate Bonnie that he enlisted in the Army. Three years into his enlistment, he was selected into the Green Berets.

During those challenging, but exhilarating three years, moving from boot camp to a string of Army bases, he had lost touch with Tray, only to encounter him in a new force created by the Department of Defense. Born out of the demise of the Navy Seals, the DEVGRU Development Group organization was formed, nominally to test weapons and tactics. Within six months, both Tray and Ferrar were fully indoctrinated into the Department's ultimate counter-terrorist group.

Ferrar had never extracted from Tray Bolton specific details about his three years with the Seals, but by the time he met up with Tray in

DEVGRU, it was clear that something in Tray had changed.

Perhaps it was Tray's checkered past in and out of juvenile hall, or his foster family upbringing, or perhaps Navy life itself didn't suit him, but Ferrar soon realized that Tray was in trouble on many fronts.

For one thing, Bonnie refused to see him any longer. Commander of her own cutter in San Francisco, California, she was a force to be reckoned with, and Tray was put in his place time and again.

Then there were the underworld figures in Tray's life. Ferrar knew them only by their sudden appearances and equally quick exits from Bolton's life. All in all, it didn't paint a pretty picture.

Ahead of him, several Bedford trucks laden with cabbage were lurching down the road. Today Bolton would be riding high upon a Pakistani Army transport vehicle to Karachi, while Ferrar swung back and forth in someone's stinking armpit on a public bus.

But their destination was the same.

It always had been.

Eight

CONGRESSMAN CONNORS had just entered his office in the Rayburn House Office Building when his receptionist handed him the phone.

"I think you'll want to take this call," she said.

He stopped below the seal of the great state of Oklahoma and took the phone. "Yes?"

"This is George Ferrar."

Connors paused to restart his heart. Behind Ferrar's hushed whisper, he heard men shouting, cranes creaking, and chains clanking.

"Where the hell are you?" he asked.

"Some place I shouldn't be," Ferrar answered. "They don't take too kindly to uninvited visitors at a seaport."

"Which seaport?"

"Sorry, can't say," Ferrar said. "If you want to hear any more, this conversation has to be off the record."

Before Connors promised anything, he had to check out Ferrar, who had become a rather unreliable source of information lately. "Tell me one thing first. Why the hell did you kill Bolton and the others at Tora Bora?"

He heard a short, incredulous laugh.

"Do you really believe that?" Ferrar asked.

"I saw them add five stars to the CIA wall. And you weren't one of them."

"I didn't kill the unit. It was Bolton who ambushed us."

"Then how come Bolton is dead and you're not?"

Connors looked around. His staff was watching him with interest.

There was a pause on Ferrar's end of the line. "How would you feel if Bolton rematerialized, alive?"

Connors lowered his voice and turned his back on the rest of the office. "I'd feel very differently, but I can't say I'd feel any better about the men who died."

"Then you just wait and see."

"I'm not waiting for anything," he whispered harshly. "I gotta know now what the hell's going on out there. We've got a timetable for another attack here, and the CIA is spinning its wheels."

"Do you still trust me?" Ferrar asked.

"It's getting harder by the day."

"I need someone in DC who trusts me."

Connors threw his free hand up. "You won't find many of us left."

"Thanks. I knew I could count on you. I'll call you later."

Connors turned and growled into the phone. "I've been through ten elections. I've been in DC longer than most Congressmen can imagine. I've worked my way up the ladder. You're talking about ruining a twenty-year career here."

The sounds of a harbor had ceased at the other end. The line was dead.

Connors looked around at his office. The entire staff was gaping at him. "So what are you looking at?" he shot out.

He relaxed his grip on the phone and set it softly in his receptionist's hand.

"You don't have to pull out your résumés just yet."

A day and a half after Ferrar's call to Connors, a smartly dressed British businessman with sandy-colored hair and wire-rimmed glasses sat on an Airbus reading an Eric Ambler suspense novel. The plane was just approaching Bahrain International Airport in the Persian Gulf.

Ferrar closed the book, leaned back, and reflected on the past thirty-six hours. From the Karachi port master, he had filed for public information and received it. The ship he had identified as bearing Pakistani bombs was bound for Bahrain and it would be arriving that day.

That had presented him with his next dilemma. How could he slip through the notoriously tight Pakistani security screen, and then avoid an international warrant for his arrest while entering Bahrain?

He was fairly adept at disguise on his own, but he had needed a friend to create alias documents for him. He realized that forged documents were a very sensitive subject and not issued lightly, but fortunately he had a long-time friend, Gerald Higgins, at the British Deputy High Commission in Karachi who was willing to go out on a limb for him.

Aside from the forged passport, a bigger problem was trying to get some visas for the region. Gerald had to use all his accrued *wasta* to procure a visa for Saudi Arabia, the nearest neighbor to Bahrain. The Saudis hassled anybody trying to enter their country, and quick twenty-four hour service to obtain a visa offset all of Gerald's stored up good-will with the Saudis.

"I'll be heavily in their debt," Gerald had reminded Ferrar. "I'll have to perform a few favors of my own now."

"And I owe you something, too," Ferrar had replied, then walked out of the heavily-guarded British compound with his new identity and all the necessary credentials to pass in and out of the region.

He felt the airplane bank in its descent, and a female flight attendant started dutifully reciting a passage from the Koran over the cabin speaker.

Looking out his window in the first class section of his Pakistan International Airlines flight, Ferrar was struck by how verdant the island of Bahrain looked in the hot, noonday sun. In a region made up of deserts, Bahrain seemed mostly oases, with mantles of lush date groves, agriculture using desalinated water, and abundant spring-fed vegetation. Perhaps it really was the Garden of Eden as some historians postulated.

No longer than thirty miles from north to south and ten miles from east to west, the relatively flat piece of land didn't look like the economic powerhouse that it was. Rich in oil, the nation had leveraged its wealth in the 1980s with savvy investments, education, and generous laws favoring banking institutions.

It had become the Switzerland of the Gulf, and a highly unlikely destination for Pakistani arms.

From the air, he noticed that the airport was adjacent to a container port, and a ship not unlike the one leaving Karachi thirty-six hours before was already berthed. In addition to the normal port facilities, a strange system of trolleys hanging from cables delivered bauxite minerals from a local smelter to the cargo port.

The plane descended low over the water and approached the landing strip. He could make out various military vehicles stationed at regular intervals around the perimeter of the airport.

If they were after him, it was time to collect on his debts.

He took the air phone from the armrest of his plush seat and dialed an anonymous number in London, followed by a number in Washington.

It was standard operating procedure for the CIA to use an electronic cloaking service that masked the caller and receiver's location, but he had rarely used it in his career.

Connors' groggy voice answered, "Who is this?"

"Sorry to wake you, old chap."

"Who is this?" Connors repeated, this time more suspicious.

"You know bloody well who this is."

"Okay, Ferrar. Drop the phony accent."

Ferrar turned serious, but retained the accent. "You've got to contact the Agency. Call off the bloodhounds that are after me, and I'll give you a piece of news that might end this al-Qaeda crisis."

The plane was dropping steadily, a minute before landing.

"Will you do this for me?" Ferrar asked urgently. "For our country?"

"Okay, what's the news?"

It was time to talk. "Yesterday, I watched a ship leave Karachi, Pakistan, steaming for Bahrain. It was carrying bombs from Pakistan."

"I wasn't aware that Pakistan was in the business of exporting arms."

"That's only one thing that makes this case unusual. I'm sure you've heard of the latest al-Qaeda plan."

"Yes," Connors grunted.

"Can you put two and two together?"

He heard Connors suck in his breath. It was common knowledge that Pakistan possessed a dangerous stockpile of weapons, including nuclear weapons, not to mention that China helped them build bombs and rockets.

Connors came back slowly, "Pakistan in possession of 'The Bomb' is a scary enough concept, but the specter of them shipping such weapons of mass destruction to some even less stable country or group is positively chilling."

"Try this on for size: they're shipping it to bloody al-Qaeda."

"Holy Mother of God."

"Now don't tell this to the Agency until I call you and let you know I'm free. First, I need proof that they've called off the chase. Then and only then will I contact you and you can divulge this information. I hate to do things this way, but otherwise they won't believe me."

"Where are you now?"

"I'm landing in Bahrain as we speak, and the place is surrounded by security."

"Okay, Bahrain."

"Now, call off the dogs, at once."

Checking out his window, he could make out that the vehicles surrounding the airport were Army Jeeps. Either the war against terrorism had brought all countries to a state of extremely high alert, or his anonymity had been compromised and his destination ascertained.

If the Bahrain military captured him, the CIA Station in Bahrain would be all over him at once. Not only were they going to nail him for the Tora Bora massacre, but worse, his lack of credibility being what it was, they might not buy his story of dangerous weapons leaking out of the region.

If Connors could get through to the CIA and they would drop their security blanket promptly and in some verifiable way, Ferrar would be free to trace the bomb shipment.

If Connors *couldn't* get through...

The flight attendant walked down the aisle for the final check. He could use a stiff drink.

"I beg your pardon, madam," he said. "Is Duty Free still open?"

"For our First Class passengers," she replied. "What would you like?"

"A bottle of Bombay Gin would hit the spot," he said, relieved that she could still take his order. He handed her a roll of rupees.

She smiled. "I'll have it waiting for you as you deplane."

After a dry country like Pakistan, he could use a drink into a reasonably moderate Muslim country like Bahrain.

They landed with a thud and taxied all the way to the end of the runway. There they came to a halt, spun abruptly, and headed back for the terminal building, a white outpost in the searing midday heat.

Several prop planes sat in a dusty tie-down area. Alongside the terminal, the only other aircraft in sight was refueling. It was a late-model Gulfstream V, perhaps Bahrain's presidential airplane.

Along the concrete fence surrounding the perimeter of the airport, the Jeeps began heading away in puffs of dust. When the Pakistan International Airline flight finally came to a halt, the only vehicle remaining was a loading ramp truck on the tarmac. It rolled up to the plane to help the passengers alight.

Ferrar stepped out into bright sunlight and an oppressive wave of heat. After Pakistan, he liked the heat.

He felt someone shove an object into his ribs and looked down. The flight attendant was handing him a bag with his gin in it.

"I'm so very grateful," he enunciated with his most precious British accent.

His only luggage was a canvas carryon, and his only clothes were a well-tailored blue business suit. He looked like one of the many bankers who flew in and out of Bahrain on quick stopovers to conceal their profits in offshore banks, or to collect cash from offshore investments.

His British passport read "Henry Swinden," and his embarkation card read "Hyatt Hotel." With nothing to claim, he was soon walking through a sliding glass door into the airport lobby.

He exited the relative cool of the terminal and stepped up to the taxi waiting line. There, a uniformed man carefully sized up his appearance and stature. For a moment, Ferrar wondered if the man were part of the country's tight security apparatus. Then the man turned abruptly and ordered a slick new Mercedes to pull out of the line of waiting Nissans and other Japanese imports.

"Hyatt Hotel in Manama, if you please," Ferrar told the driver in his best imitation of a British business tycoon.

He handed the attendant a tip, consisting of his remaining Pakistani rupees, and climbed into the air-conditioned cab.

The driver, a man in Arab headgear and reflective sunglasses, eased the Mercedes away from the curb.

"Turn off the air con," Ferrar requested, and rolled down his window.

December was mild and slightly wet in Bahrain, but nothing like the cold dampness of Peshawar. The breeze felt pleasant as they drove, and Ferrar relaxed even more.

Office buildings in Bahrain were clearly not like the high-rises of Dubai. They were relatively low to the ground and sedate, though trimmed with gold.

Most people seemed to live in family compounds. High above the three-story, gray walls, palm trees emerged from central courtyards.

The countryside grew more rural, and he was interested to see how relatively poor people looked on the roads. Much of the country's wealth had yet to trickle down to the man on the street.

The four-lane soon turned to a two-lane, and buildings began to peter out. Ferrar gradually realized that they must not be heading for the capital city at all.

"I didn't mean a resort," he said. "I meant downtown."

The driver nodded, and continued driving implacably. "We will get there, *inshah Allah.*"

The wire fence of a military base appeared ahead. It was flying an American flag! Ferrar remembered all at once that the U.S. military used Bahrain as a major military outpost in the Gulf.

And, the driver was slowing down.

Instantly, Ferrar threw an arm around the driver's neck and pulled back. The man gasped and clawed at the fabric ceiling of the Mercedes. His feet kicking the wheel of the car, they began to swerve off the pavement onto loose gravel.

Ferrar dragged the man fully into the back seat and pinned his arm behind his back.

"Who are you?" he shouted.

The man only howled.

As the car decelerated, Ferrar pulled open the side door and rolled the man into the rocky desert.

The car was heading straight for a line of palm trees along the side of the road. Ferrar launched himself into the front seat and landed with both hands on the steering wheel.

He spun the wheel and the door slammed shut. The treads shot out gravel, and he found himself driving on the road again, this time headed back into town.

Gingerly, he slid himself fully into the driver's seat. In the rearview mirror, he spotted a line of military Jeeps catching up rapidly, yellow lights flashing on their roofs, American flags fluttering from their hoods.

The Mercedes taxi had good pickup, and soon he had outdistanced the Jeeps. But surely they would call in reinforcements.

He had to get rid of these guys and make his way to the container port. As he approached the airport, he saw that his only option besides the airport parking lot was a service road that led around the airport, following the perimeter wall.

As he circled around on the dusty access road, he glanced through gates into the airfield. He was surprised to notice that another jet had landed. It was loading up at the cargo apron.

A truck bearing the name "Port Management, Ltd." was just departing through the gate.

At the next heavily guarded gate, he caught a glimpse of the aircraft's internal winch beginning to pull two containers into its airplane's belly. The containers were strapped with red tape!

Suddenly yellow lights appeared before him. The Jeeps had circled the airport in the opposite direction and were approaching him at full speed.

He pulled to a halt and took a closer look at the lettering on the side of the cargo plane. "Canary Islands Express."

"Canary Islands my ass," he muttered.

Connors was not getting through to Langley. The Director's office had not returned his calls all the previous day, and now had him on hold three attempts in a row.

Finally, the line picked up.

"Yeah, Connors, I know it's you," CIA Director Lester Friedman said, a certain smugness in his voice. "I'm a busy man, you know."

"And I've got something important to tell you."

"Like what?"

"Okay, here goes. I got a phone call from Ferrar less than an hour ago," Connors said, and waited for a reaction.

"I'm still listening."

"He gave me some news for you about al-Qaeda, but I can't divulge it to you until you call off the manhunt."

"We don't negotiate with terrorists. We capture them and put them behind bars."

"Hold on, Lester. Now hear me out," Connors said angrily and dropped into his desk chair to calm down. "You call your attack dogs off Ferrar and I'll tell you what al-Qaeda is up to."

"I'll have Ferrar in detention in a matter of minutes. He can explain himself to me personally."

"There are limits on how far you can go to coerce someone these days. Why, you might not get the information you need in weeks. On the other hand, if you let him go free, I'm prepared to blab the whole story to you in a heartbeat."

Friedman paused, then came back, this time sounding more serious. "So he was willing to trade information for his freedom."

"That's the size of it."

"He'll sell anybody out. There is no depth to which that man will not stoop."

"Are you interested or not?" Connors fumed.

"Okay, I'm interested."

"You call off your hit men, and Ferrar will call me once he feels he's safe. At that point, I'll give you his information."

"I can't believe I'm being blackmailed by a Congressman," Friedman said.

"I think that this information will be worth it. For our country," he added.

He hung up, sat back, and closed his eyes, a twenty-year career on the line.

Ferrar watched the row of American military Jeeps coming to a halt before him.

He stood on his brakes and skidded to a halt.

Behind him, the pursuit Jeeps pulled up cautiously.

Ferrar opened his car door and stepped onto the dry, rocky ground. The roar of turbine engines increased from the airstrip.

As he stood up, the Canary Islands Express rocketed down the runway in his direction, its black nose shimmering in the waves of heat.

A moment later, the jet with its cargo of bombs launched itself over his head and took a wide, banking turn to the north and west.

Packs of soldiers approached him from the front and rear, their rifles drawn. Ferrar turned to them and straightened his necktie.

"Halt," a voice ordered from behind the men.

The soldiers froze, their bayonets poised mere inches from Ferrar's throat.

Ferrar lifted an eyebrow and looked at the commander who stood on the step of his Jeep, a radiophone to his ear.

The man threw his phone down with disgust.

"Let him go, boys."

Stripping down for a swim at the al-Khubar beach resort in Saudi Arabia, Ferrar paused a moment to lean back on his colorful beach towel.

After the American troops had let him go in Bahrain, he decided he needed a bit more separation from the Yanks. He had taken a bus fifteen miles across the King Fahd Causeway, a bridge over the blue waters separating Bahrain from Saudi Arabia.

All the passengers were ordered by border control to climb out of the bus with all of their possessions. Standing in direct sunlight for over an hour while each passenger was thoroughly scrutinized, Ferrar had tried to decide how to hide his bottle of gin. He'd heard of foreigners sneaking into Saudi with goatskins wrapped around their ankles and alcohol concealed in shampoo bottles. In the end, he decided that the gin would serve better to divert attention away from his passport. And indeed it did.

In the end, he had surrendered the unopened bottle to the customs official, who dressed him down in Arabic, looked sternly at the bottle as if it contained an evil genie, and roughly pushed him through passport control. The flap had caught the attention of the immigration officer. He shook his head at Ferrar's ignorance, and gave only a perfunctory glance at his passport and visa and waved him through.

Ferrar pulled some suntan oil and a cell phone from his bag. He set aside the oil and first dialed Congressman Connors.

"Connors, it's me. They let me go."

"Thank God. Can I call the CIA back?"

"You bet. Tell them the news about bombs leaving Pakistan, and give them one more piece of information. The bombs are on a Canary Islands Express cargo flight from Bahrain. I don't know where the plane's bound, but I'm sure our boys in Bahrain can pick up the trail."

"What great information, Ferrar. Our nation owes you one."

"Let's hope the Agency can get to those bombs before they're turned loose on us. I have a sneaking suspicion that they might be more than your run-of-the-mill explosives."

"You think they might be…"

"That's right," Ferrar said. "Nuclear weapons." He began to smear sun protection across his bare chest.

"But isn't Pakistan supposed to be on our side in the war against terrorism? Who could make them pull such a stunt?"

"I'll tell you who. His first name is Tray and his last name rhymes with *revoltin'*."

"Lester Friedman is not going to buy that."

"Then don't tell him."

"He's scarcely gonna believe anything I tell him anyway, what with Pakistani nuclear weapons, Canary Islands, etc."

"Just call him up," Ferrar said with a smile, turning off his phone and setting it in the sand beside his sweating bottle of Evian.

Nine

THE SUN WAS setting over Université du Québec, and dinner smelled as good as usual in the cafeteria kitchen. But the cafeteria itself wouldn't be cleaned that night. Instead, the rooms housing the maintenance staff would be spotless. And nobody cleaned more tidily than a terrorist cell trying to cover its tracks.

The men circled like animals in a lair, looking for tidbits of evidence that might tip off police as to exactly who had lived below the campus cafeteria for the past two years.

The overcast sky was dark by seven p.m. as the men stood on the curb beside their suitcases. A white van pulled up, and the group boarded without a word. Within a minute, the six men were traveling south through busy evening traffic.

On the outskirts of the city, the van pulled into a shopping strip. The driver hopped out and slipped a bankcard from his wallet. At the outdoor cash machine, he punched in a PIN, and took out the full limit of three hundred Canadian dollars. Then he slipped a second card into the machine and withdrew another three hundred dollars.

He stuffed the money into his shirt pocket under his windbreaker and returned to the van.

At midnight, the van was still on the road, drifting over the gently rolling hills of southern Quebec. They passed unnoticed through many small towns, each with its snug little community, insulated by miles of farmland and protected by a long border from events in the United States.

The van's zigzag route took a generally eastern track, and soon they were passing over a bridge with a large sign that read, "Welcome to New Brunswick."

It was not yet morning in the Friendship Heights neighborhood of Washington, DC, and Congressman Connors had to get Ferrar's life-or-death information to the CIA before the Canary Island Express flight landed somewhere and offloaded the bombs.

But, he reasoned, the only way to get Director Friedman's full attention was to take the news directly to him at Langley, and to hit him with it the moment he arrived in his office.

That gave him an hour to shower, shave, and dress.

Outside, the sky was still pitch black when he sat down to a plate of bacon and eggs.

"Thanks, Sweetie," he told his wife Lucy, thanking her for the early breakfast.

She nodded across the table and continued reading the *Washington Post*. Headlines speculated about when the stock market might recover and announced scientific breakthroughs on the mouse genome. No news about an impending terrorist attack somewhere in the United States.

For a small town Okie girl, Lucy Connors had grown mighty sophisticated over the years. Flooded by the mass media, she trusted everything she read. Their daughter Melinda had suffered from the same hubris, thinking that the southern Philippines would be the perfect place to vacation and get away from it all. She had nearly lost her life to kidnappers, and so had Lucy trying to rescue her in the impenetrable Muslim-held jungles.

When the lives of the Connors family were at stake, George Ferrar had come through. Now America was on the line, and Ferrar was coming through again.

The two yellow yolks stared up at him for a long time. He had no appetite. He had work to do.

He leaned over to kiss his wife good-bye, and she looked up with surprise.

Without explanation, he jogged out into the cold, hopped in his car, nursed its engine to life, switched on the headlights, and peeled rubber heading off for Chain Bridge and Langley.

The Director would hear it straight from his mouth.

Lester Friedman paced angrily up and down the length of his oak-paneled Langley office. He never should have trusted Congressman Connors. Every fiber of his being told him that he should have apprehended Ferrar. But the traitorous weasel got away, and for the past seven hours, Lester had nothing to show for it.

If Connors didn't come up with some solid piece of intelligence, Lester knew that his ass was on the line.

"It'll all work out, sir," Charles White, his aide, tried to comfort him.

"Like hell it will. I'll spend the next twenty years of my life shoveling shit in San Quentin for letting our only shred of evidence on this attack slip through my fingers."

"Congressman Connors has a lot to lose, too."

"Yeah, but he doesn't run the goddamned CIA."

Just then his receptionist stepped into the room. "Congressman Connors is here to see you."

"Let him in, for God's sake."

Connors walked in and sensed the mood in the room. Apparently thinking better of offering a handshake, he took a seat opposite Lester's desk.

"Thanks for coming in personally," Lester said, trying to contain his impatience and his annoyance at himself. "Now what's the information?"

"First of all, thanks for not taking Ferrar into custody. I think we have a workable relationship with him now."

"I did my bit, now you do yours," Lester snapped.

Connors nodded. "There are Pakistani bombs, possibly nuclear weapons, leaving Bahrain via an air cargo service called Canary Islands Express, on its way to do al-Qaeda's bidding."

"What are you talking about? Pakistan wouldn't contribute any kind of weapons to the terrorists. They've gone out on a limb to take our side."

"That's the word from Ferrar."

"Then it's a diversion, a smoke screen. I'm going to get that son-of-a-bitch if it kills me."

"Lester, get hold of yourself," Connors admonished. "You've lost all objectivity. I'm not so sure you're focusing on the real problem at hand."

"Ferrar and Ferrar alone will lead us to the killers," Lester said. "And I was wrong to let you persuade me otherwise and let him slip through my fingers."

"I'm sorry you don't believe him."

"Believe him? I've got all my men and the entire Pakistani ISI behind this investigation trying to track down what the hell Beaver Tail is and what al-Qaeda can possibly pull off by December 11. How in the world could Ferrar possibly come up with more solid intelligence than all these people put together? He's in hiding, for God's sake. He's merely trying to save his own skin. The only reason he wants to contact us is to shake us off his trail."

"Well, at least look into this Canary Islands Express that's flying around with Pakistani-made bombs."

"*You* want to send me on a wild goose chase, too? What do the Canary Islands have to do with anything?"

"Maybe you don't want to hear how he came by this valuable piece of information that could save our nation," Connors said, clearly trying to dig under his skin.

"I don't care to hear any of his disinformation. You can take it with you out of this office."

Connors stood up, livid, but kept his voice under control. "He said that your son is still alive…"

Lester smashed his fist onto his desk. "Will he stop at nothing?"

"…and that Tray is behind the bomb shipment."

"You may leave this building at once."

"I'm sorry to be the one to tell you this," Connors said, shaking his head. "But I thought you would be relieved."

Then he slowly dragged himself out of the office.

Lester glared at his aide.

"Nuclear weapons from Pakistan? What kind of fool does he think I am?"

Connors reached the Rayburn House Office Building by mid-morning, went straight to his office, and closed the door. From his pocket, he pulled out Ferrar's untraceable international mobile phone number.

"Yes?" a voice answered on the other end of the line. Again it was that annoying British accent.

"It's me," Connors said. "He didn't buy it."

There was a long pause. "Ratchet it up a notch. Call the Pentagon, or the President." Ferrar had dropped his phony accent and sounded troubled.

"Ferrar, you don't get it. This whole thing is looking crazier by the minute. I'm afraid your lead is going nowhere."

"Mr. Congressman, there's a plane flying around up there with possible nuclear weapons on board. Are you gonna just stand by and watch it slam into the United States?"

"I'm sorry," Connors said. "I've done all I can."

He set the phone down gently.

Perhaps Friedman was right.

Ten

AFTER THEIR long night on the road, the six custodians in their white van turned into a gravel parking lot. An illuminated sign over the low structure read "Rigby Motel."

The driver pulled up beside a short, flatbed truck and came to a halt. The truck carried two metal cargo containers, each wrapped in red tape.

He shut off his engine, popped his door open, and slid off his seat. He shook the kinks out of his legs and confidently approached Room Number 11.

The door opened before he reached it, and he walked straight in, disappearing for a moment into the darkness.

A minute later, he reemerged jingling a key between his fingers. He walked along the front of the building and unlocked the door to Room Number 12. The light turned on inside as he checked it out.

Then he returned to the doorway and motioned for the others to follow.

The van's door slid open, and the five young, dark-haired men walked silently across the short distance into the room.

In al-Khubar, Saudi Arabia, the red disk of a setting sun bathed the dry landscape around Ferrar's hotel in a pink glow. He sat on his balcony sipping from a bottle of warm Evian and watching a flock of cranes migrate south.

Winter in Saudi Arabia was not harsh. Maybe the birds knew something that he didn't.

It was time to call in reinforcements.

He slid the balcony door open and stepped into the air-conditioned cool of his room. He picked up the room phone and placed an international call through the anonymous number in London.

The call finally passed through to Virginia.

"Central Intelligence Agency, may I help you?" an operator answered. Ferrar wondered if she were more of an operative than an operator.

"Get me Deke Houston, please."

"One moment. I'll connect you with his home number."

A moment later, Deke's sleepy voice answered. "Deke, here."

"Okay, Deke, old buddy, it's time to rise and shine. This is George Ferrar."

"Ferrar? Is this some kind of joke?"

"Believe it or not, you're our lucky winner tonight on 'Dialing for Desperados.'"

Deke had spent some good years in Lebanon and Cyprus. Then, after his marriage hit the rocks in Caracas, he had plummeted into the trenches of Virginia to live out the rest of his tattered career and shattered life. Like many disillusioned case officers hanging around the halls at Langley, Deke had only one goal in mind: to avoid down-sizing or getting canned before he reached the minimum retirement age when he could take the money and run.

"Still monitoring the UN embargo on Iraq?" Ferrar asked.

He had last operated with Deke during the Gulf War. At the outbreak of that conflict, Deke was still in the hot seat as a specialist in the regional office for the Iran-Iraq War. It didn't help Deke's career much when the horse America was backing in the long-term, bloody conflict suddenly bucked on the West and charged into Kuwait. It left the desk jockeys with their petards way down.

Nevertheless, George knew him for what he was. A damn fine mind, capable of making sense out of a royally screwed-up world. Deke was a kindred spirit, and thus a friend.

"Naw, I'm burning classified documents from our economic blockade of Pakistan right now," Deke replied.

"I wouldn't be so confident about Pakistan."

"I hear you're doing even worse than I am. Word has it you've gone off the reservation, if not off the deep end."

"Actually, I'm trying to undo an al-Qaeda plot."

"Ah-ha."

He seemed to have Deke's attention. "In fact, my plate's rather full, and I'd like to dish some of the small potatoes off to you."

"Exactly what are you trying to accomplish?"

"First, I need to intercept a weapons shipment, possibly nuclear bombs, that al-Qaeda is smuggling into the United States."

"A noble and worthy cause."

"And second, I'm trying to track down Tray Bolton and figure out where these weapons are headed."

"So you're chasing ghosts now. Or haven't you heard? You killed the man."

"Deke, listen. Bolton's still alive, but he's turned. He's in deep with the Pakistani ISI, shipping bombs out of Karachi. I need you to intercept those bombs."

"Why not alert the Director?"

"I tried that. But nobody seems to believe me these days. In a way, I can see why. Maybe once I elude all of our own hit men, I can try to clear my name. But that's a long way down the road right now. In fact, tracking down Bolton and eliminating him would go a long way toward solving all my problems."

"If Bolton's alive, you don't have to kill him, you know. Sounds like if you find him, that's proof enough of your innocence."

"I'm not really looking for revenge," Ferrar said. "I have seen him alive, and I have reason to believe that he's up to something big and bad."

"So what did you have in mind for me?"

"How'd you like to intercept the bombs? While you're at it, you might scout out the rest of Maine on a pre-retirement mission."

"That's where they'll be hitting our shores?"

"Exactly. It's a logical gateway to enter the States. Lots of islands and boat traffic. They've got two container loads of bombs headed for Beaver Tail Island, a small islet off of Bar Harbor. I'm betting that there's a bomb or two onboard that shipment."

"So you want me to follow a tip from a totally debunked ex-spy."

"I know my credibility is shot to hell. Let's call it an anonymous tip."

"Who would ever send me on official travel based on an anonymous tip?"

"Just ask for some time off. You've got tons of vacation leave, I'm sure. I've got a cottage on Beaver Tail. You can use it. Just ask a local to get you to the island. The cottage is the smaller of two family cottages there. You can't miss it."

"I suppose I could use a little diversion," Dele conceded. "How do I get into this cottage of yours? You got a key under the doormat?"

"Hey Deke. It's Maine. We don't use keys." Then on a more serious note, he said, "Can you bring someone for backup?"

"Hey, Ferrar, we all know *you're* out of your mind. Do you want everyone to think *I'm* nuts, too?"

"Okay. Have a nice vacation. I'll try and meet you there."

Eleven

TRAY BOLTON stepped out of his motel room, a leather briefcase swinging from one hand. Daylight was breaking slowly over the lonely stretch of road outside Fredericton, New Brunswick. He lingered a moment to study the layers of roiling clouds. His flannel shirt and denim jeans might not be enough for the cold. He shivered slightly and headed for the next motel room. There, he gave two short raps on the door.

The door flew open, and the six occupants filed out, splitting into two groups. Two jumped in the white van, and the other four slipped into the cab of the truck.

He hiked himself up into the driver's seat of the truck and gunned the engine to life.

He put the truck in gear and began to lead the small caravan out of the motel parking lot. In his rear-view mirror, he checked that the two steel containers were still well secured to his trailer.

At a turn-off before the capital city of Saint John, the van split off and sped to the west. Ahead of Bolton, the Atlantic Ocean lay seething on the horizon.

He headed the truck on a northeastern route toward Sussex.

Within half an hour, he arrived at a ferry landing. It was perfect. Just as the published timetable had read, the double-decker car ferry was waiting there, ready to depart on schedule.

"Hey there, Skip," he called crisply, hailing the car ferry operator, who was refueling his forlorn-looking ship.

Bolton had chosen the departure point well. They were at a wharf east of Saint John, and the van had entered a terminal due west of the port city.

The twin steel boxes, each four feet tall by eight feet wide, were typical half-height containers. Their short length of ten feet indicated European or military origins, the smallest of their kind among intermodal

65

containers. Due to their small size, they fit easily on airplanes and stacked nicely on highway trailers and rail cars. And they just barely fit into the lower deck of the coastal ferries used in the Maritime Provinces.

While he waited for the ferry to lower its loading ramp, he double-checked the registration number of the first container, the more important one. The number LFDU24425436 correctly identified the owner as a Dutch shipping firm, but falsely identified the contents as metal pipes. In fact, inside was a ten-megaton nuclear device from Pakistan.

The second container, ending with the number 47, denoted the same owner and type of contents. In fact, it did contain metal pipes, of a weight equal to that of the bomb.

The alphabetic part of the number satisfied the AAR rolling stock registration requirements, the U meaning "container." He smiled with satisfaction. All together, the containers fit nicely into the Official Intermodal Equipment Register databank. They were legit.

"Pushing off soon?" he asked as he studied the captain, a smartly dressed young man in a merchant marine uniform.

The captain hauled the fuel line off the deck and hung it on the diesel pump. "Soon as you get loaded."

"Looks like I'm your only customer today."

"Going to Halifax?"

Bolton nodded. They might start out for Nova Scotia, but he had another destination in mind.

He backed up the flatbed trailer onto the lower deck. Then he jumped out and disconnected the electrical plugs attached to the cab. Behind him, the four men jumped from the cab and cranked down a set of legs to stabilize the trailer. As a final precaution, they kicked wooden blocks around the tires.

"The bay's getting rough out there," the captain warned, indicating the waves. "There's a Category Five hurricane moving up the Atlantic Seaboard. Make sure you secure her tight."

Bolton drove the cab out of the ferry and parked it on a dirt shoulder of the road that led to the landing.

"Last call for Halifax," a voice said over the Canadian ferry company's loudspeaker.

There were no other vehicles or passengers waiting to board that morning. Bolton swung his briefcase ahead of him and stepped onboard.

"All set?" the captain asked from the ramp.

"Ready," Bolton replied with a friendly grin.

He climbed a set of internal steps to the upper deck. There he found his men waiting indoors in a passenger cabin located just behind the wheelhouse.

He stood and faced them. "I want two of you below deck with the trailer at all times."

The ringleader of the group signaled for two men to go down and take up positions.

"Okay, here we go," the captain muttered as he walked past. "I want to beat the storm. You can pay your fares once we're underway." He entered the wheelhouse and pulled on the air horn. At the stern, the ship's only deckhand hauled in the loading ramp. Then Bolton felt the engine surge to life.

Deke Houston tried to relax as he wandered through the terminal at Maine's Portland International Jetport. It had been a rough flight from DC, with the pilot battling turbulence the whole way.

Windy and gray, Portland had the added bonus of an early-December cold snap. He walked along examining displays of fur-lined boots and down-filled parkas.

He glanced at his extra-large Redskins windbreaker and baggy jeans. It was a lot of clothes for a guy who had lived his entire adult life near the equator. But not enough for Maine.

As he passed under surveillance cameras mounted around the concourse, he felt an additional chill run down his spine. He was walking through the same terminal that Mohammed Atta, the mastermind behind the terrorist attack on New York and Washington, had taken just three short months before.

At the rental car desk, he stopped to pick up the key for the car he had reserved. The young woman behind the desk seemed cheerful and trusting enough, and barely needed to glance at his driver's license.

"Have a nice trip, Mr. Houston," she said with a friendly smile, and handed him the keys and a map.

He stepped outside into the blustery wind, and knew for sure that he wasn't adequately dressed, particularly for a week on an isolated island off the coast. He jogged alongside the terminal building until he reached a blue sedan that he was renting.

Circling out of the airport and onto Highway 95 heading northeast, he saw empty bird and squirrels' nests in barren tree branches. Oak, elm, and maple leaves lay flat on rain-soaked lawns that were marked off by white picket fences.

He breezed northward passing the outlet town that had sprung up around L.L. Bean.

L.L. Bean! Just what he was looking for.

He spun into the nearest parking lot, and trotted to the famous clothing store, now a modern complex with entire wings devoted to different apparel.

In a quiet, carpeted corner, he found a section lined with racks of winter jackets.

Too much choice could pose a problem and slow him down.

He walked up to a saleswoman and pulled her aside.

"I'm sorry, ma'am, but I've got five minutes in this town before I have to head out, and I need a jacket for this kind of weather. Can you grab me one, any color, and I'll just be on my way."

Two minutes later, he was walking out of the multi-level store wearing a maroon ski jacket. Not exactly his style, but a definite improvement against the weather.

The highway rose and fell over gentle hills, flirting with the shoreline, but never touching it. He passed through small towns, one with a tiny college and another with a state penitentiary that would be an historical landmark in any other part of the country.

On his way, he felt himself returning to a period of history when his colonial forefathers might have sat on the doorsteps of their houses smoking pipes before returning to the woods to fight the French and Indian War.

Maine was not a bad retirement option. Cheap real estate. Then he turned up his collar and shivered.

Following the map given him by the car rental clerk, he turned south and east at Ellsworth and found himself driving over a low bridge onto a large island. After some hills and forests, a small airport, and a few hotels, he reached the clapboard, bric-a-brac, tourist haven of Bar Harbor.

He parked near the marina beside a seafood restaurant. Seafood. That would do just about then.

When he opened his car door, in wafted the buttery aroma of steamed lobster and clams. His stomach gave a loud gurgle.

He wadded up the bag of salty bits and pieces of potato chips that was on his lap and tossed it on the floor of the car.

He stepped outside and studied the restaurant. It was called "The Trap," a simple enough name, and not too threatening. A quick check of his watch indicated that he had several hours before nightfall.

Looking the car seemed needless given the quiet, isolated location, but considering the stash of weapons inside his luggage, it might be prudent for the sake of public safety.

He pressed the "Lock" button on the keychain, the car honked loudly and flashed its headlights, and then was locked.

Now, for a good meal.

Heavy rain washed against the large windows of London's Heathrow Airport as Ferrar, disguised as Mr. Henry Swinden, stepped off a long flight from Riyadh.

Twilight barely illuminated the corners of the terminal. Using his British passport obtained in Karachi, he briskly checked through the EU citizen line.

Immediately upon passing through customs, he headed for a bank of telephones.

The most remote booth was available. He paused for a moment looking at the keypad. What was that number in California? The numbers came back to him like a distant tune, and he dialed it.

The familiar clicking of telephones connecting internationally made his heart skip a beat. He tried to swallow away the dryness in this throat.

He had dialed Bonnie Taylor's number. A number that he had not allowed himself to call for years, out of respect for Tray and fear of his own emotional attachment to that girl from Maine, that can-do gal who was now a cutter commander.

But he had to put aside his past fears. He needed news on Tray Bolton.

Lightning streaked from the sky as the telephone rang at the other end. There was no immediate answer.

Bonnie might be on duty.

It rang a couple more times with no pick-up.

She might even have been reassigned out of the area. When had they last communicated? Five years ago? Ten?

Would she still jokingly call him her Lancelot? Their college conversations had been full of simple talk of his role as knight errant ruining the preordained union of King Arthur and Gwenevere, of a renewed age of chivalry, of life's big deceits, of grand schemes for living life backwards, of questing at windmills.

How juvenile it all seemed in retrospect. In their minds, they were living life large. In reality, they were making out behind Tray's back.

Then, when she left him and Tray for good, the opposite became true. His thoughts had become grounded in reality while he took on larger responsibilities.

More rings.

He began to outline his next step. If she didn't answer, he could call the U.S. Coast Guard and ask for her work number.

Then suddenly, unexpectedly, the phone picked up. He heard a few clicks, then a recorded voice came on the line. "You have reached my iMac. Kindly leave a message."

Through a nearby rumble of thunder, he strained to hear the voice. As tinny as it sounded over the long distance connection, it was full of life, full of richness. Full of Bonnie Taylor.

He hung up without leaving a message.

"British Airways Flight 609 to Montreal is now boarding," the PA intoned.

They were announcing his flight.

Deke Houston entered The Trap in Bar Harbor. After his eyes adjusted to the dim lighting, he saw the reason for the restaurant's name.

Lobster pots and traps hung from all four walls. And he was the only customer caught inside.

Self-consciously, he eased himself into a booth and waited.

Shortly, a waitress in her early forties tied an apron around her slim waist and approached him with a quirky smile.

"What ah you hah-ving today?" she asked, pulling a pencil from her black, pinned-up hair.

"I'm hungry. You serving dinner yet?" he asked.

"Shu-a," she said, indicating the menu on the table.

"I take it you recommend the lobster?"

"Boiled. The red-a the bet-a," she said with another funny smile.

"How about your best plate?"

"Coming right up," she said. "Can I get you a drink first?"

He looked at his coaster. "Bar Harbor Blueberry Ale?"

She shook her head. "I wouldn't recommend it. Try the amb-a."

"I'll try the amber."

She took away the menu and left for the kitchen.

He let out a low whistle. Where had she been all his life?

They sure had the restaurant-ordering banter down pat. It was almost like shorthand, like speaking in code.

A minute later, she dropped off a mug of foaming beer.

He thought he would grab her attention. "This town seems a bit sleepy this time of year."

"Thah-t's the way I like it," she said, giving him a warm, ironic smile. Her even row of teeth made her look a good deal younger than she probably was. "Whe-a ah you from?"

"DC."

She nodded knowingly.

"Know anybody from DC?" he asked.

She slid onto the bench across from him, a conspiratorial look on her face.

"Do I ev-a."

Twelve

HERRING GULLS winged toward land as Tray Bolton's ferry headed into the swells of the Bay of Fundy between New Brunswick and Nova Scotia.

As soon as they were clear of other boat traffic, Bolton signaled the ringleader, and the two men silently advanced toward the captain's wheelhouse, the small room in front of the snug passenger compartment.

The captain kept a firm eye on the horizon as Bolton approached and raised a thick hand. With one swift blow to the young man's neck, he crushed several vertebrae, severing the spine. It was a clean and sudden death.

Bolton kicked the body out of the wheelhouse and took the helm.

Wordlessly, the al-Qaeda ringleader hauled the body over to the railing and dumped it into the foaming sea. Then he took up a position just outside the wheelhouse. The deckhand was still below, but when he appeared, he would be dealt a similar fate.

Bolton took one look at a nautical map of the area and swept it off the table. He didn't need to know the islands of the Canadian Maritimes. He set his compass due south, and headed out to open sea.

Within a few minutes, the mobile phone attached to his belt began to ring.

That would be the other part of the al-Qaeda cell.

"So who do you know down there in DC?" Deke Houston asked The Trap's waitress, with whom he was rapidly becoming on intimate terms. So intimate, in fact, that he wondered if he had unwittingly stumbled into one of Ferrar's plants.

"Two guys, actually."

"Two?" He looked around the room cautiously.

"One's name is Bolton, and the oth-a's name is Ferr-a."

Deke put a finger to his lips. "You want to keep it down?"

71

"Naw, why?" she said, looking about the empty place. "They were two football play-as in my high school class. Two very choice men. Both competed at everything, Bolton like it meant life and death, and Ferr-a because he couldn't let go of a challenge."

Deke took a sip of beer and decided that she was only a harmless gossip. "Let me tell you," he said, warming up to the topic. "They're still at it."

"Grown men," she said, shaking her head.

"Grown up problems, too."

The woman sighed. "I he-a about them from time to time. Neith-a comes back anymo-a, although their families show up at The Trap every summ-a. I he-a things about those two."

"Most of it's true, I'm sure," he said. "You wouldn't happen to know the name of Ferrar's place, would you?"

"He's got a family cottage called 'Boat House,' on Beav-a Tail Island. It's the same island whe-a Tray's family has a cottage, which is called 'Yacht House.'"

"Do I sense some competition there?"

The cook stuck his head out the kitchen door and whistled for her.

"I'll get your dinn-a," the waitress said.

By the time he had finished his dinner, he had gleaned valuable intelligence. The only approach to Ferrar and Bolton's island was by a tiny isthmus that was covered by water every high tide and was impassable during storms. In that weather, he would have to charter a boat to get there.

He offered to buy the waitress a beer, but she refused. "I'll take a rain check next time you-a back in town," she said with a grin.

He paid the bill and dropped an extra twenty on the table. Then he stuffed himself into his ski jacket, and blew her a kiss from the door.

He'd be back.

Deke figured that he was the only person in the entire town of Bar Harbor that time of year that was not a resident.

Nor was he the typical tourist. Though officially on vacation, he was packing a suitcase full of large and small firearms.

Looking around, he could tell that Bar Harbor had far more pastoral attractions than hunting down international criminals.

Summertime vacationers to the island's Acadia National Park could ride the numerous bike trails, visit the lighthouses, and bake on the beaches. But those hordes had long since packed up their gear and headed back to Boston and other points south.

Now the cross-country skiing crowd would be waiting in their city condos for the first snow to fall.

And it looked like that might happen soon.

On the deserted streets and in the warmly lit tourist shops that lined Main Street, all he saw were locals visiting with each other and hurrying against the strong offshore wind.

He walked quickly along the marina looking for a boat to charter to Beaver Tail Island.

One young man, who seemed to be a recent high school graduate, was manning the fuel pump on the dock.

"Chart-a a boat, huh?" the boy responded to Deke's query. He looked at the long rows of empty berths. "Won't find anybody to do that this time of ye-a."

To have come so far… Then he spotted a fishing trawler pulling into port.

"How about that boat?"

"If you-a nice about it, he might take you. But the-a's no hotel on Beav-a Tail. Whe-a will you stay?"

"I've got a place," Deke said.

The trawler pulled up directly to the pump, and the boy hopped nimbly onto the deck to access the fuel cap.

A gray-haired old captain emerged from the wheelhouse, his mackintosh glistening wet. "A new storm's blowing in," he announced to the boy. "Bett-a warn people away."

The boy indicated Deke. "This man wants to go to Beav-a Tail. Can you give him a lift?"

The captain studied Deke, who stuck out his hand to shake. The captain shook it grimly.

"I don't recommend going the-a," he said. "With this storm brewing, you'd be strahn-ded the-a a good three days."

"I'll take the risk," Deke said. "Of course, I'd pay you for your trouble."

The captain shook it off. "I'm going to take a leak and grab a coffee. I'll meet you back he-a in hahf an hou-a."

"Thanks," Deke said with a grin.

As the captain trudged down the wharf, Deke shouted up to the boy, "I'll pay for the gas."

With three days on an island, he would need to stock up on food.

He found a large grocery store a few blocks into town. The aisles were empty of people, but the shelves were well stocked. He picked out some bread, coffee, juice, summer sausage, Oreos, and various fruits and vegetables.

He had no idea what to expect in the way of a stove or cookware at Ferrar's family cottage, so he mostly bought ready-to-eat food.

A half hour went by quickly, and the captain was already waiting for him in the wheelhouse. He looked skeptically at Deke's suitcase and two grocery bags. "Three days *at least*," he repeated with emphasis.

"I know," Deke said. He paid the boy for the fuel and stepped aboard.

The boy helped them cast off, and Deke found himself staggering to keep his balance on the rolling deck.

He perched on a fishy-smelling toolbox and stowed the bags under a canvas flap over the engine.

The trawler's bow rose out of the cold, clear water and soon they were heading out of the harbor. The rollers at sea were considerably larger. Would al-Qaeda risk a voyage from Canada on such a day?

He reached for his jacket pocket and pulled out his mobile phone. Even if it were ringing, he couldn't hear it above the roaring surf.

The phone's LCD panel told him that he had no unanswered calls.

Settling back, he determined to try and memorize the littoral topography.

In the mist, he made out bluffs on the shoreline. The boat skirted several small islands just off the big island, Mt. Desert Island. They were rocky outcroppings covered with dense forests of pine and deciduous trees, currently barren of leaves.

By the time they passed the fourth such island, he realized that no natural features could help him distinguish one island from the next.

He rose warily to his feet and made his way against a strong gust into the wheelhouse. "How do you remember which island is which?" he asked the captain.

The man squinted through the window. "You want Beav-a Tail? That's Beav-a Tail."

Deke followed the captain's gaze through the raindrop-splattered windscreen. Sure enough, ahead of them rose the large, pine-covered back of a beaver, complete with a snout facing out to sea and a long, rounded tail extending, wave-swept, toward the coastline.

"You mean I could have walked out there?" Deke asked.

"It's low tide now. But by the time you got the-a, the tide would cov-a it up. You'd be waiting in the rain for some six hou-as before you could get onto it."

"I get your point," Deke said.

The surrounding coastline was rocky, uninhabited forest several miles from the nearest dwelling. Bar Harbor was nowhere in sight.

It was the perfect place to infiltrate the United States of America.

Tray Bolton let his hand slide off the helm long enough to grab the mobile phone ringing on his belt.

"Yes?" he answered, his voice deep and resonant.

"We've acquired our ferry, sir," came the accented response from the white van.

"Good," Bolton said, allowing himself a smile. He had seized his own ferry as well. "Head her south into American waters."

"These are rough seas today," the voice complained.

"So much the better for us."

He clicked the phone off. His timing had been perfect so far. The other ferry's encroachment would alert the U.S. Coast Guard before his ship did. With luck, he and the bomb could pass undetected through the tight security net thrown around America.

In any event, he would soon be entering busy shipping lanes where Coast Guard patrols had no chance of stopping and inspecting every vessel that passed into their waters.

"Hey, what's–?" a startled voice said from just outside the wheelhouse.

Bolton heard the smack of a fist on skin, then a body thumping against a wall and dropping to the deck.

Out of the corner of his eye, he caught his compatriot drawing a pistol, and blasting away half the deckhand's head.

Messy, but it would have to do.

He noted with approval that the body fell into the sea before too much blood had spurted onto the deck. Maybe a shark would smell the blood and devour the corpse before it washed ashore.

He liked to cover his tracks.

The United States Coast Guard cutter *Reliant* was patrolling the northern edge of America's territorial waters off Maine when a strained voice crackled over the emergency frequency.

"Mayday. Mayday," the voice said with a heavy accent. "This is the *Harry Bassett*, NB2403. Heavy seas are swamping our ship. Need assistance urgently."

Commander Doug Fuller swiveled in his dark blue windbreaker and visored cap to look at his radioman. "Coordinates?"

The radioman, also in winter dress blues, leaned over his microphone and spoke in a matter-of-fact voice. "*Harry Bassett*, this is U.S. Coast Guard *Reliant*. Please state your coordinates."

The voice came back immediately with a precise location.

Commander Fuller calculated quickly. "Sounds like she's in American waters." He turned to his quartermaster, a chief petty officer, at the helm. "How soon before we reach them?"

The quartermaster checked his map. "Fifteen minutes, sir."

Fuller turned to his radioman. "And what kind of ship is she?" The call letters told him that the ship was from New Brunswick, but he had never heard the name *Harry Bassett* before.

The radioman clicked on his microphone, "*Harry Bassett*, please describe your kind of vessel."

The voice came back at once. "Twenty-ton car ferry. Two hundred feet long."

Fuller frowned. The Canadian car ferry had drifted far off course. But his cutter could handle the incident without backup, not that there were any other cutters available in that Coast Guard District. And the situation didn't warrant his other option, a helicopter search and rescue squad.

The Coast Guard was being stretched thin, even with the reservist and auxiliary troops fully mobilized. The service was part of the Department of Transportation during peacetime, but due to the recent terrorist attacks, it was on wartime footing and he reported to the Department of Defense. Thank God this sounded like a routine shipping incident and he wouldn't have to call on the Navy.

"Tell 'em to hang on. We'll be there in fifteen minutes."

He trained his eyes on the heaving bow of his fine patrol and rescue boat. Waves crashed against her hull, masking the dull roar of her twin engines at full power. It would not be an easy rescue.

Just as his quartermaster predicted, within fifteen minutes they reached the crippled ship. But, what a strange sight. Sure, the *Harry Bassett* sat floating like a cork in the water, but the heavy seas certainly weren't "swamping the ship" as her crewman had reported on the radio. Perhaps her engine was broken, but she certainly wasn't taking on water or even listing.

"Be on your guard, men," Fuller shouted over his intercom. "Something seems wrong with this picture."

On the top deck of the *Harry Bassett*, two men dressed as passengers with knit winter caps waved their arms frantically.

Fuller stepped into the cold, salty spray and lifted a bullhorn to his lips.

"State your problem."

There seemed to be no other passengers onboard, no vehicles, and no captain or crew. Aside from the two nuts running about on deck flailing their arms, the *Harry Bassett* was a ghost ship.

The two men seemed unable to hear or interpret his words, and they had already left the wheelhouse, so he had no chance of reaching them by radio.

"Okay," he said decisively. "We'll have to send out the motor surf boat. But I want our men fully armed."

The designated boarding team consisted of a petty officer second class and a seaman first class. Highly trained and experienced in drug interdiction and stopping illegal migrants on the high seas, the two men had seen their fair share of hostile action all around U.S. territorial waters.

They donned cold weather caps, bulletproof Kevlar vests, and fifteen-pound weapons belts, and began to insert rounds into their rifles and handguns.

Clad in their dark blue winter uniforms and body armor, they clambered down into a buoyant speedboat that had been lowered over the side, and started the powerful motor.

As the team approached the *Harry Bassett*, the crazies disappeared below deck.

"I want your rifles ready," he murmured to his crew as he eyed the silent ship.

An expert marksman, the quartermaster took up a sniper's rifle and trained it on the ferry bobbing just twenty yards off the *Reliant's* port bow.

Fuller tipped his cap back and raised a pair of high-powered binoculars. "Do you see anybody?" he asked, studying the dark ship.

"Nobody now," the quartermaster said, peering through his sniper scope.

"Strange. Very strange. It's like some sort of decoy."

The two-man boarding team tied up to the *Harry Bassett* and cautiously climbed aboard. Weapons drawn, they crouched low to the afterdeck and approached the wheelhouse. Not finding anyone there, they slipped into the passenger cabin, their shadowy forms disappearing from view.

Fuller's knees nearly buckling under the heavy rollers, he strained to peer into the gloom of the unlit ship.

Suddenly, a gunshot rang from the *Harry Bassett*. Then a second report.

That was all. No damage to the *Reliant*. No further firing. No activity above or below deck.

He dropped to one knee behind his bulwark and picked up his bullhorn. "Heave to and prepare to be boarded. We are taking command of your vessel."

Five minutes passed, and no response.

The boarding team might have been shot, and there wasn't a damn thing he could think of to breach the impasse.

"Should we sink the ship?" the quartermaster asked, setting down his rifle and reaching for a shoulder-mount rocket launcher.

"No. Put that away. I don't want to sink her, but I don't feel like boarding her either. I don't want to resort to our rigid inflatable boat."

The quartermaster nodded. That would be in as much peril as the first boat.

"We've got to draw up to her and board her directly," Fuller said. "I'll take the helm."

He rushed up into the bridge and announced over the cutter's internal intercom, "We're going to approach and board the *Harry Bassett*. Prepare to tie her fast."

Below his window, two of his seamen in orange U.S. COAST GUARD life vests crouched with heaving lines, ready to tie the ships fast once he drew near.

He eased the throttle forward and guided the *Reliant* closer, wave by wave, then yard by yard.

Suddenly a rogue wave hit from astern. The two ships pitched up on their prows.

"Hold on," he screamed down at his men. The entire world seemed tipped up on end. The *Reliant* would ram the *Bassett*.

Peering straight down at the other ship's quarterdeck, he wanted to steer his cutter clear. But with his rudder high in the air, the ship was subject only to the control of gravity.

Then the prow of his cutter slashed down, glancing off the *Bassett's* stern. The impact threw him forward, his ribs bashing against the helm. Gasping to regain his breath, he watched an orange and blue ball of seamen sprawling down the deck toward the bow.

He had no time to take a second breath. On the next wave, the two ships heaved upward again. Outlined against the sky, the *Bassett* had sustained a sizeable gash in her stern. Aside from some mangled chrome work, the *Reliant's* bow seemed relatively intact.

Their chance had come.

"Board her now," he cried into the intercom, and cut back on the throttle. He pulled his cap down low over his eyes and whipped out an automatic pistol. Then, clutching his sore ribs his gun hand, he climbed down from the bridge.

Two seamen managed to snare the *Bassett* by her lifeboat davits and drew her close. Fuller vaulted over his gunwale onto the eerily quiet *Bassett*. His quartermaster and radioman followed close behind with weapons drawn.

He crossed the open deck and flattened himself against the wheel-house, then peered inside it.

A uniformed skipper lay dead, his head blown off by a single shot.

"Jesus," Fuller muttered, letting out his breath. From the looks of the dark, thick pool of blood, the skipper wasn't killed by one of the recent shots.

"Look here," the quartermaster shouted. He was nudging another body with his rifle.

Fuller gasped. It was a deckhand tied to a post in the passenger cabin. The poor victim seemed to have been bound and deliberately mutilated by a sharp blade before his throat was slit.

"Sadists," he muttered.

He and his men crept farther back into the passenger area. There, behind a row of benches, he found the bodies of his two servicemen, their faces ripped off by bullets to reveal a gory view of their facial bones.

He tried to choke back his revulsion and focus on the remaining members of his crew. He had been drawn as far into the *Bassett* as he could go. Now he was leaving his own ship vulnerable.

"Back to the *Reliant*," he whispered hoarsely.

His two compatriots scrambled out of the enclosed passenger area and headed for the stern where the *Reliant* was tied up to the *Bassett*.

Behind the wheelhouse, they found the two assailants attempting to release the slipknots that held the two ships fast.

There was no resistance from his crew still aboard the *Reliant*. Then he saw why. A pistol with a smoking silencer lay by one of the terrorist's feet, and the crumpled forms of two coast guardsmen slid limply down the *Bassett's* slanting deck. He had lost two more men.

"Freeze right there," he shouted, crouching with a quick, sweeping motion of his automatic pistol.

The men ceased their feverish work on the ropes, straightened upright, and turned around to face him.

Their wide-open eyes were white against the dark of their skin, and their lips curled back in spontaneous grins.

Fuller was incredulous. Terrorists?

Maybe his crew had been part of some training exercise, an unannounced preparedness drill.

His quartermaster and radioman were fanning out behind him.

"Should we shoot these bastards?" the quartermaster asked.

With the lurch of another powerful wave hitting them broadside, the dead skipper's hand rolled across his boot, like a child stroking a small pet.

"No. Check it out below," he said coolly to his men, while keeping the two assassins in full view.

His men disappeared below deck.

Now was he chance. He could put an end to these bastards' reign of terror. Put them in a court room and the terror would linger in the news for months. Kill them, and nobody would suspect he killed them in cold blood. No board of inquiry. No recriminations.

And no regrets.

But they probably had a bigger story to tell. They were worth more alive than dead.

"One false move," he said, vowing to blow their heads off at the slightest provocation.

A moment later, his men came back.

"All clear below deck," the quartermaster reported. "But there's a complete weapons arsenal in a white van."

"What kind of weapons?" he demanded.

"Mostly submachine guns and rounds of ammunition, sir."

Yes, there was as bigger story.

"Well, we won't be needing your guns any longer, will we, boys?" he said to his two captives. "All right, you scum. I want both of you flat on your stomachs with your hands behind your heads."

He had heard of suicide bombers. Maybe they would try to cover their tracks by throwing themselves overboard, self-detonating, or refusing to obey his commands.

Either way they were dead.

Instead, the two men obliged, and were soon clasped in handcuffs while the quartermaster read them their rights. Meanwhile, Fuller frisked their bodies carefully for side arms, knives, and explosives, and their teeth for cyanide capsules. They were clean.

"Get on the radio," he ordered his radioman. "Call in support. I think we may have stumbled upon something important here."

"Sir," the radioman called a minute later as he returned from the *Reliant*. "I just checked the radar. There's a second ship entering our waters to the east. Should we go after it?"

Fuller looked around at all the carnage and his two captured trophies. "Let it go. I believe this is the catch of the day."

Deke Houston's captain approached Beaver Tail Island and had no problem locating the small dock belonging to Boat House.

Once Deke unloaded his suitcase and plastic grocery bags onto terra firma, he threw the captain a salute. The trawler backed away into the storm leaving him behind.

He glanced warily around his new surroundings.

He was down a short stretch of beach from the white clapboard Boat House. Approaching it, he tried the door handle. It opened easily. Ferrar wasn't joking; people didn't use keys in Maine.

Finally out of the wind, he dropped his groceries in a corner of the single, large room. It served as a kitchen, dining room, living room, and bedroom. Beside the bunk bed in another corner, he carefully set his suitcase that was loaded with weapons and several rounds of ammunition.

The room was dark, and he was surprised to find no light switch. The cottage could only be illuminated by oil lamps set on various surfaces.

Fair enough.

He found a box of waterproof matches and lit a wick. The yellow glow lent warmth to the bare room as dusk approached.

He glanced out the window. The storm was picking up, but before dark, he wanted to find Yacht House where presumably the al-Qaeda infiltrators would take refuge.

His ski jacket hadn't proven effective against the driving rain. Thank God he found raincoats, one black and one yellow, hanging on a peg by the door. He pulled on the black raincoat, then headed out into the fresh, pine-scented rainfall.

The island was no larger than a couple of football fields, but the old growth forest was thick, and wherever the other cottage was located, he couldn't see it from Ferrar's place. He had noticed a second, longer dock on the near side of the island upon their approach. He would head back in that direction.

He decided to pick his way through the forest rather than risk exposure on the rocky shoreline. Eventually, he reached a clearing. There he made out the dim outline of a two-story house. Two wires, one telephone and the other electrical, ran toward the house, but no lights were on.

During a brief lull in the downpour, he was able to survey the grounds in greater detail. There was a fine view out to the dock from the house's wraparound porch. The chairs on the porch were neatly stacked on top of each other. It appeared that the terrorist group hadn't yet arrived with the bomb.

He returned to Boat House along a different route, a path that followed the western, landward rim of the island. There appeared to be no other buildings on the island. The land bridge to the mainland was impassable, completely awash in waves.

After living for twenty years in the bustling metropolis of Washington, DC, he suddenly felt quite alone.

Darkness had hit U.S. territorial waters off Maine, and Bolton began navigating the commandeered ferry by dead reckoning. Battling heavy seas, he followed a broken string of lighthouse signals along the shore.

"Are the containers secure?" he shouted to the men below deck.

"Both secure, sir," an Arabic-accented voice reported weakly.

"How about my briefcase?"

"All fine, sir."

"Well, keep them dry."

Landlubbers. The Arabs in his group came from desert regions. He stood straight behind the helm, driving the ferry forward against the waves with a proud smile. He was at home on the sea.

Shortly after midnight, the lights of Bar Harbor appeared, just where he predicted he would find them. He was within minutes of his destination.

He shouted down the stairs, "Look lively, down there."

He was greeted by sick groans and green faces.

"We'll hit American shores in a few minutes."

The men were silent. Their relief was palpable, eclipsed only by a hushed awe.

They pulled up to a long, weathered pier that stretched far out from a dark and mysterious chunk of land.

They had landed on Beaver Tail Island.

He ducked below and grabbed his briefcase. Then he mounted the steps again to the upper deck and leaped onto the pier.

There, he teetered awkwardly on his sea legs. He spread his feet wide on the unmoving planks for balance.

"Welcome to my island, lads. Tie her up."

Four men jumped off and landed beside him, their clothes soaked in vomit. They staggered about, gathering and fastening ropes by flashlight.

"This is my home," Bolton continued, inhaling the pine-scented wind that whipped in his face.

He slapped the last man on the back.

"Welcome to the US of A."

The man wretched into the sea.

Thirteen

DAWN BROKE cold and stormy on Beaver Tail Island.

Deke hadn't slept well all night, having woken up repeatedly to check that his two automatic pistols and short-barreled rapid-fire assault rifle were fully loaded and that the rounds were chambered.

The fact that there was no lock on the cottage door didn't help.

Giving up on sleep around six in the morning, he shoveled down some dry cereal and drank half a carton of apple juice.

A mug of hot coffee would feel good in his hands, but scouting out the island would have to take precedence.

Strapping on his gun holsters, he created a fairly intimidating spectacle. He just hoped that there were no unsuspecting vacationers on the island that day.

He pulled on the black raincoat and stepped outside.

A bullet whacked the door, ripping it out of his hand.

"Holy shit."

He fell to his knees and rolled back inside the cottage.

More bullets tore the door to shreds.

Reaching to one side, he withdrew the assault rifle from under his arm. When the firing stopped, he rolled back toward the shattered door and unleashed a spray of bullets toward the source of the gunfire.

No cries resulted. No one ran away.

Was there a back door? He turned around. No. Only the front door. He was cornered.

Then he smelled fire. He glanced around the cottage. Had one of the oil lamps had caught a curtain on fire?

It smelled like burning wood, but he hadn't built a fire in the fireplace. Then he saw smoke drifting down from the open rafters. Rain spat against flames. Suddenly the awful truth sank in. Someone was burning down the cottage.

During the night, the terrorists must have arrived, and they were smoking him out. Perhaps they thought he was Ferrar. Had Ferrar set him up?

Just then, he heard a jingle by his leg. His cell phone was ringing. Still prone on the floor, he rolled back into the dimness and reached for his phone. "Shit, what is it?" he whispered. He couldn't believe he was taking a phone call in the middle of a gun battle.

"This is Ferrar," a voice said against an airy whistle.

"Ferrar, what the hell did you sent me into?"

"Are you okay?"

"Okay? If you call burning down your cottage and spraying me with bullets as I try to escape okay, then I guess you could say I'm okay."

There was silence on the other end.

Deke cried, "Are you coming, or not?" Maybe Ferrar was approaching by boat at that very moment.

"I'm in the air heading your way," Ferrar said.

"The *air*. Like what air? Overhead in a helicopter, or drinking martinis on a jetliner?"

"More like Bombay Gin. You're on your own for now."

"For God's sake, don't abandon me here."

"I'm coming. Don't worry about that. Listen, there's no place to hide in the house. You'll have to get yourself into the woods and hope they don't stalk you down."

"Ferrar, this was not my idea of a vacation."

He switched off his phone and turned off the power. How could he worry about conserving the battery's life when his own life was in peril?

No, he wasn't worrying about batteries. He just didn't want to give away his position by receiving another damned phone call.

Grabbing a kitchen chair as a shield in one hand, and clutching his rifle in the other, he kicked the front door open.

A bolt of pain shot up his leg.

He launched himself toward the nearest stand of trees, hobbling some ten yards across a weedy clearing.

Gunfire followed just behind him as he ran.

Spruce needles and chipped bark flew around his head as he was swallowed up by the woods. The gunfire sounded like two assault rifles or submachine guns unloading their entire magazines on him. For a moment their mechanical chattering drowned out the rain.

Then a lightning bolt streaked from the sky. A tremendous thunderclap split the air. He stopped. His face streaming with freezing rain, he picked out the charred scent of burning wood.

The smoke was too dense to come from the fire on the roof of Ferrar's cottage. Glancing around in the mist, he felt sparks landing on his hood.

The lightning had struck the tree just above him.

Another clap of thunder rolled higher in the sky.

Maine sure had intense electrical storms. That and the gunfire mitigated against Maine as a retirement place.

He leaned forward on his sore leg and kept moving. As long as he stayed ahead of his assailants, he was safe. But on such a tiny island, he couldn't avoid them forever.

And wasn't *he* supposed to be eliminating *them*?

The last leg of Ferrar's trip, from Montreal to Bangor, Maine, seemed to take forever. The mid-sized, commercial jetliner battled heavy turbulence the entire flight, and Deke's frightened voice still rang in his ears.

When the aircraft finally touched down in Bangor with a wet skitter, the passengers let out a cheer. The ailerons and flaps stood straight up as the pilot fought to bring the plane to a halt before the end of the runway.

After a long complaining whine, the brakes finally took hold and the plane fishtailed and came to a stop.

He closed his eyes. There would be a long taxi to the terminal. Then Customs and Immigration clearance. It could take an hour before he was in a rental car heading out on the forty-five-minute drive down to Bar Harbor.

On the way to the terminal, the plane passed several hangars with private seaplanes. One of those would be perfect.

Forget the formalities of immigration and customs. The moment the jet's hatch opened, he jumped out. His feet hit the tarmac at a full gallop.

He raced against a gale-force wind to the first hangar.

There he found a man in a glass booth that served as both an office and a warming shed.

"Get me one of these planes, quick," Ferrar said, reaching for his Federal Government identification card. "I'm with the Central Intelligence Agency, and we've got al-Qaeda terrorists smuggling ashore."

"Al who?"

"Al-Qaeda. You know, Osama bin Laden."

"Oh, boy," the man said with a hoot. He flipped a set of keys to Ferrar. "Take the second plane. It's fully fueled. But watch out, it's kind-er tight on the turns."

Ferrar slipped under the first plane's fuselage and reached for the door of the second, a J3 Piper Cub with water-landing pontoons.

"I wouldn't try to land on the wah-ta in this kind-er weath-a," the man called. "That's a hundred doll-as an hou-a."

Ferrar gave him a thumbs up, then slipped on the lap belt and shoulder harness.

"The CIA wouldn't happen to use credit cahds now, would it?" the man shouted.

Ferrar shook his head and gunned the engine to life.

"How about a down payment, mist-a?"

Ferrar closed the door. He looked around the cabin while the propeller gained speed. A diver's wetsuit hung from a hook. Fishing tackle lay neatly arranged in the rear.

The man shrugged and returned to the warmth of his office.

The propeller whipped up the air until it was a dim, white blur. Then he released the brake and the plane started bouncing across uneven asphalt. He headed for the nearest end of the runway.

He switched on the radio and pressed the microphone switch. "This is a Piper Cub requesting immediate emergency clearance for takeoff."

"What's your call number, Piper Cub?" came back an authoritative voice.

He glanced back at the wings just outside his window. "A1045," he read aloud.

"Roger that. A1045, you have clearance to take off, but you-a heading with the wind. You might want to work you-a way to the oth-a end of the runway first."

"I would if I had time," he muttered off radio.

He blew down the runway. Gusts buffeted him from behind, driving his nose hard into the ground. A strong downdraft pressed on him as he approached a ten-foot-high fence. He yanked up on the stick, struggling to keep the wings level. Out his window, his ailerons pointed straight downward. The nose popped up in a near stall.

He threaded in the throttle to full speed and pushed down on the elevators at the tail. For a few seconds, the Cub hung nearly motionless, carried along by the wind.

Seeking lift, he glanced down at his indicator panel. Ground speed was a hundred miles an hour. Air speed was half of that.

He turned the plane hard to starboard. Thank God it was "kind-er tight on the turns." He found himself in a strong headwind, with all the lift he needed to fly to the moon. But none of the speed.

He dipped the nose down and plunged toward the ground. Picking up speed, he lifted the nose gently and skimmed over the grass.

With a light touch and a banking turn, he cleared the airfield once again.

They didn't teach that maneuver at flight school.

Seeking a reasonable altitude, he skewed against the wind in the direction of Bar Harbor.

The radio crackled. "A1045, that was some takeoff. Where are you headed?"

"Out to sea," he replied, intentionally keeping it vague.

"Ah you crazy? The-a's a Force Four gale wah-ning in effect," the tower informed him.

"I know."

"Don't try to set down in the high waves out the-a."

"I'll keep that in mind. Over and out."

After fifteen minutes of hustling from rock to rock in the forest of Beaver Tail Island, Deke had had enough.

Yet, behind him came the constant rustle of branches, the thud of a pair of feet, and the occasional report of a rifle followed by an errant bullet whistling past his ear.

He had tried circling back to Bolton's Yacht House, thinking that his pursuers would scarcely expect him to approach their own headquarters. But they hunted him down nonetheless.

It was time for a new direction. Breathless and weary and his leg screaming in pain, he would be overtaken in seconds.

He had to turn the tables on them and counterattack.

Yacht House came into view, lights blazing inside. Beyond that, a large ferry-like ship was docked at the pier.

If the men brought nuclear weapons, the bombs might still be onboard the ship.

He charged into the open, heading toward the pier. Winded, he pumped icy air that nearly froze his lungs.

As he sprinted, he sprayed the windows of Yacht House with a hail of bullets. His pursuers fired at him from the woods. Fragments of dirt bit the backs of his legs. These turned to wood splinters as he dashed down the pier.

What the hell was he going to do?

A reasonable swimmer, he might make it to shore despite the frigid water and high waves. But first, he had to destroy the bombs.

With his rifle, he drilled several holes in the hull of the car ferry just below waterline. Then he hurdled over the side of the ship and emptied bullets down a staircase straight into the floorboards of the lower deck. Water gurgled into the ship.

Against a veil of rain, the shadows of his pursuers ran toward him down the pier. He knelt behind the wheelhouse on the rocking ship and opened up on the men with his rifle. It was his first chance to get a look at them.

The first was Middle Eastern, clean-shaven, agile, and wearing a flak jacket. Deke's first blast mowed him down, sending the man somersaulting into the waves.

The next attacker was tall, bulky, blond, and wore a red lumberjack's shirt. He moved erratically, making it hard for Deke to lock on a target. The rain-obscured figure approached quickly, small sidearm fire spitting at Deke.

Behind him, Deke was barely aware of a distant engine roaring over the water. It sounded like another attack.

He rolled across the deck to avoid gunfire, and let another round loose against the assailant. This time he saw the terrorist's face.

It was Tray Bolton.

The noise of the approaching engine grew too loud to ignore. He whipped out a pistol and turned around.

A small prop plane was swooping down at him just a few yards above the waves.

Ferrar saw Deke fighting a lonely battle on the deck of the ferry. Over the water, wind drag increased considerably, and he struggled just to keep aloft.

He had but one hope of saving Deke.

He unfastened his seatbelt and stood up behind the controls. He aimed the nose directly over the ferry at an assailant firing at Deke from the end of the pier.

Then, he grabbed the diver's wet suit that hung behind him, stepped back in the cabin, yanked upward on the safety latch, and forced the exit open. Below him, water rushed by in a dizzying blur.

He jumped.

The roar of the plane diminished, replaced by the rush of wind in his ears, then the crash of waves below.

Over his shoulder, he caught a glimpse of the plane skimming over the water straight for the pier. It sheared off the top of the ship, and smashed into the end of the pier, creating a brilliant ball of fire.

Straightening at the last moment into a human torpedo, he plummeted feet first into the surf. He hit it like a ramrod through a plate glass window. After shattering the surface, he was lost in a swirl of dark bubbles. It took a moment to regain his orientation, at last finding the surface, a churning mass of light above him.

Holding his breath, he found the zipper to the wet suit and struggled into it. Icy water trapped in the rubbery suit, soon matched his body temperature. But his face and hands began to seize up in the blunt cold of the water.

He propelled himself upward in the familiar, stinging salt water. Popping his hooded head above the surface, he gasped for air. The end of the pier was engulfed in flames from his full gas tank. The ferry hung off a single tether, its stern aflame and its upper deck listing precariously. Deke was balancing on the foredeck, looking around in wonder. Ferrar put his face in the onslaught of waves and began to swim toward the orange glow. Panting, he reached the vessel. But above him, Deke was hard at work. More gunfire had erupted nearby from the shore, and Deke was responding sporadically, perhaps saving his ammunition.

The ferry tilted even further as Ferrar grabbed a ladder with numb fingers and began to crawl on deck.

"Deke," he yelled. "I'm here."

"They're all over the place," Deke yelled back. "I think I got two of 'em. One was Bolton."

Ferrar pulled himself up the backwards-tilting ladder.

A hand grabbed his suit from underwater.

He heard a splash as someone broke the surface.

"What took you so long?" a deep voice said.

It was Bolton, pulling him off the ferry.

Ferrar's fingers slipped off the ladder, and he tumbled back into the surf.

Damn it all.

Bolton had him pinned back in a headlock. Even if he could struggle free and catch a breath, he was underwater.

He jabbed backwards with an elbow and struck Bolton in the abdomen. The blow was blunted by a cushion of water.

Ferrar turned their two bodies until his right arm was free of the water, and lashed out behind him through the air into Bolton's right kidney. The grip on his neck loosened enough for him to squirm free.

Instead of heading up for air, he plunged downward and away from his powerful foe. He kept swimming until he could see the smoking ferry above him. To his surprise, he found a circle of light above. Deke had carved a hole in the hull with bullets. He swam upward toward the light.

He emerged headfirst on the lower deck of the ship and sucked in air. Dizzy, he saw Deke just ahead.

He struggled to get his arms up through the splintered hole. Then, he caught sight of two containers in the ship's hold. Each was wrapped in red tape, like the ones he had seen loaded onto the plane in Bahrain. They were the bombs from Pakistan.

Meanwhile, Deke was staggering backward toward him, Bolton had emerged, waterlogged on deck and had leaped down the steps onto the lower deck, a hunting knife drawn.

"Tray," Deke shouted in alarm and surprise. "It's me, Deke Houston."

Bolton continued his threatening advance, and Deke edged backward. Ferrar ducked into the water, but it was too late. Deke stumbled over him.

Ferrar ripped an arm through the last remaining board, and grabbed for Bolton's passing boot. Suddenly, he heard a loud creaking noise as the ship listed even further. The abrupt change in angle sucked him back under.

On his way down, he took a last gulp of air and slid below the boat. Missing the boot with his free hand, he felt a second boot brushing past. He grabbed for it with fingers that barely worked, and found himself clutching the ends of a shoelace.

He yanked on it and held it for all he was worth.

There was a low thud above him, and the light became obscured. A body had fallen to the floorboards of the hold.

Was it Bolton or Deke who fell?

His lungs bursting, he planted both feet on the hull and kicked. He shot to the surface and found himself awash on the crest of a wave that began to drag him toward shore.

Flailing helplessly on his back in a wash of foam, he watched several men untie the flaming ship. They began the desperate job of hauling it to shore before it would sink, detonate, or be consumed by fire.

Out of the flames, a cold, stiff figure stepped off the ship and onto the pier, a bloody blade glistening in his hand. He stood in a red plaid shirt, hugging himself for warmth and shouting commands to his men to hurry. Ferrar knew the voice well. It was Tray Bolton.

Oh God, Deke.

Anguished and numb, Ferrar turned to face his fate, a jagged promontory at high tide, during a gale.

Several times, breakers threw his crumpled body against the rock bluff until at last he grasped an edge with his frozen fingers. A foot found a toehold. Gradually pulling himself out of the pounding surf, he climbed up the cliff one hand at a time, until he finally reached a grassy knoll.

There he buried himself in leaves, barely breathing, the sandy-colored dye in his hair leaching in yellow icicles from his black hair. Above him, the sky opened up in vicious cracks of lightning.

And through an opening in the clouds, he thought he glimpsed Deke Houston's soul ascending toward heaven.

Late that afternoon, Congressman Connors returned to his office after a floor vote on emergency aid to the airline industry. His telephone was ringing.

He felt at peace with himself as he picked it up. "This is Ralph Connors."

"Connors? This is Ferrar."

"You again?"

"Me again," Ferrar said with a cough.

"You sound like hell."

"I feel like hell," Ferrar said, his voice grave. "Al-Qaeda has come ashore."

"Like hell they have," Connors said. "The Coast Guard has just intercepted a shipment of weapons from Canada. The two men they caught aren't singing yet, but I think the Coast Guard has the situation well in hand."

"Try again, old pal," Ferrar said. "I'm watching a couple of containers from Pakistan rolling across our fair land on the back of a railroad car."

"Ferrar, I'm telling you you're nuts. These terrorists shot up half the crew of a Coast Guard cutter off Maine before they were apprehended. End of story. I'm not buying anything else."

"That must have been a diversion to let the real shipment slip past the Coast Guard."

"So why would they allow us to capture them if they have something to hide? These guys are suicide bombers. Get it? Suicide. They would have killed themselves long before divulging information. Your story just doesn't hold water, Ferrar."

"Connors, these are clever people. Do you remember when Melinda's captors told us to go to Davao?"

"That's not fair bringing up my daughter. I'm not doing this because I owe you something."

"No. Hear me out. They wanted us to go to Davao so that they could strip us of the ransom and keep Melinda. We called their bluff and made sure we had your daughter first. It's a mistake to assume these guys are stupid."

"Okay," Connors said with a sigh. "So say you're right that they got more weapons past the Coast Guard. Director Friedman won't buy it."

"Screw Friedman. Go straight to the President."

"We're not exactly on speaking terms. I guess I could try Hank."

"Hank Gibson at the FBI? Now you're talking. Terrorists traveling around inside our borders is an FBI matter after all, not the CIA."

"Too bad," Connors said, holding his head in his hands. "Hank and I made great golfing partners. I guess it's not too late to make one more enemy in the Administration."

"I want the Department of Justice all over this," Ferrar said over the line. "I'm going to turn on my radio. Once I hear Hank's boss, the Attorney General issuing a warning to the nation, I'll call you back with more details. But only if you come through with the Attorney General."

"Attorney General? What's he got to do with this?"

"Hey, we're fighting a publicity battle here. People can't be lulled into thinking that we've seen the last of al-Qaeda. Our entire nation must be on guard."

"Okay, I'll work on it," Connors said lamely, and set down the phone.

Fourteen

ALL THE LEAVES had fallen, but a mild winter seemed in store for Upstate New York as Ferrar sped along a country road in a hotwired pickup. Late afternoon sunlight flashed off the piggybacked metal containers sitting atop a freight train. From the state highway, he could even make out the red tape on the twin containers. The rest of the train was made up of drab twenty- and thirty-foot-long containers, boxcars, tank cars, and other types of rolling stock.

If the contents of the containers hadn't been so deadly, the scene might have made a perfect advertisement for American railways.

Country tunes rose and faded on the FM radio as he moved from one isolated town to the next, tracking the train on its westward course. Whenever one station faded out, he found the next strong signal and tuned in.

Finally, in Chautauqua County in far western New York, as he headed under a viaduct that intersected the railway line, the voice of a disc jockey broke in to the current hit song.

"I apologize for this interruption to our regularly scheduled programming, but we have an Emergency Broadcast Network announcement direct from Washington. Please stand by."

A moment later, the voice of United States Attorney General Douglas Laidlaw came over the speaker with his squeaky Texan twang.

"My fellow Americans. During these tragic and dangerous times, we are doing our utmost at the Department of Justice to track down new leads that may defuse more terrorist attempts on our nation. In this regard, I hereby issue this special warning for all citizens to be vigilant over the coming week for a possible terrorist strike within our borders."

The sound of reporters' excited questions rose and abated.

"I'm sorry," Douglas Laidlaw said. "I cannot be more specific about place, method, or time. I simply want our nation to step up its vigilance and take special precautions over the coming week."

93

The signal feed broke from Washington, and the disc jockey came back on.

"There you have it, a new announcement out of our nation's capital. Apparently there are no specific details..."

Ferrar turned off the radio. That was all the detail he needed.

Now, if he could only make a left turn through the Mayville gas station, head his stolen pickup down a long alley, and honk his way through a line of cars at a drive-through restaurant, he just might find a way out of town and back to the railroad tracks.

It was dusk at CIA Director Lester Friedman's personal residence in Washington's posh Georgetown neighborhood.

"Becky, dear, I've got to turn the investigation over to the FBI," he informed his wife as he stripped off his tie and entered their bedroom after a long day at the office.

Rebecca reached toward her dresser, picked up a college graduation photograph of their foster son, and caressed it with a gentle hand. "I assume you can still keep on top of this problem," she said.

"Of course I can. And I will."

"I won't rest easy until you put Ferrar behind bars. I want to look our son's murderer in the eye."

He nodded and left for his study. There, he picked up the secure telephone and sat down heavily behind his desk.

FBI Director Hank Gibson picked up the phone on the first ring.

"Hank," he said without preliminaries. "Ferrar has entered the United States. He's no longer within our jurisdiction. The case is yours."

"I'm well briefed on the case against Ferrar," Hank said. "In fact, we've already obtained wiretap permission from the DC court. Our men are in place."

"You'll have to find a way to take care of Connors," Lester warned.

"Don't worry. I know him well. I play golf with him on occasion. Just you relax now. I've seen the evidence against Ferrar, and it's compelling. He's as guilty as sin."

"I'll have to rely on you, Hank."

"I know what you have at stake in this."

Lester closed his eyes. His marriage, among other things.

Congressman Connors waited at his elegantly set dinner table as Lucy served platters of ham and sweet potatoes to him, and five FBI agents and technicians.

"Sweetie," she said. "Is all this necessary? Don't you trust George?"

"I *do* trust George," he said. "But this is the compromise I came to with Hank."

"I apologize for the inconvenience," the lead FBI agent said, reaching for the sweet potatoes.

Suddenly the phone rang atop an old-fashioned telephone table.

The five FBI men scrambled into the living room and positioned themselves behind their phones, a telephone tracking machine, and a tape recorder. Then the lead agent signaled to Connors that he could pick up.

It was Ferrar, his voice partially masked by the rumble of heavy traffic. "The bombs are heading west into Ohio by railroad," Ferrar said. "I suggest that you halt all railway transport immediately. At that point, I will tell you what specific train and containers to look for."

Connors slammed his fist against the table. Ferrar was still being cagey. "Isn't there any kind of evidence you can give me to prove that you're not blowing smoke up my ass?"

"What if I can prove that Bolton is still alive? Would that change anything?"

"What do you mean? It would change everything."

After all, the radio transmission from Tora Bora had clearly implicated Ferrar. Bolton had described the ambush before his own chilling scream and death. If he weren't dead, then what was he up to?

"But you told me that already," Connors insisted. "And I haven't seen squat."

"If you want to know where Bolton's been in the past twenty-four hours," Ferrar said, "just have the FBI stop by Beaver Tail Island in Maine off of Bar Harbor. They'll find Deke Houston's body there. He was a good friend from the Agency. They'll also find a stolen ferry from Canada that transported the bombs."

"Evidence. I need *evidence*."

"Connors, this sunken boat is beside the dock of Tray Bolton's family cottage on Beaver Tail Island. You'll find Bolton's fingerprints all over the place. You remember the al-Qaeda plot uncovered in documents in Tora Bora? It's well underway."

"How did you know about those documents? That's classified—"

The phone went dead.

Connors set down the receiver and turned to an FBI technician sitting by the coffee table with earphones. The technician nodded. "We've got him on tape, and we've got the call traced to western New York. A town called Mayville."

The lead FBI agent was already on the phone to the field office in Cleveland.

"You gonna close in on Ferrar?" Connors asked over his shoulder.

The lead agent shrugged. "Why not?" Then he finished his call and hung up.

Lucy shot a terrified look at her husband.

"How about stopping the train first?" Connors asked.

"Word from on top is we've got to stop Ferrar."

Fifteen

DINNER WITH his FBI watchers would have to wait. Congressman Connors was pissed off. By allowing the FBI to eavesdrop on his telephone conversation with Ferrar, he had sold Ferrar out. He had thought that the FBI would surely be after the bombs, but instead, they seemed to be after Ferrar.

Lucy tried to stop him as he stormed from the dining room and out of the house.

"Wait," she cried, grabbing him by the elbow. "Don't get yourself in trouble, too. You can't stop an FBI investigation."

"Lucy, this is not about stopping an investigation. This is about believing in George Ferrar. We trusted him with Melinda, and thank God our daughter is safe and sound and in grad school right now instead of decapitated on a Philippine beach. That wouldn't have happened without Ferrar."

"What's that?" the lead FBI agent inquired, leaning out the front door toward them. "Saving your daughter from that al-Qaeda group in the Philippines? Don't think for an instant that he's legit."

Connors stopped dead in his tracks. "What do you mean an al-Qaeda group? It was Abu Sayyaf."

"Yeah, well haven't you been listening to the news lately? The Abu Sayyaf kidnaps people for ransom to fund al-Qaeda. Most likely the money you gave Ferrar as ransom for your daughter went straight into bin Laden's pocket."

Connors stared into the blackness of the residential street. His whole world had turned upside down.

He felt his wife's fingers gently tugging him back into the house.

"Sweetie," she was saying. "All this has to stop sometime."

He hung his head. "Ferrar said that al-Qaeda smuggled a Canadian ship with the bombs right to Bolton's cottage in Maine."

The FBI agent snorted. "Ferrar chose the spot well. He's still trying

97

to implicate Bolton."

"But that's the location on the Tora Bora documents," Connors protested.

"Sir, didn't Ferrar just divulge that he knew about those documents? He could have written them himself."

A shudder went down Connors' spine. A cold wind was blowing his whole world empty.

"Sweetie," his wife said with gentle persistence. "Just let them bring in George for questioning."

"I don't think bringing him in will solve anything," the agent said. "We have explicit orders to shoot him on sight."

Connors closed his eyes tight. It was Ferrar against the world.

"I know what's happening here," he said at last. "This country is about to kill the only man that can save it."

Ferrar became so frustrated trying to follow the railroad line through the nighttime streets of Columbus, Ohio, that he stopped by a convenience store to buy a roadmap.

"Got freight train tracks on this map?" he asked the attendant as the train rumbled past, shaking the windows of the store.

"Doubt it," the gray-haired man said, scratching the back of her head.

Ferrar bought the map anyway, and returned to his stolen pickup. During red lights and at railway crossings, he took it out and studied it.

A full hour had ticked by since his call to Congressman Connors, and still the damn train hadn't come to a stop.

If the federal government was going to stop all the trains, it could do so using a communication network of stationmasters and signals around the country. If the nation didn't have the will to do what it took to stop terrorists, the train before him could roll on forever.

Ohio was once the nation's switchyard, and still resembled one to him. The possibility of the twenty-car train veering onto any other set of tracks at any time kept him on constant alert.

According to the map, the road was approaching a small river. For a stretch of fifteen miles or so, the highway ran parallel to the river, with the train probably running alongside. He would have a chance to relax and drive straight for that short while.

It was amazing how the universes of railways and roadways coexisted so independently. He must have started and stopped a hundred times that day and evening, while the train never changed its speed or direction, barreling southwest toward some destination he couldn't fathom.

Suddenly, he spotted flashing blue lights ahead on the nearly deserted two-lane. Who were the cops after? Him? He had been careful not to pass the speed limit or break any rules or laws. Okay, so there was that car theft back in Maine.

And he must have broken God-knows-how-many federal laws just to get back into America.

As he converged on the revolving lights, he realized it was a roadblock. Two squad cars sat perpendicular to his lane, blocking his pickup.

The cops served only as a checkpoint, because as he approached, he realized that both shoulders of the road were open to allow vehicles to pass. Two cars ahead of him slowed down.

At the same time, the caboose raced past, its red lights taunting him as they glared in his eyes.

He didn't have time to play games with the police. The left shoulder was clear, and he headed for that. In a swirl of dust, he skirted around the checkpoint only to face an oncoming car, its headlights flashing angrily at him.

He pulled a hard right and fishtailed back into his lane.

Behind him, the cops jumped into their squad cars and set their sirens blaring.

Meanwhile, the train grew smaller in the distance ahead of him.

He stepped on the gas and burned a line of rubber onto the pavement. Soon, he was zipping through the night, streaking around slow-moving traffic in his lane.

Despite his frequent, risky forays into oncoming traffic, the cops were gaining steadily on him.

Then a shattering explosion burst into the cab from behind. Fragments of glass hit the back of his skull like a wooden board. They were firing live ammunition. And they weren't shooting out his tires. They were aiming for his head.

His eyes nearly burst from the pain. He could barely see for a moment. The pickup careened toward an onrush of more police cars. They were closing in on him from both directions.

The train rumbled alongside him as he drifted closer and closer to the tracks, dodging the occasional telephone pole.

Suddenly he realized that he was driving parallel to the twin containers with the red tape—the containers that held untold danger to his country. And the train wasn't going to stop for anything.

He opened his door, jamming it ajar against the onrushing wind with the toe of his shoe. Cop cars sped past him, unwilling to sacrifice themselves by throwing themselves in his way.

He swerved to avoid hitting another telephone pole.

The red tape flapping in the wind was just within reach. He nudged his front wheels closer to the tracks.

Then he noticed a railway crossing sign ahead, a flashing yellow light with no drop-down arm to stop traffic. The train was heading across the street at an oblique angle.

He slowed slightly, pulled up beside a bouncing boxcar, and caught hold of a rusty ladder affixed to its side. That would do.

Wind tore at his face, nearly suffocating him as he stepped out of his speeding pickup and planted a foot firmly on the first rung of the ladder.

He released his hold of the truck's door, and climbed the metal rungs. He scrambled as fast as he could to avoid the swerving pickup, its flapping door slamming repeatedly against the train in a shower of sparks. Suddenly, the truck veered away from the train, then back into it, screeching metal against metal. He turned to see it plow into a storefront as the railroad tracks threaded between two buildings.

He pulled himself onto the roof of the speeding boxcar. Reinforcement seams were his only handholds as he flattened himself to avoid bridges with low clearance and low-hanging wires.

His only protection from the icy pellets of frozen rain that began to sting his face was a windbreaker and corduroys that he had stolen from a Laundromat in Maine.

He squeezed his eyes shut and tried to catch his breath. The image that arose out of his dizziness was the enigmatic, interested face of Bonnie Taylor. The last he had seen of her was on college Graduation Day. It was an image forever etched in his memory.

He shook his head to clear his thoughts. Was he truly out of his mind? Why was he really after Tray Bolton?

Then he lifted his eyes and squinted at the two containers ahead of him.

He had to decouple the car.

The FBI agents and technicians and a downcast Connors were settling into the dining room for Lucy's dessert when Connors received another call.

They assumed their positions and grabbed their earphones. Then Connors picked up the phone.

"Hello?"

"Ralph, it's Hank."

"Yeah, Hank," Connors said dejectedly. "We're all listening."

"Bad news. Ferrar eluded us."

"What did you expect, that he'd come all this way from Kabul to surrender without a fight?"

"All this way for what reason? To set off a nuclear bomb?"

"Who said anything about a nuclear bomb?" Connors shot back. "I thought you weren't buying his story."

"Well, now that we know what train he's on, we were able to quickly track down the origins of all the containers onboard."

"He's *on* the train?"

"Long story," Hank said. "Don't ask."

Connors bit his tongue and suppressed a laugh.

"It turns out that two of the containers onboard are owned by a Dutch shipping company, which is neither here nor there. But they originated from Pakistan, and traveled through Bahrain—"

"And Canada," Connors finished.

"That's right. So, it looks like we might be talking about major weapons here, perhaps a nuclear bomb or two."

"That's what I've been telling you all along," he said with exasperation.

"Let me finish. And for what purpose? Whose plan is this?" Hank asked rhetorically. "Ferrar's or al-Qaeda's?"

"I thought the assumption was that Ferrar was working for them."

"I think it might take more than a few days to untangle all the communications you've had with him over the past few days to ascertain where the truth lies."

"And we don't have a few days."

"That's right. It's already the evening of December 9th, which gives us two days or less until the strike. So our only option is to stop the train and confiscate the bombs before Ferrar gets away with them."

"Don't you see?" Connors insisted, with a sudden surge of triumph. "He's already trying to stop the bastards."

Sixteen

IN HIS PENNSYLVANIA AVENUE office overlooking the White House, Hank Gibson, Director of the Federal Bureau of Investigation, had his secretary place a call to Police Chief Stewart Powers, head of the Springfield Ohio Police Department.

"Chief Powers, this is Hank Gibson, at the Federal Bureau of Investigation."

"We're awfully sorry we lost your man," Powers apologized immediately. "God knows we had him within our grasp. He just sorta—"

"Never mind that, sir. I heard the report. What I need now is for your men to bring the train that Ferrar is on to a halt. Stop it at all costs. It might be hijacked, which means it could continue barreling its way across Ohio until it explodes."

"Explodes?"

"Yes. As in a nuclear device."

"Good God. Then we'll just have to set the railroad signals to stop her."

Gibson shook his head. "That's not good enough. She may not respond. You'll have to set up a roadblock."

"Roadblock? How do you set up a roadblock for a train? You'd be better off sending up a fighter jet to take her out."

Gibson allowed a smile. "Look, the point is we want her stopped in order to board her. But we can't derail her because it might cause leakage."

"Well, we could shut off the power if she's electric, otherwise, we could sidetrack her, but that might end up a dead end, at which point she'd crash."

"You work it out. I'm dispatching agents right now to Springfield to take away the felons onboard."

"Okay, Mr. Director. Over and out."

Hank hung up, not entirely confident that the job would be done right, or could be done at all.

How *does* one stop a runaway train, anyway? Maybe the Chief was right about the fighter jet.

He lifted the phone, and said to his secretary, "Get me the Secretary of Defense."

Chief Stewart Powers was a soft-spoken, round-bellied man, who had just become a grandfather. He loved Springfield, and by gum he was there to protect it, no matter what the feds tried to make him do.

He pondered a wall map in his office. Springfield was a small city, spread for ten miles along the Interstate and the Conrail railroad tracks. The map confirmed what he knew already. There were no switch offs onto other railway lines. The freight train could take only one route, straight through the heart of the business district.

First, he needed to reach Art Gantry, Springfield's stationmaster.

He consulted a city directory and found the number of the main station.

A ticket clerk answered the phone.

"Get me Art, please. This is the Chief of Police."

A moment later, a gruff voice came over the line. "Yes, Chief?"

"Listen, Art, we've got a commandeered freight train pulling through town."

"Commandeered?"

"Hijacked, whatever. Right now it's just entering the eastern end of town."

"That would be the CSX coke train. I've got them on Track 2."

"Is there any way to contact the engineer so we can stop the train?"

"Sure. I can radio him right away."

"Good. If that doesn't work, do you know of a way to stop that train yourself? For instance, is it electric or what?"

"No, it's diesel. It runs by itself."

"Can you stop it physically?"

"Not without derailing it or making it rear end another train. First, I'd illuminate my stop signals."

"Okay, turn on your stop signals. I'll also try to have my men flag it down. Whatever you do, don't derail or wreck it."

"I'll get on the case, Chief. If I get through to the engineer, I'll patch him through to you."

"Okay. I'm at the police headquarters number."

He hung up the phone and stepped out of his fluorescent-lit office into the office cubicle area. There, he waved aside the dispatcher, slid into his chair, and grabbed the microphone that reached all the squad cars in town.

"All points bulletin. This is the chief speaking. All right, team, listen up. The Federal Government wants us to stop this train, without making it crash. Here's the plan. I've looked over the map, and there are no switches we can set to send the train off course until it reaches Dayton. And we're definitely not gonna let that happen, so we need you to set up flagmen on Burnett Road and Spring Street. You'll attempt to flag down the train to make it stop. If it doesn't stop by Highway 68, then we'll consider it duly warned. At that point we'll attempt to shoot at the engineer and bring the train to a stop. In any event, to protect our citizenry from any risk of 'hazardous material,' we don't want a train wreck here in Springfield."

He released the transmit button for a moment and studied a map under the glass on the desk.

Then he spoke into the microphone again. "If she hasn't come to a stop by the entrance to the quarry, you can open fire. Now go to it, team. This is our moment to shine."

The dispatcher was holding his hand over his phone and waving at him.

He stepped over to the phone. "Yes, who is this?"

In the background, he heard a rumbling cadence coming from the inside of a moving train.

"This is CSX train number K 350 10. What do you want?"

"I want you to stop immediately. You have a wanted man onboard, and we need to apprehend him."

"Oh, a *wanted man?*" the voice said with a note of amusement. "So that's what you're calling me these days. It sounds like a TV show."

"Have you hijacked the train?"

"I'm just borrowing it for a short ride."

"Stop her at once. You have dangerous material onboard."

"Oh, dangerous material? Like what."

Powers bit his tongue. He would give away no more. "If you don't stop the train voluntarily, I'll open fire on you."

The dispatcher was whispering to him, "He didn't stop at Burnett. There's a man on the roof of the train working his way forward. He's about five cars back of the locomotive. It's probably Ferrar."

"We're attempting to flag you down to stop," Powers barked. "Now pull the brakes at once."

"Why don't you make me," the voice taunted with a laugh, before signing off.

"Damn it," Powers spat out, slamming down the receiver. Who the hell was he just talking to? It didn't sound like any kind of engineer he knew. "He's going to plow straight through town."

He ran back to the detailed map in his office. The next major crossroad would be Spring Street, followed by a long stretch of industrial zone to Highway 68. Then beyond that lay Sugar Grove, a commuter development outside of town where his daughter's family lived with their newborn daughter.

The dispatcher reported in. "Spring Street, sir."

"Boy, he's moving fast."

"Should reach Sugar Grove area in ten minutes at this rate, sir."

"Is Ferrar still atop the train?"

"Our officers spotted him several cars back of the locomotive, moving forward."

Powers stood up. "Have our men ready after Sugar Grove. Shoot at the engineer and Ferrar to kill them both. Damn, they'll outrun us at this rate."

"After Sugar Grove, we could try to demolish the trestle bridge at the quarry, sir."

Powers pursed his lips. Not a bad idea. The train would have left his jurisdiction, and his responsibility. Just after Sugar Grove, the tracks crossed a deep limestone quarry. With the bridge gone, the train would plummet into the lake at the bottom.

Or it might explode and melt down his daughter's development like another Three Mile Island.

"Don't knock over any bridge. Just blast away at the engineer."

He sat down heavily.

Who did these men think they were, transporting nukes through his town?

Ferrar staggered forward a few more steps, his feet spread wide, as he swayed back and forth atop the twin containers.

He could not afford to take his eyes off the horizon for long. A low bridge or tunnel could decapitate him in an instant.

Falling to his knees, he unzipped the waterproof waist pouch that he had obtained in Pakistan, and removed the small plastic transponder. Fumbling in the wind and darkness, he flipped on the switch so that it began transmitting its homing beacon. Then he removed the adhesive covering and attached the transponder to an indentation in the container's surface.

Now to try and decouple the car.

As he regained his feet, he was instantly smothered by more wind in his face. Pushing forward step by step, he bent his head down every few seconds to breath. He inhaled the fumes of a coke oven at a steel mill. That explained the sudden darkness of the landscape. They were passing through industrial wasteland.

He lowered himself onto the wooden planks of the container's flatbed car.

Below him, the railroad ties and gravel roadbed zipped by illuminated by sparks from the train's undercarriage. The noise was deafening. The train seemed to exceed a safe speed for the tracks.

He lay down at the end of the car and gripped the edge.

In the darkness, he couldn't make out the mechanism that coupled the two train cars. Suddenly, decoupling moving train cars seemed like something one could only do in a movie.

He had a better chance of reaching the locomotive and overpowering the engineer.

Leaning over the side of the car, he counted the train cars ahead. He had two boxcars to go before the locomotive. He could make it.

Keeping an eye on the ladder of the boxcar in front of him, he launched himself into space and landed with a resounding clang on the nearest rung.

He moved forward again, sensing for the first time that the sway of the car was slackening off. As the rhythm slowed down, the icy wind also ceased to blast in his face.

For some reason, the train was creeping to a halt.

Within a minute, the brakes were hissing, and they had come to a complete standstill in the middle of a grouping of warehouses and shacks, perhaps part of the steel mill.

An image of the rushing ground was still imprinted in his eyes. He began to climb down the front end of the boxcar when he heard a gunshot. It was a single report near the front of the train, perhaps inside the engine itself.

He peered forward between the cars and saw the silhouette of a man jumping out of the engine.

The headlights of some vehicle flashed over the train and caught the man full in the face. Before jerking his head back out of sight, Ferrar saw the man's broad face, strong jaw, lined cheeks, and blond hair. It was Tray Bolton.

A second later, Bolton's footsteps raced past him, his winter boots kicking up gravel.

Ferrar took a chance and peered toward the end of the train. A small forklift truck was lifting the first of the two containers off the train car. It swiveled and set the container onto an eighteen-wheel, tractor-trailer truck.

"Careful," Bolton shouted. Then a moment later, "Got it?"

"Yes," a voice came back as the truck's motor roared to life.

Bolton flew past Ferrar again and jumped into the engine.

Moments later, the train cars pulled taut and they began gathering speed. Paralyzed, Ferrar suddenly realized that he had to make a decision: follow the eighteen-wheeler or get to Bolton.

He held onto the freight car as it lurched forward, and soon the train was rocketing across flatlands toward a distant cluster of lights. It looked like a housing development in the middle of nowhere.

Hank Gibson sat bolt upright as the Secretary of Defense, Murrow Hughes, spoke with him over the telephone.

"Okay, Hank," Hughes intoned coolly. "We've scrambled an F-16 Fighting Falcon from nearby Wright-Patterson Air Force Base in Dayton. He should have the train in his sights in a few minutes."

"What is his target?" Hank asked.

"We could aim for the train, or for a bridge that lies just outside of the town of Springfield. It appears to span a rock quarry."

"First let me get back to the Chief of Police. Hold on."

Hank dialed Chief Powers. "Did you stop the train?"

"Weird thing," Powers said. "It ignored all our flagmen. I talked to the engineer. He said he wouldn't stop, and that we should try to catch him. Creepy sounding guy. So I set up men at the next crossroad, and it still hasn't shown up."

"When's it due?"

"Should have been there several minutes ago. Maybe it slowed down. I might have to send my men back up the tracks to see what happened... No, wait."

The line was muffled for a few seconds while new information came in.

"It's moving. It's approaching a development called Sugar Grove right now. Gathering speed."

"Is it going to stop?" Hank asked. In the background, Powers relayed the question to the field.

"No, sir. It's not stopping. I gave my force permission to open fire once the train passes the populated area."

"Understood," Hank said. He hung up the line to Springfield, Ohio, and returned to the Secretary of Defense.

"The train is proceeding slower now, but gathering speed. I can't permit any collateral damage, so don't blow away the train while it's among houses. Might as well just take out the bridge."

"Roger that," the Secretary said. The line clicked dead, leaving Hank Gibson alone to his thoughts. He contemplated the illuminated profile of the White House down the broad avenue.

He couldn't believe that he had just ordered a military strike against a target on American soil.

Where that bomb was heading, he might never know.

Police Lieutenant Barry Fox and three other officers kneeled behind their squad cars amid corn stubble on the edge of Sugar Grove.

They had given the engineer fair warning. Now the niceties were over. No more red signals. No more flagmen. No more roadblocks. The bastards had it coming.

But where was the train?

At last, Barry heard the distinctive rumble of empty boxcars.

Then he saw the yellow engine and red cars in the distance. It was approaching slowly, its wheels barely grinding away. He felt the agonizingly long wait that drivers feel at a railway crossing when a train is just barely creeping past.

Finally he had the side window of the locomotive within his gun sight. The interior lights were off, and he couldn't make out the engineer.

As the train pulled closer, he realized that it was gaining significant speed. He and his riflemen would only have three or four seconds to take out the driver.

"Open fire," he ordered.

So the law enforcement officers did exactly that, shattering the front and side windows, denting the metal door, and riddling the cab. The flashes and thundering from the dark, fallow field looked and sounded like a military barrage.

But the train's progress continued unabated.

"Lieutenant," an officer shouted as the massive train rumbled past. "I can see a man on the roof of the second car."

"That's Ferrar," Barry shouted. "Gun him down."

Ferrar was busy maintaining his balance on the swaying train while choking on the fumes of the locomotive just half a car ahead.

Suddenly over his right shoulder came the roar of a fast-moving jet.

Also to his right, a burst of gunfire erupted from an empty field. A wall of squad cars was outlined in the smoke, as police pumped lead into the locomotive.

Maybe they would get Bolton for him.

But the train continued chugging along. In fact, its speed increased.

Uneven railway tracks nearly toppled him. He leaned over to cough in the asphyxiating fumes.

Bullets started ripping up the metal boxcar on which he stood fighting for balance.

The police were aiming at *him*. Hell, he wasn't the engineer. What could possibly be on their minds?

He fell to the cold, hard surface and hugged the rattling frame. He could just barely keep out of sight of the policemen firing at will from the field. The locomotive's hot exhaust whipped through his hair. Bullet tips smacked the roof below him, denting the metal under his hands. The surface turned searing hot. Other bullets burst through the sheathing and left smoldering holes just inches from his face.

He had to change his position, and scrambled forward on hands and knees into the black cloud of diesel fumes.

Suddenly the jet entered his field of vision. From its delta-wing profile and bubble canopy, it appeared to be an F-16 fighter jet streaking out of the night sky, straight for the train.

It was approaching too fast. It would pass just seconds before the locomotive.

Then a brilliant white flash illuminated the entire landscape. Before him, to either side of the plume of diesel smoke, loomed a deep, black canyon. A red fireball rose hot and blinding directly in front of him. Scraps of metal spun and flew overhead.

He dropped to his stomach once more, and forced himself to observe what was happening.

The snout of the locomotive dropped below his line of sight. The sound of its engine diminished as if suddenly muffled.

The F-16's single glowing tailpipe disappeared among the stars. Gun blasts had ceased from the field.

He was riding a shimmying mechanical beast. Ahead, the burning timbers of some sort of structure fell away. A bridge!

The train was flying off a blown-away bridge into a dark, gaping void.

He wouldn't follow it there, land in a scrap heap and be buried by tons of metal as more train cars piled on top of him.

Instead, he reversed himself and sprinted toward the back end of the boxcar. At the last second, he veered to the right and threw himself into the dark, still air, the train falling off to his left, his arms flailing to keep him upright.

He looked down. The bottom of the gorge was a distant forty yards below. Straight below looked particularly dark. Metal and wooden beams hit the bottom and flames were instantly extinguished.

He was over water.

He braced himself for impact.

Pointing his feet straight down and holding his crotch, he tightened his buttocks.

The last image from the air was that of a broken, burning trestle and the train arcing downward with him at the same speed.

He hit the water like an I-beam, just beside where the bridge had fallen, and just before where train cars had begun to pile up.

The moment he hit the water, he spread out his arms and legs, flapping them wildly to cause resistance before he hit the bottom of the lake.

He needn't have worried, for he never reached the bottom. Instead, he found himself in frigid, wet stillness. He was weightless and, for a moment, safe.

Chief Stewart Powers stood on the rim of the quarry at Rock Way, Ohio. Forty yards below, he looked into a deep, wide pit of flaming wreckage that floated in a black lake.

"What's the situation?" he inquired of Lieutenant Barry Fox, the ranking officer on the scene.

Barry pointed to a rescue crew working below on the fringes of the lake. "We've recovered one container, sir. If the other has fallen into a deeper recess in the lake bottom, we might not find it for some time. It would require deep water diving equipment to search the lowest part of the quarry."

"And what did you find in the container?"

"Pipes, sir. Plain metal tubes. You know, like water pipes for a sewer."

"That's just great," Powers said. "We've been spending all our time setting up roadblocks, firing on people, bombing bridges, and destroying entire trains for a box of sewage pipes? I can't wait to tell the Director of the FBI that."

"I thought you'd be relieved, sir."

"Why's that?"

"That there was no hazardous material onboard."

Powers had to agree. All he needed was a little perspective on the events of that evening. Things did not turn out as badly as they might have.

"Did you turn up Ferrar?"

"No. Again, he may have died under all that wreckage, and we'll never know it unless his body bloats up, frees itself, and floats to the surface. On the other hand, he just might have managed to escape alive."

"A fool like that, ramming his truck into a moving train, then trying to walk along the top of train cars. I know a wacko when I see one. He's watched one too many cop shows on television. How about the engineer?"

"Not recovered either, sir. Actually, the engine is still buried under all that wreckage and water, so I seriously doubt if we'll turn up any evidence until we get a heavy crane down there."

"Okay. Good work, son. I'll wait until you turn something up before I get back to Washington."

He turned away from the glowing sight. He had never seen anything quite so ghastly in his life. An entire freight train half-submerged at the bottom his town's limestone quarry.

Yet, Springfield should feel proud. They had just spared the nation another unspeakable act.

Seventeen

SEATED BEFORE THE Congress' Joint Intelligence Committee at the Dirksen Senate Office Building, FBI Director Hank Gibson tried to control the quaver in his voice. He was recounting the final heroic moments when the U.S. Air Force teamed with local law enforcement personnel to defeat the al-Qaeda terrorist cell.

At the end of the table, CIA Director Lester Friedman listened with satisfaction, nodding from time to time.

Just as Hank delivered his concluding remarks, Congressman Connors stumbled in, late as usual.

"Sorry, gentlemen," Connors said, dropping his briefcase on the stack of papers before him and opening the latch. "Hank, may I ask you a question or two?" he said, staring straight down at him.

Hank nodded. "It would be my pleasure."

"Okay, I've heard the news reports," Connors started. "It looks like congratulations are due. But let me clear up a point or two. First, have you recovered the bombs from the train yet?"

"Ah no, sir. If you had been here earlier, you would have heard me testifying that due to the depth of the lake and the amount of wreckage and debris, the authorities on the scene have not yet been able to retrieve any sort of weapons, nuclear or otherwise."

"What a shame," Connors said. "Secondly, did you capture George Ferrar?"

"Again, sir, I would refer you to my earlier testimony this morning that we have neither apprehended Ferrar, nor found his remains at this time due to the immense amount of debris."

Connors closed his briefcase with a smile.

"Can you tell me why you're grinning, Congressman Connors?" the CIA Director leaned into his microphone and asked.

"Because that means Ferrar is still on the case."

It was midmorning in Ohio. With one hand draped over the steering wheel of a stolen minivan, Ferrar turned the digital tracking device on. No signal crossed the orange-backlit screen. Damn it.

He immediately turned it off.

Where might the container be?

He reviewed the sequence of events atop the train. He had attached the transponder to the top container, and he had switched on the transponder's homing beacon. Then the small forklift had taken the container off the train and set it onto a tractor-trailer.

The truck couldn't be that far away, but he had failed to pick up the signal all morning.

He rubbed the stubble of a beard on his jaw and stared straight ahead out the minivan's windshield as he sped through western Ohio. The train had been heading westward. It seemed logical to assume that the eighteen-wheeler transporting the container would be heading in the same direction as the train.

He had lost an hour and a half of valuable time climbing out of the quarry, scaling its fence, and hotwiring a minivan that was parked in the cement company's parking lot. Perhaps he wasn't close enough to the truck yet for the signal to pick up.

He checked his speedometer. Seventy miles per hour on a speed limit-enforced Interstate in a stolen vehicle was pushing his luck. He eased off the accelerator slightly.

Highway signs indicated that he was angling toward southern Indiana: Indiana border 35 miles, Indianapolis 259 miles, Springfield, Illinois, 411 miles, St. Louis 635 miles. He couldn't imagine a possible terrorist target in Indiana except for the Indy 500 Speedway, where half a million spectators gathered for the annual race. But that race wasn't until May as he recalled, and it was December.

December 10th to be exact.

The next day would bring a cataclysm to rival that of the World Trade Center and Pentagon attacks. Surely nothing had that high a profile in the asparagus fields and maple groves of Indiana.

Beyond Indiana lay southern Illinois. Again, no major targets there.

The truck could have changed direction and headed up to Chicago or down to Memphis. He could use a full rack of Carson's ribs in the Windy City. A plate of blackened catfish in Memphis wouldn't be all that bad either.

Drowsy from several sleepless nights, he let his attention wander. The idea of Bolton dead in the train crash struck him as somewhat incongruous. Why would Bolton have offloaded the bombs onto a truck only to proceed onward with the train that he surely knew authorities would be tracking?

Nevertheless, chances were fairly high that Bolton didn't expect an F-16 to strike out of the sky and drop the bridge in front of him.

He picked up his cell phone and punched in Bonnie Taylor's number in San Francisco. If Tray Bolton were still alive, he might try to contact her.

FBI Director Hank Gibson was just zipping up his pants in a men's room at the Rayburn House Office Building when his CIA counterpart grabbed him by the shoulder.

"Hank," Lester Friedman said. "I'm afraid that we might be making a terrible blunder here."

"Yeah, getting my dick stuck in my zipper would be a problem."

"I won't let this go until I see Ferrar dead."

Hank looked down and examined his zipper. All his body parts seemed intact. "We've got divers out there right now."

"That's not good enough," Lester said, following him to the sink. "It could take days before they decide there's nobody down there to find. In the meantime, Ferrar could be out there orchestrating our country's demise. Remember al-Qaeda's doomsday prediction? December 11. And that's tomorrow. I don't want to tell you how many nuclear power plants, dams, capital buildings, monuments, skyscrapers, stadiums and other dangerous and high profile targets we have spread around this country. We need to find Ferrar."

Hank stared at Lester in the large wall mirror as he washed his hands. "Well, we are following up on one possible lead."

"Which is?"

"An employee at the quarry in Ohio reported his vehicle stolen as his shift ended early this morning."

"And?" Lester asked excitedly.

"Jesus, Lester, calm down," he said, shaking his hands dry. "You shouldn't be losing sleep over this thing. There are terrorists all over the world plotting the destruction of our republic. Don't get hung up on one little case that isn't even yours any longer." He ripped a couple of paper towels out of the dispenser.

"You're right. I am losing too much sleep. My wife and I are even worried that with Ferrar still unaccounted for, since he killed our son Tray, he might hunt us down next."

"Nonsense."

"I know it's nonsense, but that's the kind of fear that makes me determined to find him before he commits some atrocity on a Biblical scale."

Hank wadded up and tossed the paper towels emphatically into the trash. "Well, we've got an alert out in several states for any vehicle that fits the description of the missing minivan. Nobody will have ever recovered a stolen minivan in so little time before. I guarantee. I hope the public doesn't expect this level of service from the FBI every day. But if we do find Ferrar, it may help us to solve the mystery of whose bombs those really were."

He swung the door open to leave.

Behind him, he heard Lester's words, "There is no mystery."

Eighteen

Bonnie Taylor leaned back during her morning shower. Blonde hair dripping wet, feet together on the shower mat, and face raised upward, she let the hot spray pound away at her shoulders.

No matter how much sleep she grabbed before another day of work, she still couldn't alleviate the tension in her body that had all started with the call from Tray two days before.

Just hearing his sonorous voice had been an odd sensation. It had brought back hundreds of memories, of high school dates watching the submarine races off the Bar Harbor piers, of campus evenings studying together in Doe Library at UC Berkeley, of his picking her up for Friday night dances, of their frequent tiffs, his raised voice, his blinding jealousy, his humble apologies, and of the long nights she spent holding him like a relic of the past when she knew that they had no future together.

After she had read that he was memorialized with a white cross at Arlington National Cemetery, the sound of his voice had produced a secondary effect. Relief. He was alive and still interested in her after those eight years of absence. Those lonesome years of juggling boyfriends, delaying her future, and nibbling gingerly at other opportunities. It relieved her to know that a rock from her past was still there to hold onto.

Unfortunately, it was the wrong rock. The wrong man from her past.

She was just trying to lose his voice in the sound of rushing water, when she heard her telephone ring.

She turned off the shower and grabbed her oversized bath towel. Duty necessitated answering every call, as the U.S. Coast Guard expected 24-hour availability.

She quickly patted down the full length of her long limbs, sculpted from years of PT Physical Training, then wrapped the towel around her regulation-length hair and padded barefoot across the lightwood floor of her bedroom.

116

The clock read 06:00. What had prompted the early call? It could be a distress call from sea, although there were no storms in the area. She was frequently summoned out of bed for an SAR Search-and-Rescue sortie. Or it could be him again—Bolton, the bolt out of the blue. She would take a capsized ship with PIW People in Water any day.

"Hello?" she answered in a somewhat defensive way.

"Bonnie?"

"Yes? Who is this?"

The man on the other end hesitated before identifying himself. She heard the sounds of a car interior—the muffled whoosh of tires, the hum of a motor, the squeak of a car seat.

"This is George."

"George who?"

"Ferrar."

Oh my God. Two men from her past in the same week. What was she, a lightning rod for disaster?

"George, why are you calling me?"

"Are you angry with me?"

"No, I'm not angry with you. I'm just curious why now, after twenty years of pursuing your own quests and me pursuing mine that you feel you must get me out of the shower at oh-six-hundred hours and make me stand here dripping wet trying to get out a coherent sentence."

"Bonnie, I'm not calling about *us*. I'm on an urgent mission and I need to know if Tray has contacted you."

She sat down, squarely on her white commander uniform that she had so carefully laid out on the bed.

"Well, I…."

"Okay, that answers my question. You've spoken to him. How recently?"

"Slow down, George. I mean, I've just sat on my newly pressed dress whites, and I need a second to formulate a response."

"How recently?" Ferrar repeated.

Through his terseness, she detected a note of concern.

"My God. Has something else gone wrong? After all, at first I thought he was dead. I'd heard that he'd just been put to rest at Arlington. Then two days ago he called me up out of the blue."

"I need to know if he's dead now."

"You mean if I've heard from him since then? No, I haven't."

"Okay. And you don't mind if I keep checking in?"

She whipped off her towel and tried to pat down her uniform. "Well, uh. No."

"Thanks." The phone clicked off.

Huh? She looked at the phone.

What was that all about? Was George on a real mission, or was he simply worried about Tray and her? It didn't matter. Those two men were as thick as thieves, and now they were using her as a telephone answering service.

To hell with them both. She had a life.

As he steered his stolen minivan onto the Indianapolis Beltway, Ferrar turned on his tracking device once again.

"Hallelujah!"

A round orange circle appeared for the first time, indicating that the transponder was somewhere in the vicinity. Thank God he was on the right course.

Just as suddenly as the orange blip appeared, however, it vanished without the device having time to calculate the truck's speed or direction.

If he were not close enough to the trailer truck bearing the bombs, the signal would tend to fade in and out. He had to pick up his speed.

He gunned the engine as he joined a steady flow of noonday traffic that circled the sprawling city. The only question he had to resolve was what direction to take. With Indianapolis a transportation hub on the Chicago-Atlanta and Cincinnati-St. Louis axis, he couldn't afford to guess wrong.

Aiming west around the northern curve of the ring, he tried to shadow fast-moving cars in the far left lane. He passed a squad car half-hidden in the grassy median. The cop didn't seem concerned with speed limit enforcement, as the average speed in the passing lane that day was nearing seventy-five miles-per-hour.

What was the cop looking for?

A moment later he checked his tracking device. Another blip, this time stronger, indicating that he was not only on the right track, but getting closer.

Another set of cars, these black and unmarked, sat alongside the road. That didn't bode well.

He needed to ascertain which direction the truck would take off the beltway before he could ditch the minivan and continue the chase by some other means.

As the highway arced counterclockwise, he peered into the glaring sunlight as far ahead as he could see. There were several trucks, but no eighteen-wheel rig bearing a half-height container. As he approached the shade of an overpass, he noticed a man leaning over the far railing.

Passing underneath, Ferrar cast a glimpse of the man in his side view mirror. He was using binoculars to study the traffic.

That did it.

Ferrar floored it. A family car with a Pokémon figure swinging in the back window blocked his lane. He swerved farther right into a slower lane. Another car, this one a small, late-model Chevy, blocked his way. He veered back left in front of the Pokémon car. There was some open ground and he sped for the horizon.

He mentally ticked off the exits, mostly local, then one big ramp diverting traffic off to Chicago. He had to decide fast.

He flipped on the tracking device. The blip was stronger than ever. The direction indicator now registered *west*.

The beltway was heading west at the time, so he didn't exit. But was the truck on the beltway circling westward, or had it already exited to the west?

Suddenly he caught the flash of red and blue strobes in his rearview mirror. The cops weren't using their sirens. They were trying a sneak attack.

Then he saw two black sedans slowing in front of him. They had him trapped. All he could do was bang his fist on the steering wheel. The silver minivan with Ohio plates that he was driving stood out in traffic like a flashing neon sign.

The next exit was within a hundred yards. He drifted out of the center lane to the right, then jerked hard right again. Thrown against the side of his car, he cut off a Greyhound bus and eased off the highway, immediately immersing himself in the steady flow of suburban traffic.

Behind him, half the cops seemed to have followed him. He took a hard right. It turned out to be a residential street that was altogether too quiet.

Damn. He needed mayhem. So he pulled a left onto a street that paralleled the main street. He passed garbage bins, restaurants, and the parking lots of two small office buildings.

At last he found what he was looking for. A gas station with a garage. He pulled directly into an empty space in the garage, shut off the motor, and jumped out. There was a red button by the garage door. Skittering across the greasy floor, he reached the button and jabbed it. Slowly, the garage door lowered, concealing the minivan.

A mechanic approached him. "Do you have an appointment?"

"No, but I saw the space open," he said, thinking quickly. "I need the tires rotated and the oil changed. But more importantly, do you mind if I use the john?"

"Key's hanging in the office."

He had eyed an extra set of dark green coveralls hanging on the wall. As he passed out of the room, he snatched them and took the men's room key.

Walking outside to the restroom, he didn't lift his head, but turned his ear to listen to the sounds of traffic. No sirens, no screeching tires. He may have temporarily lost the cops.

He unlocked the men's room door, stepped in, and shut it quickly. In the cramped, unheated space, he changed clothes quickly, burying his damp clothes from the quarry at the bottom of the trash.

He emerged wearing the clean grease-monkey suit.

Out by the pumps, an elderly man leaned from his Lincoln Continental while he waited for the gas to finish pumping.

Perfect.

"Excuse me, sir," Ferrar said, jogging up to him. "I noticed some blue smoke pouring from your exhaust pipe."

"No kidding," the old guy growled.

"It could mean damage to a catalytic system like yours. Do you mind if I check her over?"

"No, go ahead," the man said morosely, flipping him the keys.

The old guy hauled himself out of the car, finished nursing the last few drops of gas into his tank, locked the gas cap, closed the door to the fuel tank, and plodded back to the pump to return the hose.

Ferrar jumped into the car, started the engine, and didn't look back as he pulled onto the busy street. He crossed several lanes and headed up the ramp back onto the expressway.

With a new car, a new license plate, new clothes, and a full tank of gas, he felt like a new man. Total time elapsed: ten minutes.

But how long before the man missed his car?

As smoothly as zipping his coveralls, he merged with the beltway traffic heading westward, still in a counterclockwise direction. It was time to check his tracking device. The display was weak, and he could barely make out the numbers. No signal. He was losing the truck.

Easing into the fast lane, he allowed the powerful car to cut loose. The exit west for Springfield, Illinois, and St. Louis was looming. He decided to take it.

The flashing lights and black sedans were a distant memory, and cars no longer lurked along the side of the road. But the flood of traffic was breaking off into two great streams.

He tried the tracking device once more. There wasn't even an orange glow. The batteries were dead.

He flicked on his blinkers and worked his way toward the Illinois-St. Louis exit, a choice he knew that would decide the fate of the nation.

Lester Friedman's bulletproof limousine was just pulling into the front gate of CIA Headquarters in Langley when he received a call.

Charles White, his faithful assistant, handed him the phone with a whisper, "It's Hank Gibson."

He grabbed it, "Yeah, Hank?"

"We found him."

Lester felt the tension drain physically from his body.

"Where is he?"

"He *was* in Indianapolis. Where he is *now*, I do not know."

Lester cursed under his breath. "How the crap did you lose him?"

"We traced the minivan to Indiana. There we chased him, he eluded us, and he ditched the minivan. We took fingerprints off the steering wheel. Sure enough, they belong to Ferrar."

Lester closed his eyes and held his forehead. "So what can we do?"

"Step up the manhunt," Hank Gibson replied tersely.

"But how do you know what to look for?"

"We know what vehicle he's driving now. Only, he's got a three-hour lead on us. And he could branch off in any direction. But we've got the regional alert updated and propagated again."

"Damn it," Lester said. "I can track a terrorist through the back streets of Istanbul. Why can't you even nail a fugitive in Indiana?"

"It's not as simple as it may sound," Hank said, and hung up the phone.

Lester tried to hand the phone back to Charles.

"Sir," he heard a voice calling from outside the car. "Sir?"

He looked up. Charles was holding the door open for him.

"We've arrived at your office, sir."

Where was that damned truck? Ferrar pounded his fist repeatedly against the leather steering wheel of the Lincoln Continental.

With the tracking device dead, desperation was beginning to mount in him. He had passed Terra Haute and the Illinois border an hour earlier. At the speed he was traveling, he should have reached the loaded truck by then. But, of course, the truck might be on a completely different road.

As he had for the past three hours, Ferrar scanned the string of vehicles for a giant semi that matched the picture in his memory of the previous night.

Then, far ahead, he made out a truck pulling a single, half-height intermodal container.

As he inched closer to the truck to pass it, he noticed that the container had a strip of red tape around it. He felt his heart pounding in his chest.

He pulled ahead of the rig and tried to match its speed. A road sign zipped by: St. Louis 150 miles, Denver 1001 miles, Los Angeles 2018 miles.

From his side view mirror, he couldn't make out the face of the driver in the semi's cab.

The sun flared off the truck's windshield. Inside, the driver wore aviator glasses. Ferrar couldn't make out the rest of his features.

Next to him in the cab were two other men, each with sunglasses as well.

Ferrar pulled into the passing lane and slowed down to get a better look at the driver. There he saw it. Through the semi's fogged-up windows, he noticed the man's hair. It was short and blond. And his red plaid shirt was none other than that of Tray Bolton.

Oh, shit. So Bolton *wasn't* on the train.

He had to jackknife the truck or tip it over. But how? Unarmed, he wouldn't stand a chance in an ensuing gun battle. He wasn't even sure that the Lincoln Continental he was driving could force the semi off the road.

For a mile, he watched rows of harvested corn, bent and broken stalks yielding to a strong westerly wind. The entire Midwest was bracing for a winter storm. Would they be ready for nuclear winter?

He couldn't risk damaging the cargo in the truck. He'd have to call in reinforcements.

What exactly was their destination? St. Louis was within two hours' reach. What was in St. Louis? The Rams. The Cardinals. The Arch. He didn't remember Tray Bolton harboring any particular dislike of the Rams or Cardinals. After all, the Patriots and Red Sox played in the AFC and American League. It had to be the Gateway Arch.

At the next exit, he pulled off the Interstate, leaving the truck roaring on ahead. He turned abruptly into a Shell station and snapped up the public phone. Dialing "0," he reached a local operator, and asked to place a collect call to Washington, DC.

"And what number would you like to reach?" the woman asked in her flat, Midwestern accent.

He gave her Connors' office number.

"And your name, sir?"

"George Ferrar."

A moment later, a receptionist answered, "This is Congressman Connors' office."

"I'm calling for Mr. George Ferrar," the operator said. "Will you accept a collect call?"

He heard a muffled discussion in the background. Suddenly, two or three phones picked up.

"Ferrar, is that you?" It was Connors.

"We'll accept the call," the receptionist said.

The operator clicked off.

"Tell your men in black to take a hike," Ferrar snarled. "Since you've got them tapping the line, I'll have to make this quick. The Gateway Arch in St. Louis is the next likely target. The terrorists are due to arrive there within two hours."

He hung up.

He missed his long, leisurely conversations with the Congressman.

Connors stood up behind his desk and glared at the FBI agents seated across from him and around the room.

"You heard him. Now act on it."

The lead FBI agent across the desk yanked off his earphones.

"He's jerking our chain. How does he come up with this bullshit?"

"I assume he's still following the shipment."

"It's at the bottom of a lake in Ohio."

"Have you found it?" Connors shot back. "You guys are the ones who buried it. Now I think you'd better call Hank. Because if you don't, I will. If you guys don't act on this tip, I'll be the first guest on Nightly News to inform the American public—*after* the bombs go off."

"I'm calling him," the lead agent said, his index finger already jabbing at the dial pad.

Nineteen

SAC JEREMY FUCHSMAN, Special Agent in Charge of the FBI's St. Louis Field Office, was a busy man. Recent captures of Taliban and al-Qaeda terrorists had yielded a bonanza of leads indicating other terrorist plots and suspects at large around the American Midwest.

In fact, for the past week, he had been on the road interviewing flight instructors, neighbors, Western Union offices, and imams in mosques up and down Missouri's eastern region.

When the call came through from the FBI Director, it was by pure chance that Jeremy was back in his office. He stood holding his breath while staring at the gleaming, stainless steel St. Louis Gateway Arch.

"Attack on the Arch?" he repeated incredulously. "How? When?"

The recognizable voice of Hank Gibson came back more forceful than ever. "We believe that they are traveling west and that they have bombs, perhaps nuclear devices, on some sort of transport, either rail, road, air or even by sea. Nothing is unthinkable these days. The attack might come within two hours. Make that an hour and forty-five minutes. Mobilize your crew and local law enforcement agencies. You're point man and you don't have a moment to lose."

"I understand, sir."

"Report back to me directly on a regular basis."

By the time Jeremy set down the phone, his flexible young mind had already determined a course of action.

Through the glass door of his office, he waved at all the available agents to gather around him. While they laid aside their work, he placed a call to the St. Louis Police Department.

Four agents, two women and two men, assembled around his desk. The two women were young, energetic, and athletic. They were highly trained, cookie-cutter products of the FBI Academy, located on the Marine training base at Quantico, Virginia.

One man was a middle-aged legal expert, and the other was an overweight investigative agent named Stanley Welles, with one year remaining before retiring from the bureau.

The four stood motionless as they listened to him speak on the phone. Their jaws were set and their lips turned grim.

"I need roadblocks on all the major arteries leading into the city: rail, highway, air, and water," Jeremy was saying to Police Commissioner Frank Wheeler. "And I need them immediately. They're due to attack in an hour and forty minutes or less. Don't let any sort of explosives through. We're talking about anything from zip guns to possible nuclear bombs, here."

There was a loud tirade on the other end of the line. Then Jeremy gave it his all.

"Frank, I know this is short notice, but this is the big one. The one we've all been waiting for. Al-Qaeda is aiming an arrow straight at our heart. The Arch is ground zero. We have to move on this on every front. I'm heading down to the riverfront this very minute to coordinate evacuation and defense."

He slammed down the receiver.

"Emerson," he continued in the same breath. "Call the National Park Service and tell them to evacuate the Arch and its surrounding area immediately. Then follow up."

One of the women slipped out of the office to make the call.

"Stanley, you are the roamer. Check out all the access routes to the Arch."

Stanley grunted and peeled away from the group.

"You two, come with me. We're clearing out of here and going down to the Arch."

He turned around for one last look at the Jefferson National Expansion Memorial Park. The sprawling green grounds and clear ponds stretched for over a mile along the low western bank of the Mississippi River. In its center stood the gleaming silver Gateway Arch, the symbol of the Gateway to America's West, to new frontiers.

If it went down, so too would the American dream.

Larry Sloan's mother was the volunteer parent on the class field trip. Larry's 3rd grade teacher, Mrs. O'Ryan, had just taken one of the ball-like tram capsules back down a leg of the Gateway Arch.

It was one in a long line of gondolas that moved up and down the Arch like a string of rosary beads. Larry's mother and three classmates were still with him at the top, waiting impatiently for the next capsule to arrive.

It never did.

Some sort of siren started blaring in the confined space of the observation deck.

Larry looked at his mother, and she tried to smile reassuringly.

He looked past her at the cramped room. Children from other schools were leaning over the slanted window ledges to look down. The river was on one side and Busch Stadium, the Old Courthouse, and the skyline were on the other.

When the alarm sounded, they all slid down from their perches and stood stock-still.

"Sounds like a fire alarm," Mrs. Sloan said pleasantly. She glanced anxiously from the tram doors that stayed shut to the exit door that led to emergency stairs. "I guess that means we'll just have to walk."

Larry sniffed the air. There was no smoke.

"I don't smell a fire," he shouted above the din of the alarm. "Can't we wait?"

Just then, an older schoolgirl jabbed a finger against the thick pane of glass. "Look down there," she cried.

Larry scrambled past his mother. Being tall for his age, he was able to jump up high enough to get a good view straight down. A series of black cars, followed by police cars and fire equipment, were pulling up to the north and south bases of the two-legged structure.

"Cool. Fire trucks," he exclaimed.

The children let out an excited cry.

"Away from the windows," his mother was saying.

"You know, Mrs. Sloan," a girl called out with a know-it-all tone. "This building is made completely out of metal."

"...so we shouldn't have to worry about fires. Now, calmly hold hands and let's go down the stairs."

"There must be a thousand gazillion steps," a boy protested.

The wail of the alarm was especially piercing by the emergency exit. As the children approached the closed door, they held their ears and began to look at each other with panic.

Mrs. Sloan struggled to push the metal door open. Children had wedged themselves against her, and she didn't want them to spill down the stairwell.

Suddenly carried away in the mad rush, she tumbled down the stairs into darkness.

"Larry!" she screamed as she fell.

Special Agent in Charge Jeremy Fuchsman arrived with his FBI team on the grounds of the Gateway Arch moments before police entered the park.

The fire truck ahead of them pulled to a stop just before the Arch, and firefighters in full gear ran directly into the base of the Arch. Good God. It was just like 9/11.

Standing in the mid-afternoon shade of the Arch, he looked at the riverfront. The *Admiral*, a long, sleek riverboat and casino, sat tied to the dock slightly downriver. Other pleasure boats had been dry-docked for the winter. The only other boats were barges plying their way up and down the great waterway.

"Check out the river access," he told Porter, the silver-haired legal expert. "And get yourself some police for backup."

He looked at Skylar, his last remaining agent.

"What am I supposed to do?" she asked.

"You tell me."

He whipped out his cell phone and punched in the number of the FBI Director in Washington. "This is Jeremy Fuchsman in St. Louis. I've got emergency crews dispatched and police setting up roadblocks. Can you give me a physical description of who or what we're looking for?"

"I don't know exactly what to look for," Hank Gibson said. "But here's the man we're after."

Jeremy heard some papers being shuffled.

"One George Ferrar, possibly traveling under an alias. 43 years of age, Army Green Beret, black hair, six feet tall, 220 pounds. Considered armed and extremely dangerous."

Jeremy jotted everything down. "Any word on how he's traveling?"

"Nothing. Let me check about the bombs, though."

Jeremy was put on hold. Yeah, the bombs would be important, too.

Hank Gibson came back within seconds. "As for the bombs, they may be traveling by container. You know those containers that ride on train cars and on the backs of trucks? I don't have an exact dimension. It does have a registration number, however. It's LFDU24425436."

"Good," Jeremy said. "That gives us something to go on."

He thanked his big boss, then got Frank Wheeler, the Police Commissioner, on the phone and relayed the descriptions.

Then he leaned back against his car, a cold wind whipping at his field jacket.

"Well, Skylar, where are we going to find this guy?"

She pressed her young red lips together, then said, "I'd try the old bridge."

"Which old bridge?"

With her light blue eyes, she cast a glance upriver at an elegant old pedestrian and railway bridge.

"Eads Bridge?"

She nodded. "Nobody will be checking that."

He squinted to the north where the bridge hopped across the Mississippi on three long spans. Beyond it lay the new Dr. Martin Luther King Jr. Memorial Bridge. "You could be right. Take a squad car and head up there."

She bounded off to an array of police cars that had pulled up to the site.

From the base of the Arch, firefighters were escorting terrified youngsters and tourists away from the structure. He wandered over to the South Tram Load Zone and nabbed a fireman. "What are the conditions like up there?"

"The trams stopped when we pulled the alarm," the fireman said. "We've got people trapped inside the trams, and at the top of the structure. We're sending up a team to escort them down. I understand that it's mostly school children."

Jeremy nodded. The Arch was a fine target indeed.

In East St. Louis, Illinois, Ferrar passed a phalanx of police cars beginning to form a roadblock across the Interstate.

In his rearview mirror, he saw the first brave policeman walk into the middle of the highway to flag down cars and trucks.

They had narrowly missed him. But if this was their only way of catching Bolton and the bombers, they would fail, for the trailer truck was just ahead of him.

If they even knew about the truck.

He squirmed uneasily in his seat, late afternoon sunlight streaming in through his windshield. At least the cops would be preoccupied with roadblocks and not chasing down speeders. He leaned harder on the accelerator.

Then he noticed a broad, curved reflection of sunlight along the horizon. There, across the bridge and just to the right of the Interstate soared an unmistakable landmark. The Gateway Arch, proud, elegant, firm.

At least for the moment.

Larry forced himself against the other children that were trying to wedge themselves into the Gateway Arch stairwell.

But they were going nowhere. Bodies had fallen ahead of them in the stampede, and no one was moving.

He looked around desperately.

There was another door at the far end of the observation deck.

A girl followed his glance.

"Let's try the other door," she shouted.

Larry looked back to where his mother lay smothered in bodies.

"Quick," the girl shouted. "There's another way. Follow me."

Several children turned to follow her. More youngsters peeled away from the crowd and hurried past him.

That was Larry's big opportunity. He clawed his way through kids to the doorway, then through it. Ahead of him lay darkness, and screaming. A low voice was groaning from fifteen feet down the steps.

"Mommy," he cried, and began pulling at the tangle of arms and legs that smothered her.

Twenty

JEREMY PULLED a ringing phone from his jacket pocket and noticed a Washington prefix on the caller's number.

"SAC Fuchsman," he answered.

"This is Hank calling. Keep on the lookout for Ferrar in a Lincoln Continental. I don't have any more details, other than it has a gold exterior."

Jeremy punched in the number of his roving agent, Stanley Welles, and relayed the news.

"Who's inside it?"

"The suspect, George Ferrar." He glanced at his notes and read off the description.

"Green Beret, eh?" Stanley repeated in a faltering voice.

"Just stop the son-of-a-bitch. Use deadly force if necessary." Then he gave Stanley the description of the container. "They might be arriving by truck, rail, air, or sea."

"I'll focus on trucks."

"Fair enough. Good luck."

Which was all Jeremy could offer.

Gold Lincoln. Deadly force, Stanley Welles repeated to himself, as he headed east toward the river.

He approached Interstate 70 and inched his black sedan the wrong way up an exit ramp. Finally at the top, he positioned his car on the shoulder, facing oncoming traffic from Illinois.

Ahead of him lay the flat expanse of Poplar St. Bridge that carried cars across the mile-wide Mississippi.

A steady stream of traffic zipped past him as he contemplated what to do next. The most he could do at the moment was to filter through all the cars and trucks he saw until the police roadblock was in place.

And what if he did get lucky? He could wait for a Lincoln or container truck to approach him, then take a shot at its tires. Or he could face the vehicle head-on and force it off the road. His best option was to drive with suicidal directness straight into oncoming traffic and intercept his target. The only problem was that he might get the wrong vehicle.

He had to narrow down the field. There were several container trucks passing him at the moment. But how many Gold Lincolns could there be?

He decided to switch to police band radio and clue the cops in on his location and intentions. He picked up the mike and called in to Jeremy.

"SAC Fuchsman, this is Stanley Welles. Come in."

Half a minute later, he heard a breathless, "This is Fuchsman."

"I'm stationed on the Interstate watching for cars that are crossing the bridge into the city," he said.

"Is the traffic still flowing?" Fuchsman's voice came back.

"Yep."

"That's not good."

"Wait. Here come some more container trucks."

"Try to read their identification numbers."

"Are you kidding? They're flashing past me."

Suddenly, some distinctive grillwork appeared on a fast-approaching car.

"Hold on. I think I've just found the Lincoln."

He clicked the radio off, and accelerated into the oncoming traffic.

As Ferrar started across the long bridge that connected Illinois with Missouri, he watched a flatbed truck bearing a single, short container. He couldn't make out the details, because it was silhouetted against the sunset.

He had to get closer to be sure it was Bolton.

They had already passed the police roadblock, and nothing stood between the truck and the Arch.

It was up to him to take it on.

Fortunately, no other traffic stood between them, and he had a clear, unobstructed view. By the time he crossed the state line, halfway across the Mississippi River, he had closed the gap to a mere fifty yards.

Sure enough. The red tape was flapping in the wind.

He sized up the low guardrail that prevented vehicles from plunging fifty feet into the river. The truck was in a vulnerable position against the rail. If he could bring it to a halt on the bridge, Bolton would have no avenue of escape.

He cruised into the center lane and began to approach the truck from the left. With luck, he could get in front of it and wedge it against the guardrail.

He needed a better angle and velocity, so he pulled to the far left lane again. Just then he saw an oncoming car weaving into his lane. They were on a collision course, and Ferrar was the target.

"What the..." He swerved behind the truck again.

The approaching car veered around the truck, aiming for him.

Ferrar continued to drift onto the shoulder. The jerk was going to smash *him* into the guardrail.

Ferrar slammed on the brakes, fishtailing at once, his rear wheels pulling to the left. He spun the wheel hard left, and found himself skidding sideways on two wheels.

The approaching driver hit his brakes and spun toward him. A terrifying screeching of tires filled the air. Ferrar battled for control of his car. Releasing the brake, he tried to steer gently to the right and return all four wheels to the pavement.

He did, and the killer sedan flew in a blur past his windshield. Ferrar straightened his front wheels and found his car hurtling toward the left bridge railing. He spun hard right, gunned the accelerator and peeled rubber as he approached the railing.

Boom.

Behind him, the black sedan rammed into the right-hand railing.

Ferrar hung on the steering wheel and squeezed his eyes shut.

He felt no jolt. Only the traction of wheels finally gripping the road. He looked up. He was carving a path straight down the Interstate. But, an orange flash illuminated every inch of his car's interior.

Behind him, a fireball rolled toward the sky. The black sedan was aflame as it hurdled over the railing and fell toward the river.

He closed his eyes again.

When he reopened them, the trailer truck was far ahead.

Prodding the engine into a higher gear, Ferrar found that the Lincoln was still operable. The wheels hummed, and the engine rose to a high-pitched drone.

To his right, the Gateway Arch stood out in all its six hundred and thirty feet of splendor. The truck was pulling into the exit lane.

Ferrar shot to the far right, several hundred yards behind the truck.

Its blinkers signaled that it was going to exit. There was no way he could catch up with the truck before it rammed into the Arch.

It would be in cinders within a minute.

Jeremy Fuchsman watched in horror as a fireball tumbled end over end off the Interstate bridge.

He yelled into the police band radio, "Stanley! Stanley come in"
Then his professional instincts took over.

As he watched police cars mobilizing in the direction of the car, he realized that the flaming vehicle could be a diversion. He had to stay behind with the Arch.

So he forced himself to turn away from the gruesome sight.

A car was rocketing around a pond and aiming straight for the foot of the Arch.

It was flashing its headlights and honking, nearly losing control on some low hills, and then slipping sideways across the grass.

He squinted into the sunset, trying to make out details on the vehicle. All he could tell was that it was a big sedan, and moving fast. He whipped out his service revolver and bent low to the ground. His legs carried him in a half-crouching sprint toward the Arch, where he rounded the sharp corner of the North stainless steel base and held his revolver steady before him.

The car straightened itself out and continued to speed straight at him.

"Stop, or I'll fire," he shouted in warning, taking aim at the driver.

Pow.

A hard edge flew in his face. He recoiled, holding a smashed forehead and crumbled to the pavement. He tried to roll over. His right shoulder snapped as he hit the ground. He looked up through a curtain of blood. Stretching the gun out before him in his left hand, he held it level to the ground and aimed at the oncoming car.

It was screeching to a halt, skidding on the hard surface.

The driver was positioning the vehicle at the base of the Arch. The front door flew open.

He took a last, exhausted breath and squeezed off a round at the person's head as it appeared, a fuzzy blob with red lips.

The gun exploded to life.

His hand recoiled limply. Cordite filled his nostrils. The smoking revolver landed with a clatter beside him.

From the open door of the Arch, the sound of small feet came pounding his way.

"Stop, Larry!"

His head rolled away against his crippled arm.

Ferrar was a mere five yards behind the trailer truck, eager to beat it to the exit ramp.

Though obscured from view, the exit ramp was right in front of them. He pulled onto the shoulder to pass the truck.

Then something strange happened. The truck swerved left at the last moment and didn't take the ramp.

Ferrar gritted his teeth as he slammed on his brakes and attempted a hard left.

He couldn't avoid the yellow crash barrels in his path. The last image he recorded in his mind was of the truck careening down the highway. He found himself hurtled forward against his seatbelt, and jerked toward the passenger's seat.

His neck snapped sideways, and blackness ensued.

A great deal of time may have passed. Or maybe none at all. Slowly, he began to focus on distant sounds, that of sirens approaching.

Lifting his head was painful, but something deep inside him said it was necessary. He saw a line of squad cars on the far side of a mountain of crash barrels. His head-on collision had prevented them from entering the highway. His monster car had saved his life.

But the truck!

His car was facing down an empty highway, the tall towers of St. Louis directly ahead of him. He blinked several times and tried to focus on the distance.

There was a single, black dot on the road. It had to be Bolton's truck.

Oddly, the Lincoln's motor was still running. His hand must have jabbed the car into neutral during the collision.

"Sorry, boys," he said, giving the cops a toss of the hand. He regretted it immediately. It was painful to move.

Then he headed into the sunset after Tray Bolton.

Twenty-one

IN THE LONG, lingering dusk, Tray's red and yellow taillights finally turned off Interstate 70. Following at a safe distance, Ferrar found himself on a truck route zigzagging through the hushed western edge of St. Louis. After the mess he had left behind, he figured that he had only one arrow left in his quiver—surprise.

The truck prowled through the quiet, green communities as if sniffing out a place to stay for the night. Whenever it came to a traffic signal, Ferrar stopped one light behind.

They passed several commercial streets with lighted storefronts, motel entrances, and gas stations. But the truck continued on to some unknown destination.

Then an illuminated blue street sign gave Ferrar the answer. They were approaching a cargo facility near the East Terminal of Lambert St. Louis International Airport.

The truck finally came to rest under a pool of light at the cargo facility. The guard on duty checked Bolton through at once, and directed him toward a set of warehouses to the right.

Ferrar pulled up next and powered down his window. The scent of airplane exhaust was overpowering.

He rubbed the sore spot in his neck. He was going to have to stay coherent a short while longer.

"Boss' car?"

"Huh?" He looked stupid for a moment until it finally dawned on him how incongruous it must look for someone in mechanic's overalls tooling around in a late model Lincoln Continental. "Yeah. I get the dirty work, but the wheels aren't bad."

"What did you do, drive her into a brick wall?"

He frowned. The whole front end must be mangled. "Came that way."

The guard nodded and blew out a lungful of air that turned to steam at once.

"What you got today, buddy?" he asked.

"Last minute drop-off for Federal Express," Ferrar said.

"Okay. That would be a left at the end of this block."

"Thanks much." Ferrar threw him a two-fingered salute.

Instead of following the man's directions, he hung an abrupt right and followed Tray's truck. He watched the guard in the rearview mirror as he turned the wrong way. The guard seemed mildly amused, but didn't otherwise object.

The container truck was parked behind a hangar. Ferrar pulled up to an office just around the corner.

There, he remained in the car and watched. A forklift slipped its prongs under the container and gently plucked it off the flatbed. The forklift backed up beeping, turned, and headed into the open hangar.

It was time to move in.

There was no need for disguise. His black growth of beard obscured half his face. His oil-stained overalls identified him as a dumpy mechanic.

Even Bolton wouldn't recognize him.

Hoping to find a side entrance, Ferrar circled the hangar. There was none, but the entire back of the building was open and a DC-7 cargo plane was just pulling out. Its four huge turboprop engines began roaring and its navigational lights began to flash.

He dodged through the opening into the shadows of the hangar. He looked around inside. The place was strangely empty. The men from the truck were gone, presumably already aboard the plane with the container.

He tried to make out the objects around him in greater detail. Nearest to him appeared to be stacks of books bundled in plastic and strapped to pallets.

Deeper in the shadows, he made out a man leaning over a table. The blond hair and chiseled physique were familiar enough. It was Tray Bolton.

Tray's briefcase lay open on the table before him, and he was inserting a needle into his forearm, just below a rubber tube that pinched off the flow of blood. With a squeeze of his thumb, he injected several cc's of a clear liquid into a vein.

Ferrar's feet bumped into a crowbar. It would make a good weapon. He picked it up.

Behind him, the airplane was taxiing into the nighttime. He checked its wings, fuselage, and tail for a company logo or insignia. Strangely, it was unmarked.

"Hi, George," a voice said in his ear.

He spun around, ducking, and came up with the hooked claw of the crowbar slashing upward through the air. It caught a sheet of plastic from the pallet and tore a hole in it.

Several Bibles spilled out onto the floor.

Bolton began laughing deeply, having stepped back to avoid the swing. His strong hands grabbed the end of the crowbar that was tangled in the plastic sleeting, and yanked it out of Ferrar's grasp.

Ferrar righted himself. He was furious, but unafraid. He gaped at Bolton's lighthearted expression.

"Bibles?" he muttered. Why did Bolton have Bibles?

"Yes, the Holy Scripture," Tray said. "Want a copy?" He tossed one toward Ferrar, who stepped back just in time. Who knew what kind of chemical agents they contained?

"You look like you've got a few questions on your mind," Bolton said.

"And from that smug look on your face, I'd say you have some answers."

"Try me."

Ferrar examined his former boyhood friend and competitor. They had both come a long way since Bar Harbor High School.

"Okay, here goes," he began. "For starters, how did you escape from Tora Bora?"

"Ah, you're still interested in tradecraft. There's always an escape route in any such cave complex. I happened to have studied a map long before our assault team arrived. Didn't you?"

"I didn't know there was such a map. So you planned the ambush long before we got there."

Bolton bowed, but didn't respond.

"What happened to Deke Houston at Bar Harbor?"

"He wasn't dead enough when I got to him."

Ferrar hung his head.

"Next question?"

"How did you escape from the train wreck?"

"Now think about it. Why would I have stayed on that train? The shipment was already offloaded onto the truck."

"But I heard you shoot the engineer, I saw you go back to check on the truck, and then run up ahead to the engine."

"I set the train in motion and jumped off. I needed to shake the police off my tail."

"Well, how did you happen to have a truck handy in Ohio?"

"I had a truck with a forklift as backup. My men shadowed me in it on the highway all the way. I kept in touch with them by CB radio. When the Chief of Police radioed me, I knew my cover was blown. So I simply told my men where to stop, and we transferred the goods from the train to the truck."

Ferrar nodded. It was a tidy, well-planned operation. "That brings me to why," he said, toeing the open pages of the Old Testament with his foot.

"Why what?" Bolton asked.

"Why are you doing this?"

Bolton untied the tourniquet from his arm and leaned against the remaining stack of Bibles, the crowbar still level before him. He sucked in his breath as if the heroin rush were coming on fast.

"Do you think this whole thing is about Islam?" he asked with contempt in his voice. "You've got to be kidding. I'm here because I know half the drug cartel in Latin America and Asia, not because of ideology. Don't you see the big picture? Al-Qaeda needs money, and what better source than drugs?"

"Where did you get this whacked out drugs-for-weapons scheme? From Ollie North?"

"Don't you see the exquisite irony of it? Osama thought it was inspired. While drugs are destroying America, the money America spends on drugs can subsidize the very terrorists whose bombs and chemical and biological agents are bringing the country to its knees. Bin Laden gave me *carte blanche* to run operations in America."

"So you're saying that America has underwritten the Islamic Holy Wars around the globe."

"Now you've got it."

"But you're not Muslim."

"Far from it. In fact I'm using them as much as they're using me. And we both know that."

"So you're in it for the money."

"Money? Ridiculous."

"Glory, then."

"Oh, there's no glory in this kind of undercover op. Only the aesthetic satisfaction of watching a perfect scheme unfold."

"Then you must have some beef with America. What do you hope to get out of this?"

"There's nothing wrong with America, and I don't expect to make a cent."

Ferrar eyed him with skepticism. "So it's not the money or the cause."

Tray smirked. "Look at the two of us. We're not drug lords or playboys or idealistic radicals. We're soldiers."

"God, so many people like you have sold this country out. It's a wonderful country, a beautiful land, people who care. What *is* it, Tray? What is it with you people?"

Tray took a deep breath, and struggled to concentrate. "It's personal, George. It all boils down to what makes us individuals, what makes us wake up in the morning, what keeps the adrenalin flowing."

"Is personal satisfaction enough of a reason to betray your country?"

"Betray? Should we talk about betrayal? Let's start with you betraying a friendship."

"Me? What did I do?"

"Bonnie. That's what you did. You did Bonnie one summer. All summer during college, at The Trap in Bar Harbor. Talk about betrayal. How about you selling out both Bonnie and me?"

"I didn't know that you and she were still an item."

"An *item*? That's teenager talk. There's so little you ever realized about us. And that blindness will cost you everything."

He felt stunned as if struck by a concussion grenade. Then slowly his mind traveled back to those wonderful, sticky, intoxicating days spent one summer with Bonnie Taylor back in Maine. For two months, they had recaptured those lost days of high school when Tray had stood between them.

Tray Bolton sure knew how to make a guy feel cheap. Not only did Ferrar temporarily steal Tray's girl, he betrayed the trust of his friend.

And if that weren't enough, Tray seemed to be making him out as the cause of al-Qaeda's attack on America. Tray had said that his blindness would cost him everything.

"Would you mind defining *everything*?"

"It will cost you everything you know and value," Tray said. His angry expression reminded Ferrar of an attacking grizzly bear. "You will die. Bonnie will die. And the country will come to its knees."

How little Ferrar had realized during that summer in Maine what enormous ramifications a tryst would have on the world.

"Okay, while I'm groveling down here in remorse, just let me ask you one last question." He eyed the Bibles. "Surely you weren't transporting Bibles out of Pakistan."

"Ah! You were onto me all the way from Pakistan?"

"Peshawar, Karachi, Bahrain…"

"…Quebec City, Bar Harbor," Tray finished for him. "I thought you would appreciate that touch, using my cottage as a transshipment point."

Ferrar saw the genius, but failed to share the triumph.

"So what do you have in there?"

"Oh, it's not in there," Bolton said, kicking the pallet of Bibles. "It's up there." His eyes traveled upward. Ferrar noticed that Tray's eyes had turned glassy. Surely not from emotion.

Just then he heard the roar of the DC-7 passing overhead.

"It's a bomb," Tray said simply, with a grandiose, sloppy gesture of the crowbar. "A ten-megaton atomic bomb."

Ferrar stopped breathing. No longer did the bomb simply exist in theory. Bolton's words had made it real. A terrorist with an atom bomb had made the long journey into the heartland of America.

"And all you want is personal satisfaction? How can your ends possibly justify such massive weapons?"

"That's the way we build them. Isn't it?"

Suddenly, a red blur streaked out of the darkness toward his head. The crowbar hit Ferrar with incredible swiftness. He was able to duck enough to avoid it whacking him directly across the brow.

But the crown of his head absorbing a crowbar didn't feel much better. He fell to the floor in a heap.

"Try and catch me now," Bolton said with a guttural laugh.

In his stupor, he felt Tray Bolton fumbling clumsily for his wallet. Inside was a wad of cash and several IDs—some false, some not.

Ferrar was losing touch with his identity anyway as he slipped off into blackness.

FBI Director Hank Gibson's office was buzzing with agents trying to coordinate with state and local law enforcement in Missouri. The manhunt was shaping up to be the biggest since the Summer Olympics bombing in Atlanta.

In the FBI's search for truth, the last thing they needed was a red herring throwing them off the trail. Hank needed a moment to clear the air with Congressman Connors.

Connors was still in his office at the far end of Pennsylvania Avenue when he picked up the phone. "Yo?" Connors answered, casually enough.

"See what I told you?" Hank began at once. "Ferrar phoned you and warned of an attack on the St. Louis Arch. Well, rush hour traffic was held up, crowds stampeded, agents were killed, and the Arch didn't fall. It was all a diversion."

"He *is* in St. Louis now," Connors reminded him. "Why would he draw attention to his own whereabouts?"

"All this fiasco tells me is that the man's not telling the truth. We're going to hunt him down and bring him to justice."

"Over my dead body."

Hank didn't care as he threw down the phone.

The guard at the air cargo facility in St. Louis heard his telephone ringing and turned. He was happy to step out of the cold into the relative warmth of his booth to take the call.

"Yeah?" he answered.

"This is the SLPD," a matter-of-fact voice said. "We're on the lookout for suspected international terrorists in the vicinity. In particular, we want you to keep an eye out for several suspicious vehicles. One's a semi truck with a container."

"Seen plenty of them today," the guard reported.

"The other's a gold-colored Lincoln Continental with a male driver, black hair, six foot."

The guard stiffened. "I just saw a man drive through my gate in a huge boat with a dent in it. It was gold, and it may have been a Lincoln Continental."

"Good. He's armed and dangerous."

"What do you mean 'good?'"

"We'll be there right away. Just don't let him leave." The phone clicked off.

The guard didn't move as he stared into the dimly lit cargo area, his fingers frozen to the receiver.

Ferrar slowly revived only to have a blurry view of his surroundings. He was lying on a slick concrete slab. Cold night air whooshed past an immense opening.

He seemed to be in a large warehouse.

In the night sky, a plane roared off. He blinked to clear his vision. Its taillights were awash in the wavering fumes of its engines.

Then he remembered the crowbar. It brought back immediate and painful sensations. He groaned and felt a numb spot on the top of his head.

Suddenly it became crystal clear to him. He had to catch Tray.

His knees wobbled as he tried to regain his feet. His head felt as big as the building.

Putting one foot in front of the other, he staggered out toward the airstrip. Along the tarmac, he found an office. He squinted to make out the sign. It read Air Cargo—as good place as any to start.

He began to feel a throbbing bump on his crown. The last stage of coming to was losing the numbness that served as a local anesthesia.

He reached up and felt something warm and sticky seeping from his hairline. His fingers were glistening red in the floodlight. They smelled of iron. At least it was blood and not cranial fluid.

He closed his eyes and staggered the short remaining distance across a patch of grass to the Air Cargo office. By the time he reached it, he felt sufficiently revived by the cool wind to hang a casual smile on his face.

Inside, blinding fluorescent lights glared down on filing cabinets and on a hot young woman who sat poised behind a desk. Veering to one side, he was rewarded with a remarkable view of her legs. She wore long brown leather boots, a miniskirt, and a blouse with a lapel that threatened to blow completely apart in the sudden gust of wind.

"Close that door, and come in here," she said.

He obliged.

She had a sweet face, with bright brown eyes that opened wide when she saw the blood.

A pair of patrolmen from the St. Louis Police Department positioned themselves on either side of the entrance to the Air Cargo office. Meanwhile, Sergeant Fontaine, his muscles rippling under his starched uniform and leather jacket, aimed for just above the knob and took a flying kick at it.

The door gave way with little resistance, and he burst into the room, stopping just short of the receptionist's desk.

There, he righted himself, his service revolver drawn. He had nothing to aim at but a pretty young woman with a funny look on her face.

He straightened his jacket and quickly holstered his gun. The receptionist smiled with relief and went back to her business, which seemed primarily to be patting down her disheveled hair and pinning it up.

"S'cuse me, ma'am," Fontaine started. "But have you see'd a man,'bout forty years old, six feet tall, black hair…"

"Muscles out to here?"

"Er, yes. That would be him."

"Well," the woman replied. "We might have had a brief encounter."

"Like, what did he want?" Fontaine asked, trying to summon all his interrogative powers. He was feeling lucky today. This case might well put him in line for a move into Investigations.

"Well, he wanted to know something about a cargo flight," she said.

"Does this have anything to do with a container shipment that went out in the past hour?"

"Yes, it does. They just barely got it on the flight and took off."

He moved in and flipped out his notepad. "And what flight might that be, ma'am?" He had been on an airplane once.

"It was chartered," she said.

"Oh." He didn't know anything about chartered.

"Let me check," she continued, turning and searching her records. "That's strange. No flight plan. I have no idea where it's headed."

He tried to read the pages over her shoulder. But his eyes couldn't help traveling down her neckline to the firm points in her bra. "Where do they usually fu— er, fly?"

"It's a tourist charter. They fly to all the normal destinations," she breathed dreamily. "Hawaii, Las Vegas, Niagara Falls, Grand Canyon, San Francisco. You name it."

He glanced at his two colleagues, stumped for what to ask next. Maybe he wasn't quite investigative material after all. "So, uh, where is the *suspect* heading?"

"Oh, I have no idea. What is he suspected of?"

"I can't tell you that, ma'am," he said, leaning forward confidentially. Maybe he couldn't make it in the detective department, but he *could* make it in the women department.

"Do you know his whereabouts at the present time?" he asked, savoring the sound of his own words. He straightened out his full torso and circled her. Boldly, he looked under the desk to see if Ferrar was hiding under her skirt.

He raised his eyes quickly. It wasn't much of a skirt.

"He's in a plane flying somewhere, I'm sure."

Fontaine furrowed his brow, humiliated. "He's got a plane?"

"This is an airport after all," she breathed.

There it was again. Her breathy voice. He drew back and nodded. She wanted him.

He reached for his belt, and slowly unhooked the radio. Barely able to contain the tremble in his voice, he told the Police Commissioner the whole story.

To Fontaine's disappointment, Commissioner Frank Wheeler didn't sound so overjoyed by the news.

"Okay, so the bombs are on one airplane and the suspect's on another," Commissioner Wheeler summed up. "I want all planes at the airport grounded, Sergeant. Commercial, military, private. We've got all sorts of injuries to children at the Arch, a pileup of police cars on I-70, an FBI agent dead from falling into the Mississippi in a ball of fire, another FBI agent with a gunshot wound to her shoulder, and the FBI's SAC down with a broken arm and severe facial lacerations. I tell you, we've got to nail this guy."

Just then, Fontaine heard the sound of a private jet soaring overhead in a takeoff profile.

It was heading west.

Twenty-two

REBECCA FRIEDMAN stopped trimming pork chops and leaned over the kitchen counter to listen to a public service announcement on the radio. It was Attorney General Douglas Laidlaw, his voice yappy as a Southern preacher, speaking in apocalyptic terms.

He told the nation that he had just learned from the FBI that the air transportation system was at immediate risk of another terrorist attack. He said that he had directed the Federal Aviation Administration to ground all air transport nationwide effective immediately. Furthermore, he advised that the public sit tight for a few hours until Federal authorities stabilized the situation.

The vagaries went on. There were "likely targets," and "potential suspects under surveillance."

"Damn it," she shouted at the radio. She pounded a fist against the counter. "You know who you're after. Give us all the details."

But he didn't. Instead, he went on to announce a general alert concerning tourist sites in the United States.

"Vague. Vague," she cried out. "Where? Florida? New York? Washington? California?"

He gave no more details, and the regular programming resumed.

At that moment, the front door popped open.

She looked around startled and grabbed the meat cleaver.

"Easy, dear." It was just her husband.

She approached him with an accusatory glare. She stopped well short of the perfunctory welcome kiss that she normally administered, and snapped at him, "Why doesn't that bastard give out Ferrar's name and physical description? Why, I could go to the *Washington Post* right now and spell out all the details that we need to nab him."

"You'd better not, dear," he said, hanging up his overcoat in the hallway closet. "What's cooking?"

"How could you even have an appetite at a time like this?"

"Because I know the FBI is on the case."

His ambivalence was an open invitation to attack.

"Lester, our son lies buried in rubble in Afghanistan because of that man. Ferrar has ruined all our lives, and now he's fixing to do something truly evil to the nation. I can feel it in my bones. What are we waiting for?"

He looked downward at her, his eyes small and hard. "Rebecca, we don't know for sure what he's up to. There are even some camps that say he's going after the real terrorists. So don't you go jumping to conclusions."

"*Some camps?* Like who? Like you?"

"No, not me at all. I've been after Ferrar from Day One. It's people like Congressman Connors who're convinced that Ferrar deserves a Medal of Honor."

"How can this kind of *crap* go on at the highest levels of government? You call up the Attorney General right now and give him a piece of your mind."

"You mean a piece of *your* mind."

She glowered at him, then suddenly realized that the cleaver was still clenched in her fist, and she was leveling it at him.

She dropped it on the counter with a clatter, and held her apron over her face. Her shoulders began to tremble involuntarily. And tears of helplessness quickly drenched the apron.

Lester put an arm around her, but she couldn't be consoled.

"Okay, I'll do it," he relented.

He sat down with her on the couch, placed himself beside her, and pulled a phone from his pocket.

"Hello? Get me Hank. We've got to release a full description of Ferrar to the press."

Flying a Gulfstream IV was normally a joy for Ferrar. The controls were simple and the small jet responded with enthusiasm.

However, flying while drowsy with a throbbing headache made it difficult. And flying during a nationwide grounding of all aircraft threatened to turn him into a nervous wreck.

As soon as the radio crackled with a general FAA directive for all aircraft to land at the nearest safe harbor, he developed a distinct discomfort at being airborne. And it didn't make him feel any better to know that he was the intended target.

Soon military aircraft would claim all the nation's airspace, and he'd be a sitting duck. Or, rather, a flying duck. No matter.

It was time to think clearly about where to land.

Nancy, the sweet young woman at the Lambert Field Air Cargo office had been most helpful. It hadn't taken much persuasion to get the DC-7's destination out of her. It was Oakland California International Airport.

She had been worried about his bleeding scalp, and had tended to him with hydrogen peroxide and some tender pressure.

Hoping to get a head start on those who were pursuing him, he had extracted a promise from her not to divulge the destination of the DC-7 to any authorities. Again, she had complied.

Then she had applied even more pressure, this time with her entire body, and soon he had found himself sandwiched between her and the water cooler. It had taken some self-control to extricate himself from the situation, and it had taken even more diplomacy to leave her while remaining in her good graces.

He looked back on the incident with detachment. How long had it been since he had had such a woman? Any woman?

The war in Afghanistan had taken a toll in many unforeseeable ways. One of them was a total lack of women on the battlefield—or in the country for that matter, except for the black gliding tents that had passed for women. Where had the ladies of the American military been when it was time to free their Afghan sisters?

He could think of one fine woman in uniform.

He pushed a button that set the jet on autopilot, heading due west over the spiked peaks of Colorado. He loosened his safety belt and slipped his cell phone out of his pocket.

He hoped it didn't throw off his navigational equipment.

Bonnie Taylor entered her cozy house in the Twin Peaks neighborhood of San Francisco, having finished a frenzied afternoon of fleet maneuvers and contingency planning. She hung her white Coast Guard hat in her closet and kicked off her boots. Then she plopped into the sofa in front of her television and clicked on the remote.

A fuzzy close-up of a man appeared on the screen. It took a moment for her to realize that she knew him. It was George Ferrar, rugged, dark, and looking like a scared rabbit.

"This CIA file photo of George Ferrar was just released minutes ago to the press. He is considered armed and very dangerous."

Her phone rang.

She ran into the kitchen and grabbed the receiver off the wall.

"Yes?" she answered, trying to mask her brusqueness.

"This is Ferrar. We're in big trouble."

"*We're* in trouble? Your wanted poster is on TV, or haven't you heard? The Bay Area is panicking with reports of an impending terrorist strike. And guess what? *You're* the terrorist. What are you gonna hit? You've got all these fine targets here, buildings, bridges, museums, Silicon Valley, tectonic faults. People are scared shitless."

"Hear me out."

She listened for several minutes, at first unsure if she wanted to continue the conversation. Ferrar contended that Bolton had murdered his own men in Tora Bora, seized an atomic bomb in Pakistan, and was going to blow some place up.

It didn't make any sense. Sure, Tray was capable of anything, but so was any other commando with a twisted mind. Take Ferrar for instance.

Then Ferrar came to the last part. "And it's all because of you."

She caught her breath. The story suddenly began to make some sense. It could easily be because of her.

"Are you still listening?" he was asking softly.

Reluctantly, she said, "Okay, you've got my attention."

She heard him take a deep breath. "I believe Bolton will show up on your radar screen within the next few hours."

"Then I'm going to leave here at once."

"Bonnie," he said with some clear difficulty. "You can't."

"What? I can't leave my own house in the face of who, no *what's*, coming here?"

"I need you to draw him in. Bait him. Otherwise I can't get him."

She gave a half-laugh, "You two men are just out to destroy me. You're a team. You've always been that way. He's destroyed my self-respect..."

"He's been abusive, hasn't he? He's a master of mental torture."

"...and you're playing with my emotions, too. You've both abused me."

This caused Ferrar a moment's hesitation. When he came back, there was a surge of emotion in his voice.

"Bonnie, listen to me closely. Bolton and I are not a team. Never have been, never will be. This is our only chance to find the bomb. Just occupy him for as long as you can. Distract him. Hell, give him what he wants."

"George, you're still living in a fantasy world. And now you want me to sacrifice myself for you..."

"We have to work together."

"...and then you'll come and slay the dragon. Ta da!"

"Okay, just call me St. George. The problem is I can't come right away. I'm in the air right now."

"Do you think I'm nuts? Wait around for a homicidal maniac to break into my house? George, I haven't heard from you for years. For all I know, these stories on TV are true."

"I am no terrorist. I want to help you."

On the fringes of her perception, she heard footsteps at her front door. She whirled around, her heart skipping a beat.

"Oh, my God," she breathed.

Tray Bolton burst through the door. He wore a broad smile and held out both arms toward her.

"Tray," she said, losing all sensation in her body. The handset fell from her grasp and swung by her knees.

Twenty-three

AT PETERSON AIR FORCE BASE east of Colorado Springs, Commander Whitey Sullivan took an important, but expected, phone call in his office. It was the head of the North American Aerospace Defense command, otherwise known as NORAD. The NORAD chief had a note of urgency in his voice.

Whitey stood at attention while he listened.

Apparently, the FBI had located a suspect. He was airborne and flying west out of Lambert in St. Louis.

He smiled at the irony. While NORAD was busy searching for incoming missiles from Russia, his base was equipped to take on the more immediate threat of attack from a domestic platform.

As part of Operation Noble Eagle, helping to defend the continental United States in the aftermath of 11 September, his base had just received an AWACS aircraft that was previously on loan to NATO. At the moment, he had her flying high above the Rocky Mountains, her sophisticated radar combined with an identification friend-or-foe subsystem picking up, identifying, and tracking all flying objects from low-flying planes to commercial airliners, even incoming missiles and UFOs.

The FAA had grounded all aircraft in the nation, so if there was a blip on the AWACS console, that would be their man. It couldn't be any easier than that.

Whitey hung up the secure telephone and got on the base intercom. "Scramble the F-15 and F-16 fleet at once. I want air reconnaissance support for the AWACS out over Utah. We have a suspect flying west from St. Louis. I want you fully armed for air-to-air combat."

Six crews were ready on strip alert, and two minutes later he heard jet engines firing up on the tarmac. He silently counted the number of planes. "One, two, three, four, five, six."

He smiled to himself, and leaned over the base's intercom mike. "Good luck, men. We're gonna shoot ourselves some terrorists tonight."

He parted the blinds in his office window and watched as the blazing arrow-shaped jets roared down the tarmac and off into the dark, empty sky.

It didn't take long for the E-3 Sentry Airborne Warning and Control System aircraft, known as AWACS, circling over Salt Lake City to spot trouble. The modified Boeing 707/320 commercial airframe's thirty-foot rotating radar dome quickly zeroed in on the only other manmade bird in the sky.

Reconnaissance Officer Burt Huett had watched with satisfaction as the blips on his graphic console followed predictable patterns of flight. No new blips appeared, and all planes in the air converged on the numerous commercial airports in the West and on the West Coast.

There were, of course the dozens of private airplanes that disappeared into a vast number of small landing strips. Those pilots ranged from ranchers, crop dusters, flight instructors, and private businessmen to the occasional weirdo in California or Colorado trying out a new type of microlight in the middle of the night.

Only one dot remained on the large console. It maintained an unswerving westward course. The blip was not accompanied by a call number, so it either didn't have an identification transponder or the system had been silenced. Another suspicious feature of the plane was its ground speed, calculated to be a good 450 miles per hour, well above the speeds attainable by prop planes.

He reached for his radio and transmitted a message over the general flight frequency. "This is the United States Air Force. We're trying to contact an aircraft flying over northeastern California. Come in."

No response.

"The FAA has grounded all flights immediately. Please identify yourself. Over."

Ominously, there was no response. While the radio blared mere static, the blip continued to move westward undeterred. It was possible that the aircraft had a radio failure and didn't receive the original FAA message to land. In that case, it wouldn't have heard Bret's second warning. More likely, the pilot was ignoring him.

Turning its transponder box off *and* maintaining radio silence added up to the small jet defying the flight ban. That had to be their man. There was only one problem. As it had just entered California airspace, it would be within striking distance of populous coastal cities within half an hour.

Meanwhile, on the bottom right of his console, he watched a cluster of blips, identified by the AWACS' receiver as friendly fighter jets. They were only now just passing from Utah into Nevada.

The Air Force should scramble fighter jets in California to intercept the bastard.

He rolled a trackball that zeroed a crosshair onto the cluster. Within seconds he had their ground speed. Seven hundred miles per hour. He pulled up a calculator on a separate console and figured out the distances. The fighter jets could still beat the terrorist to California's coast with minutes to spare.

It was time to give his commander an update on the rogue plane. He selected the scrambled military frequency on his radio and spoke into his lip mike.

"Our target is passing over northeastern California, cruising due west at 450 miles per hour. It's headed in the direction of San Francisco, and should reach there in 27 minutes. Over."

"Roger that," several voices came back.

"I calculate that our fighters should reach him before he makes the coast," Huett said.

Then from a longer distance away, "I'll convey this information to Army, Navy, Coast Guard, and FBI."

It was the Chairman of the Joint Chiefs of Staff at the Pentagon.

Leo Pollo was a five-star Army general, highly decorated in Korea and later in Vietnam. He had every reason to be the Pentagon's Chairman of the Joint Chiefs of Staff, and he was.

As the nation's top-ranking military officer, he didn't exactly command all branches of America's military, but he came damn close. The connection point between the administration and the services, he was in a nuts and bolts position. Just the way he liked it.

Standing in the Pentagon's Operations Center, he took the secure radio transmission from the AWACS with an air of calm. But the short hairs on the back of his neck still bristled against his uniform's collar.

The Ops Center had direct lines to the President, the Secretary of Defense, and all the other cabinet posts related to national security.

And one of the buttons connected him directly with Hank Gibson, head of the FBI.

"Hank," Leo thundered. He knew no other way of speaking. "Our AWACS over the Rockies has detected what we presume to be the terrorist George Ferrar heading for San Francisco. He is either piloting or has commandeered a jet. His ETA is approximately twenty-three minutes."

"San Francisco," Hank repeated thoughtfully. "Where's he landing?"

"Landing? We've scrambled half a dozen fighter jets to intercept him and shoot him down. He's not landing anywhere."

"Leo, this is important," Hank said angrily. "Now listen to me carefully."

Leo adjusted his military stance. He wasn't used to being dressed down by anyone, especially a civilian.

Hank tore into him. "Police interviewed an eyewitness in St. Louis. She confirmed that Ferrar doesn't, I repeat does *not*, have the bombs. They left St. Louis on another plane. *He's* on a smaller plane and he's not going to blow anything up. What we need are the bombs. And he's our only lead now to finding those bombs."

Leo shook his head. "What other plane? There's only one in the air."

"It is a larger jet and it departed earlier. It probably already arrived at its destination."

"Okay, then let's work with what we've got. We don't have the bombs, but we have the terrorist's ringleader, and that's Ferrar. What the terrorists still need is the brains to position and detonate the bombs, and we've got that man under our thumb. We can stop Ferrar from setting these things off. My boys are under orders to knock him out of the sky."

Ferrar sat in the pilot's seat looking down at the dark Sierra Nevada range when he felt a buffeting sensation.

It felt like a blast of wind.

He checked his wind indicator. No shift in wind direction, and no wind sheer or updraft.

His cell phone hadn't thrown off the altitude and navigational equipment. Oakland lay dead ahead in twenty minutes.

Then another blast rocked him in the other direction.

What the hell?

Two more jolts sent him flopping against the instrument panel. Looking up, he suddenly realized what was happening. He was being buzzed by a handful of fighter jets.

One by one, their sizzling tail flames shot by overhead, nearly melting the Gulfstream's glass canopy above him. They were toying with him, like sadistic hawks swooping on a smaller bird mercilessly until it died of fright.

He leaned on the control yoke, dipping the nose straight toward the mountaintops. His entire weight leaning forward against his shoulder harness was compensated by the gathering g force load. Within several seconds he would be weightless.

He wondered what velocity the aircraft could take before breaking apart.

Evasive maneuvers in a civilian airplane couldn't outrun a fighter jet. He didn't have a prayer.

Leo Pollo detected a slow burn on the other end of the line. The Director of the FBI was close to shouting.

"I am not going to lose my prime suspect to a bunch of overeager airmen."

"Okay," Leo finally relented. "I get your point. Let me see if I can call off the engagement."

"Great," Hank said. "This will give me a chance to scramble my field offices in the Bay Area."

"We'll escort Ferrar from a safe distance, and you can start looking for the bombs."

"Yeah, chances are they arrived from St. Louis in the past hour," Hank said. "I'll have my men start by checking the airports."

Leo's mind was already on the next call he would have to make. Letting go of a tight leash did not come naturally.

After alerting his field office in San Francisco, Hank Gibson felt it was his duty, but not his pleasure, to phone Lester Friedman with an update on the chase after the CIA's fugitive employee.

Hank's secretary phoned around and found Lester at home.

Hank began his briefing at once. "Ferrar appears to be heading for San Francisco."

"And the bombs?"

"They seem to be heading independently to some sort of tourist destination," Hank said. "That's the best information we have at present."

"That's excellent information," Lester replied. "If Ferrar is heading to San Francisco, then you can bet the bombs are heading for San Francisco, too." He seemed to wait for confirmation from Hank.

Hank couldn't dispute the probability. Of course Ferrar would be heading where the bombs were going, but possibly not for the same reason that Friedman assumed.

As head of the operation, Hank couldn't trust Ferrar to do the right thing. He couldn't take the risk of allowing Ferrar to diffuse the situation. But he could rely on Ferrar to lead them to the bombs and the FBI could take it from there.

"How are you going to capture Ferrar?"

Hank told him about the fighter jets scrambled from Colorado and chasing the lone jet over California.

"Then you can blast him out of the air," Lester said with glee.

"We're not taking that approach," Hand said. "The fighter jets will escort the plane to its final destination. At that point, our men will apprehend Ferrar."

Lester tried several times to start a sentence. Finally, he spluttered, "Has Ralph Connors gotten to you or what?"

"Let's just say that cooler heads must prevail."

He set down the phone before Lester could unburden all of his emotional baggage once again.

Five hundred and fifty miles per hour was pushing it, Ferrar decided as he plunged two thousand feet to evade the fighters on his tail.

How many g's could the Gulfstream IV take in pulling out of its rapid descent?

He quickly checked the night sky for the fighter jets. They had abandoned him during his freefall. Maybe they didn't care to play such dangerous games, or they had time to spare before acquiring their target and firing on him.

It took more than arm strength to pull upward on the yoke. In his weightless state, he needed a brace against which to pry back the nose of the jet.

He freed his left foot and wedged it against the instrument panel, crushing a glass fuel gauge with his heel. Then he raised his other foot, relinquishing all control of the jet's ailerons and flaps. With that leg, he braced himself further against the instrument panel, then began to stretch gently backward.

The jet's trajectory slowly began to change. The mountains, now distinguishable through the front glass panel, were rushing up toward him, a black mass of peaks and ravines and trees.

The acceleration began to decrease. He suddenly found himself flung full force against his harness. He stretched backward, his knees flexing, his thigh muscles bulging, his back nearly cracking under the strain

The control yoke moved slightly. He strained his biceps and forearms, curled his fingers tightly and closed his eyes. He didn't want to see what would happen next.

As the plane's pitch altered further, deceleration increased and the wings began to torque to the port side.

He dropped his legs under the panel and adjusted the ailerons and flaps, instantly compensating for the slight roll. But his lunge for the foot pedals had overcompensated into a roll to the starboard. He eased down on the other pedal and the jet straightened out, level with the ground.

He had checked his fall.

It was time to take another look out into the night.

He was flying through a forest. Trees swept by out his portside window.

He yanked upward on the controls. Needing more speed for control, he pulled the throttle full out. The plane zoomed to 520 miles per hour. The glint of a stream flashed below. The jet ran parallel to it for a few hundred yards. He flew past rounded boulders, then alongside a cliff.

Then, gently, he began to ascend.

He fought to make out the twists and turns of the canyon. He skewed left and right, following the terrain immediately to his left. Then he looked up.

A stone mountain lay dead ahead.

Lester came to the chilling realization that Hank Gibson and the FBI had been put solely in charge of national defense. He ordered his limo to pull up directly to the front of his house. He had to get to the Pentagon, fast.

"And get me Ferrar's personnel file."

He was waiting on the curb when the car arrived.

Inside the limo, his aide Charles White was just receiving a faxed multi-page printout of Ferrar's complete service record.

The rear wheels spun out on slick, fallen leaves as Lester grabbed the faxed pages and began to flip through them.

The file contained every official detail about Ferrar's life since his inception into the Agency, from his promotions to his citations, both good and bad.

Lester immediately turned to Ferrar's security check, where page after page of interviews with persons who knew him had been carefully assembled. There was his mother's account, his high school counselor's interview, his residential advisor's comments from Berkeley. Then Lester's eyes fell on a more familiar name. Tray had given a full accounting of his high school buddy.

As the limo angled downhill toward the Potomac, Lester adjusted his reading light and let the page speak to him. Tray had known George Ferrar as a high school sophomore when the Friedmans had moved to the submarine base near Bar Harbor. Tray had spoken highly of Ferrar's athletic ability, and commended his friend's steadfastness throughout high school. It brought a tear to Lester's eye. How deceived Tray had been at the time.

Within minutes, they were passing over Key Bridge into Virginia.

Tray's depiction of Ferrar became more detailed during their college years at the University of California. The two had competed at Arabic studies, both earning the highest grade point averages possible for a full three years. Their tastes ran to Persian cuisine, lamb kebabs, and hummus. Then things seemed to go sour between them, according to Tray's account of events.

Ferrar had turned hostile and predatory, unpredictable and unreliable. Tray had regretted this change in his friend's nature, but had allowed Ferrar his freedom to explore the other side of his personality.

Circling the Pentagon on the expressway, Lester saw where floodlights illuminated the gaping hole and construction crews were hard at work. Less than three months earlier, hundreds had died there from the al-Qaeda attack.

Tomorrow, the nation was facing a different attack.

Quietly, he vowed that such a tragedy would never take place again on American soil.

Then his attention returned to Tray's interview. When asked what had brought about the changes in his friend, Tray had given a simple answer: "women." When asked to elucidate, Tray had added the stinging comment, "He stole my woman, he took her to bed for an entire summer back in Maine, and he turned against me in every way. With such shifting loyalties, I would not trust his patriotism in the least."

It was amazing that the CIA had hired Ferrar at all.

The driver eased off the highway and ramped down toward the Pentagon. Security let them pass through the parking lot without reducing speed. But they weren't stopping at the parking lot. Another military policeman waved them through to a ramp that led under the building, directly into the executive parking garage.

Lester snapped the folder shut. He knew the woman in question. Her name was Bonnie something-or-other, the love of Tray's life.

Soon Lester and Charles were traveling up the elevator to the office of Murrow Hughes, the Secretary of Defense.

He wasn't going to leave America's defense to the FBI.

Ferrar couldn't raise the Gulfstream's nose fast enough to avoid the dark mountain that loomed ahead.

But did he have a choice? He scanned the murky horizon for some sort of an escape.

Then a series of lights twinkled over the shoulder of the mountain. It was a city.

He pulled hard to starboard, toward the lights. If he could clear the tops of the trees, he might find himself hurtling over a valley, or even a plain.

The sound of his twin engines reverberated off the canyon walls. The fuselage vibrated from the excessive speed. Pressed deep in his rattling seat, he gently banked the small jet away from the mountain, over the treetops, and toward the grid of streetlights.

With a last whoosh, he swept past the mountainside, treetops scraping against the underbelly of his fuselage. At the last moment, when it seemed that he might have finally freed himself, a loud bang shook the jet. Then he heard a ripping sound. A rush of air sucked out of the cabin.

A tree or boulder must have torn a hole in the fuselage.

He eased back on the throttle. Trying to maintain his speed, he gently prodded the jet for lift. If he could avoid crashing into the city, he would be a lucky man. It might spare a life or two below as well. It might even allow him to rescue the nation from another stunning terrorist attack.

Get off it, Ferrar. Just keep alive.

Then he began to drift to a higher altitude. There was hope.

He took the luxury of scanning the skies.

The fighter jets were gone.

Twenty-four

MURROW HUGHES was normally an impassive Secretary of Defense. But not after the personality profile that Lester showed him.

His face turned beet red, and he stormed into the Ops Center, slamming Ferrar's record down on a table before his Chief of Staff.

"Leo, This George Ferrar is a complete psycho. We've got to stop him at once, no matter what the cost. Even if he's hijacked a civilian airliner, we've got to shoot him down."

Lester was about to add a description of Ferrar's performance at Tora Bora when they were interrupted by another radio message.

"This is Whiskey Five Two," the voice sounded over the speaker. "We've lost our man."

"Lost Ferrar?" Lester said incredulous.

Leo Pollo took the news with his usual calm. "Boys," he ordered over the radio. "I want you to find him, and you've got new orders. Shoot at will. I want you to kill the target."

Seated at his station aboard the large AWACS jet flying from Nevada into California, Reconnaissance Officer Burt Huett anxiously scanned the humming radar console. Where was the anomalous blip?

Then, finally, near the capital city of Sacramento, he picked up a faint signal. He stared a second time at the altitude reading. Could Ferrar be flying at just twenty yards above the terrain?

"We've picked him up, sir," he said into his microphone, and read out the exact coordinates.

"That's Sacramento," Leo Pollo exclaimed.

"That's right, sir. Sacramento, California."

Two bright stars shone on the western horizon, tracking Ferrar's every turn.

158

And they were glowing brighter.

The fighter jets had found him, and were forming a familiar attack formation, one group off the starboard wing and the other off the port wing, both slightly above and behind him.

He calculated that the fighter jets were just clearing the crest of the mountain range, two miles behind.

"Okay, baby, take her away," he told the trusty Gulfstream as he pulled her nose upward and jabbed the autopilot button. Then he unsnapped the pilot's seat belt and headed back in the icy, sucking wind of the damaged cabin.

Lester Friedman and Defense Secretary Hughes watched the Pentagon's top general, Leo Pollo, stand over a sweating signals officer as one frantic message after another came over the speakers.

First it was a pilot's voice as intimate and clear as a lover's whisper, "This is Whiskey Five Two. We've acquired the target."

"Whiskey Five Two, you have permission to fire," Leo said, stepping forward.

"We've engaged the target. It is dust."

Lester turned to Murrow Hughes with an exuberant, "Yes!"

Leo raised an eyebrow, but managed to maintain his composure.

Then the AWACS came over the airwaves. "The target has just disappeared off the radar screen."

Leo turned to the Secretary of Defense and the Director of the CIA with a satisfied smile. "I believe that'll do it for the evening."

Lester was trying to contain his excitement and maintain some sort of professional dignity. "And I thank you from the bottom of my heart. America thanks you."

Then he sank into a chair and closed his eyes with relief.

Congressman Connors didn't have the time or desire that evening to dress properly before driving off to the Pentagon.

The Secretary of Defense had just phoned him with devastating news. Their pilots had found Ferrar and shot his plane out of the sky.

As he wheeled through the streets of DC, Connors grabbed the cell phone out of his flannel shirt pocket and dialed the head office of the FBI.

"Since when are we firing rockets at Ferrar?" Connors yelled over the phone at Hank Gibson.

"I wasn't aware—" Hank began.

"How could you not be aware? You're leading this operation, aren't you?"

"Apparently the military thought it was their call."

"Like hell it is," Connors shot back. "They don't have all the pages of the game book. What kind of an operation are you guys running over there anyway?"

"I'm at a loss—"

"Yeah? Well let me tell you something right now. I want to see the FBI, the CIA, and the military top brass all assembled in one place, singing from one song sheet at the Pentagon in twenty minutes. This is no way to run a railroad."

After Connors suffered a few hassles with the guards at the Pentagon parking lot, a call from Leo Pollo helped extricate his car, and he drove straight into the basement, screeching to a halt at the elevator lobby. To hell with striped parking spots.

Then he noticed Lester Friedman's limo already there. "Now we know who's been pulling the strings around here."

He burst into the Ops Center from one door just as Hank Gibson entered from the opposite direction. Between them stood Leo and Lester like two cats savoring the aftertaste of a canary dinner. Behind them sat the Secretary of Defense, an eternally serious look written across his furrowed brow.

"Where is the President in all this mess?" Connors demanded.

The three others gathered together shoulder to shoulder in front of the Secretary of Defense, as if to form a united front.

"Why the sudden charm offensive, Connors?" Leo asked.

"Charm? You haven't seen charm yet. Now who's leading this screwed-up operation?"

From behind the wall of men, Murrow Hughes spoke quietly. "The President has made it abundantly clear to myself and to the Attorney General that this sort of work is at an operational level, and he doesn't want to get involved with the details. Not only does he want deniability if the press gets involved, but he wants to maintain a calm veneer for the public. It's a question of civil order, of not causing panic."

Connors could see the President's dilemma. He was caged in. If he went public, the terrorists would win. If he kept it under wraps, the terrorists would be able to enact their evil plan.

"If the President's out of this," he said, "I suggest that your three agencies work out whose job this is. We've got a CIA officer running a mission within the United States with the FBI on his back and the full might of the American military trying to blast him off the face of the earth."

"No," Lester corrected. "We've got a turned CIA special operations commando leading an al-Qaeda operation to nuke the United States."

Secretary Hughes stood up and walked into the full light. "I'm afraid that we have a problem here. We need the input of all our agencies, and we don't have anybody taking leadership in this matter. May I suggest that this remain a case for the FBI? They can work with state, county, and local law enforcement, liaise with the CIA on an as-needed basis, and keep the Pentagon apprised at all times. Here at the Ops Center, we will evaluate every piece of information and determine the proper and prudent course of action from the standpoint of national defense." He looked at Hank and Lester for consensus.

Hank nodded. "This is principally an FBI matter now. I've already called the Energy Secretary to dispatch his Nuclear Emergency Search Team from Nevada to San Francisco."

"See," the Secretary said, turning to leave the room. "The bombs are the last piece to the puzzle, and Hank already has the situation well in hand."

Just then a voice squawked over the speaker. "Sir, we've got a slight discrepancy." It was the head of NORAD calling the Secretary of Defense from his bunker deep within a granite mountain outside Colorado Springs. "We have a slight conflict of information here. It appears that the target was heading straight for a range of mountains when it was struck. It would have crashed anyway."

The room fell silent.

"What does that mean?" Connors demanded.

"It means he's dead," Lester said. "He would have died anyway."

"No," Leo spat out. "It appears that Mr. Ferrar has flown the coop once again."

"How could that be?" Lester asked, his voice suddenly sounding dry.

"It means," Leo interpreted, "that he bailed out somewhere between the Mississippi and the Pacific Ocean."

Perry O'Donnell shivered in his modern office on the 13th floor overlooking Golden Gate Avenue.

It was midnight on the West Coast. He watched nervously as the date on his wall clock flipped over to December 11.

Fog had rolled over the bay and smothered San Francisco in another of its frosty winter nights.

But it wasn't the lack of heat that caused Perry's involuntary shiver. In fact, he was feeling plenty of heat from Washington to find the al-Qaeda bombers before the end of the day. It was the sheer impossibility of the task—finding a handful of terrorists in twenty-four hours in so huge a metropolitan area—that made his blood run cold.

As Special Agent in Charge of the FBI's San Francisco office, he was point man for a massive manhunt. And everyone was descending on his city.

A native of Brooklyn, he had spent a career moving from one field office to another around the country, getting to know each jurisdiction like the thick veins on the back of his hands. And he knew San Francisco like a seasoned cop.

He had agents at the airports. He had staff calling all the police precincts from Oakland to San Jose. The only thing he had to go on was the physical description of a metal container four feet high, eight feet wide, and ten feet long. Against his training to avoid ethnic bias, he threw in a description made out of whole cloth: look for Middle Easterners.

The call from Hank Gibson in Washington had been the final blow. A rogue CIA operative was also on the loose, potentially masterminding the plot. At least Perry had a name, a photo, and a description of the suspect: one George Ferrar, a handsome looking guy, from his most recent security photo. Black hair, square jaw, blue eyes, rugged physique.

But looking for one man in the vast urban sprawl of the Bay Area and the untamed forests of Northern California was going to be more than tough. It was next to impossible.

Nevertheless, he had given Ferrar's name to Eddie Lucas, his Assistant Special Agent in Charge of Organized Crime, Drugs, and Terrorism to look into connections with Ferrar.

Perry's office was working the phones feverishly for leads on the bombs and fugitive, and thus far, nothing had materialized. They had every associated agency working the problem for them. They had contacted the California Highway Patrol, the Federal Aviation Administration, the Immigration & Naturalization Service, the United States Customs Service, and all the city police departments within the area of his jurisdiction. He was getting calls every other minute from the FBI divisions in Sacramento, Los Angeles, and San Diego as well.

But he still didn't have the feeling that the net was tightening.

Eddie Lucas had dug up the only promising lead, and was going at it full tilt. Eddie had phoned the CIA and learned from Ferrar's personnel file that he had once been a student at the University of California at Berkeley during the Seventies. He had had a girlfriend there named Bonnie. If she still lived in Berkeley, admittedly a small chance, Ferrar might be holed up there.

Eddie had called the FBI's Resident Agent in Oakland to look for all former Berkeley coeds named Bonnie specifically in Ferrar's age range and to crosscheck the names against the Bay Area phone book.

Perry O'Donnell sighed. It was a slim chance, but his only hope.

Twenty-five

FERRAR STOOD waiting at the bus stop on Castro Street in San Francisco, muscle-worn and weary from a night spent flying evasive maneuvers, parachuting over rocky terrain, and hitchhiking in a beat-up pickup. He had spent the last few hours in transit also fighting the demons of his past with Bonnie.

He remembered the bus stop from a previous, aborted trip to see her. He had tracked her down several years earlier, found her phone number, jotted down her address from a telephone book, screwed up his courage, and ventured out to discover what had become of Bonnie Taylor.

He had gotten to the foot of a set of stairs that led to a mysterious house in the affluent neighborhood of Twin Peaks. He remembered that he had taken one glance up the steps and kept on walking. After all, what if she had seen him? He had had no right to barge back into her life and potentially damage any permanent relationships she might have formed with somebody else. For all he knew, she was married. He was no home-wrecker.

It was amazing how little he knew about her life for the past two decades. The last he had seen her was saying good-bye to her on campus as she headed off to Connecticut for the Coast Guard. Or was *she* saying good-bye to *him*?

How could she have forgotten that brilliant summer in Bar Harbor when everything had been so perfect? He would pick her up after work at The Trap, where she was spending the summer waitressing for rich Bostonians on their vacations. They would sneak down the back alley and avoid the souvenir shops and lobster joints and head for her house for a stimulatingly new, but inevitable romp between the sheets.

On weekends, they would escape the flotilla of ferries and whale watching boats and row out to his family's deserted cottage. Barefoot, braless, her hair down, she had come on to him in the woods, on the shoreline, on the pier. He had tried repeatedly to direct her thoughts toward the future, but she had sprung back from his ideas like a trampoline artist, chasing him back into the present. The future was something she never dealt with very well.

And after she had left college, she had never looked back. She had never written or tried to contact him in any way. She was off living in her eternal present.

But as he stood there, the fumes of commuter cars gathering in his face, he realized that the future had finally arrived. And so had her past.

All he had left in his pocket to catch the early morning bus up the hill was a pair of quarters, jingling in his pocket against his cell phone and a roll of Lifesavers, the digital spy camera from the listening post in Peshawar.

Spry young men walked up and down the street, their bright teeth shining at him. He heard the clatter of coffee cups in Starbucks, the rich gourmet aroma helping him return to the present.

Across the street, the dark Castro Theater was featuring John Wayne in a revival of *The Green Berets*. The incongruity of that movie playing in the heart of the gay capital of the nation brought a smile. Perhaps Bonnie had reveled in that very sort of irony, being a female serviceman living in a sea of men with cotton candy-pink hair.

His eyes traveled upward to a steady stream of headlights trickling down the hill. He checked for a bus once again. No luck. He'd have to climb up to her house.

Fifteen minutes later and his legs aching, he was lost on a winding road. He was beyond the busy streets and wrapped in a thick blanket of fog.

Stopping beneath a dim streetlight, he read the street sign attached to the pole. Corbette. His heart suddenly paused. He had been there before. It was Bonnie's road. Her house lay somewhere up above him in the darkness and mist.

He asked himself one last time. Was he doing this for Bonnie? He and Tray made a terrible one-two punch. The only thing she would get out of him stepping out of the fog and into her life was that the bomb might not go off. She would have her life back, but in emotional shambles.

However, the city would not end up in shambles. He was doing this to stop the bomb.

Walking slowly, he ran his fingers over the pebbly surface of a concrete wall. San Francisco had many such walls holding back the hillsides. But this was no ordinary wall. It was Bonnie's wall.

He shuffled several feet further until he felt a break in the wall.

Shivering in the impenetrable fog that poured over Twin Peaks, he began to climb the steep steps. Near the top, he reached some thickets.

He stopped and felt around. There was a small wooden gate.

A light glimmered through the bushes.

There had to be a back entrance with a garage, some more accessible way for people to enter the house. He slipped along the low wooden fence and circled the property. Reaching the far side, he saw a floodlight burning from a garage onto a stone path that led to a back door.

The door was just opening. A man in Coast Guard dress whites and a service cap stepped out and turned back briskly to close the door. Her husband perhaps?

The man turned, his shoulder boards reflecting in the light.

It was Tray Bolton.

Ferrar slipped the roll of Lifesavers from his pocket and was fortunate enough to snap off a few pictures before Tray passed him.

Tray popped up the door of a silver 512 Testarosa with its distinctive wing-shaped doors and side air-intake system. It didn't look good, a terrorist in Coast Guard uniform driving a twelve-cylinder drug-trafficker's car.

The automobile roared to life, waking some nearby birds, and zoomed away down through the mist.

Ferrar advanced on the house at once and rang the doorbell.

No answer. Lights still burned inside. Bonnie had to be there.

He rang again, pressing the bell insistently.

Still no answer.

Fine. He leaned a shoulder against the door and shoved. It was locked. Pressing himself between bushes that fronted the house, he made his way to a window. Prying upward on one, he found it locked as well.

He took off a leather shoe and hammered the glass near the lock. It shattered neatly without much sound.

He slipped the shoe back on, unlocked the window, and slid it open. Within seconds, he was inside.

The house was spacious and simply furnished with a cleanly swept fireplace.

He moved swiftly from room to room, calling out Bonnie's name. Again, no response. She was nowhere to be found.

But something helpful did catch his eye. A computer sat in a small office just off her bedroom.

Assistant Special Agent in Charge Eddie Lucas spun away from his computer and caught his own reflection in the nighttime window. He had a determined look on his weary round face.

"Whatcha got there?" his boss Perry O'Donnell shouted across the room.

"Pay dirt," Eddie said, and waved a single sheet of paper. He crossed the room to explain.

He had spent most of the night hunting down Ferrar's former girlfriend, Bonnie X. It had taken him an hour to compile a list of "Bonnies" among University of California alumni. Comparing that list of names with Bay Area phone lists produced an even longer list, numbering in the hundreds. Armed with several sheets of phone numbers and street addresses, he then had to find a way of narrowing the list, rather than expanding it.

At that point, he had started putting the staff to work calling every number. The standard question of "Do you know a George Ferrar?" met with more than a dozen "Do you know what time it is?" replies. But it did yield several positives and some maybes.

As he explained to Perry, he would have to personally handle it from there.

"Okay, take some men with you and hit the streets," Perry advised. "The time bomb is ticking."

"Where should I start?" Eddie asked.

"Any in Berkeley?"

"None. I've got four in San Jose."

"Computer geeks. Forget 'em."

"Two in Palo Alto."

"Eggheads. Leave 'em for last."

"Three in Marin County."

"Rich. Maybe."

"A couple in San Francisco."

"Bingo," Perry said. "That's where you'll start."

Ferrar lost no time attaching the spy camera to Bonnie's Macintosh. She had a cable hanging out of her computer, and he simply plugged it into the USB port on his roll of Lifesavers.

Seconds later, all three photos had automatically appeared on her machine. Ferrar leaned in close to examine the pictures. The date had been stamped in the corner of each snapshot. All they needed was a little more brightness and contrast, which he was able to add quickly using her software. Within half an hour, he was ready to transmit them to Congressman Connor's office.

He typed in Connors' fax number and stood up, about to click the Send button when he heard a car pull up.

From the sound of the footsteps, several people had jumped out.

"Shit."

He clicked the button to send the photos, and quickly left the office. Bonnie's bed lay unmade. Beyond it was a bathroom. The other door took him out to the living room. Only the kitchen separated him from the approaching footsteps.

The doorbell rang impatiently.

He treaded lightly to the front door that led down the long path to Corbette Avenue below. Suddenly, the back door crashed open.

His movements masked by the sound, he let himself out the front door, shut it behind him, and raced down the dark path. A shadowy object rose up in front of him, and before he could swerve, he had mowed down a man. He threw the man back against the wooden gate, where he cart wheeled over backward and landed with a moist splash in the grass.

Ferrar continued charging forward, vaulting over the fence, and slipped down the stone steps toward Corbette. He encountered no resistance, and the man lying in the garden behind him had not yet pulled himself together.

Sprinting down the curved, dewy road, he tried to put as much distance between himself and the intruders as he could. He soon found himself on a major street where commuters were descending from Twin Peaks into town for another day of work.

A bus pulled up to a stop, and he poured on the speed to catch it.

He threw his two quarters into the hopper beside the driver, and turned to find a seat. The interior was well illuminated, and many seats were empty. As the bus pulled away from the curb, he felt alone and exposed to the world.

"Broken window, sir," an agent called to Eddie from the back bedroom of the house on Twin Peaks.

The team of agents had fanned out in the lighted house, calling out traces of evidence.

"Front door is unlocked."

"The perp may have been in the computer room," a voice rang out.

Eddie rushed toward the agent who had said that. He found an egg-shaped iMac connected to a strange-looking thing. It was a roll of Tropical Fruit Lifesavers.

On the screen, the last image in a column of three was being sent over the computer line.

Eddie leaned in close and jotted down the telephone number in the onscreen message box. It had a DC area code.

The connection finished, and the fax line clicked off.

An agent came limping into the office holding his head.

"I got jumped," he explained, groaning as he tried to explain what happened. "He came out the front door like a flash of lightning and bowled me over in the front yard. I must have cracked several vertebrae falling over the fence out there. I landed on my head. I swear it's about to explode."

"Did you catch his face?" Eddie asked as the agent began to sway backward.

"Ohh," he yowled as two other men caught him by the arms and gently pulled him back onto the queen-sized bed.

One agent leaned over the stricken man and tried to pat his face, but got no response. Another agent brought in a dripping towel from the bathroom.

The injured man had gone completely pale, and his eyelids were fluttering. This had to be the work of Ferrar.

Eddie shook his head at the pitiful domestic scene. "Call da ambulance," he ordered. "I'm going after Ferrar."

He pocketed his notepad, sprang out of the room, and let himself cautiously out onto the front yard. The first blue of daylight filtered through foliage in the silent, dripping garden.

He eased himself over the splinters of the fence where his agent had fallen, and followed the steps down to the road below. Encountering nobody, he headed for the main street, his thick legs churning furiously.

As he reached the thoroughfare, a bus was just pulling away from the curb. He could make out several people onboard: an older woman in a woolen cap, some Hispanic cleaning ladies, a couple of men getting friendly with one another, and a young girl in a school uniform.

A typical city bus.

He leaned over, gasping for breath, and finally let his eyes drop to the notepad hanging from his pocket. Whose fax number was that in Washington?

By the time the bus reached the second stop on Castro Street, the man was trying to force his tongue down Ferrar's throat.

Ferrar slapped him on the face. "Don't get fresh," he said. "Where is your sense of decency?"

"Hey," the young guy said, watching Ferrar stand to leave. "Where's your prick?"

Ferrar pressed outward on the side door and let himself off the bus and onto the sidewalk.

An indigo streak was beginning to glow in the eastern sky.

He had a lot of work to do that day, and strode briskly toward Union

Square. In the refreshing breeze, he tried to focus on what to say to Congressman Connors, and how to approach the military.

But it took a long time for the image of the young man with the milky breath and smooth chin to disappear from his mind.

Using his cell phone, Eddie called the number he had jotted down. He held the phone away from his ear while the fax picked up on the other end and began its piercing squeal, an attempt at an electronic handshake.

The squeal stopped and the fax machine began to ring like a telephone. he had to be patient. It was already office hours on the East Coast, and eventually someone would answer the ringing fax.

But he was surprised by the reply he finally received. "Congressman Connors's office. You're calling his fax machine."

"Congressman, huh?" he said. The FBI hierarchy had a strict pecking order, and Assistant Special Agents did not talk directly with U.S. Congressmen. "I think I'd better bump this baby upstairs."

"What is this in regards to?" the woman asked.

"Does the Congressman know someone named George Ferrar?"

"Are you the press?"

"No. FBI."

"Hold on. The Congressman is at the Pentagon right now. I'll patch you through."

In a few short seconds, the Assistant SAC found himself talking with the illustrious Chairman of the House Permanent Select Committee on Intelligence.

"What's happening?" Connors shouted out.

Eddie identified himself.

"Have you seen Ferrar?" Connors asked.

"Hey, let me ax the questions," Eddie said. He had immediately lost control of the conversation, and his cool. Maybe that's why the bureau only allowed top brass to talk with the Hill.

"I don't want to repeat myself," Connors said.

"Yes, sir. He was just here, at this house in San Francisco. Did you just receive a fax?"

"Not that I'm aware."

In the background, he heard someone call, "Hey Ralph. Your secretary just sent us a fax."

"Check the fax," Eddie said.

He heard Connors walking over to a fax machine. A print head was chattering and paper was spitting out.

"Holy shit."

"Yes, Congressman?"

"This is Tray Bolton. Where did you get these pictures?"

"It appears that George Ferrar sent them to you. We just missed him as he left Bonnie Taylor's house."

"Bonnie Taylor, huh?"

"Know her?"

"Yeah, I've heard Ferrar talk about a Bonnie," he said. "He'd get a little Chianti in him and talk about the mistakes of his past. She seems to have been one of them."

"Sounds like *he* was a mistake in *her* past. He just struck a Federal agent and ran from the scene of the crime."

"That wouldn't be the first time," Connor said with a chuckle.

"I fail to see the humor in this, sir," Eddie said as an ambulance shot past him, its siren wailing.

"*You* may not, but this gives *me* an enormous sense of relief," Connors said. "If you'll please excuse me, I have a picture to show to the Director of the CIA."

Twenty-six

"GET IN HERE, buddy," a female voice said from a passing car on Castro Street.

Ferrar waved off the advance.

"George. Get the hell in here."

He whirled around. In a small brown Toyota, a woman wearing a gray sweat suit was leaning over from the driver's seat.

"Bonnie?"

"How'd you guess? Now jump in here before I catch you making out with another buck."

"Oh, Lord," he said, rolling his eyes. He pulled the passenger door open and slid in.

"I'm going to report you as a peeping Tom," he warned.

"And I'll report you for lewd behavior in public, not to mention breaking and entering my house."

"You've got me there," Ferrar said, holding up both hands. "How did you know I was here?"

She steered into the flow of commuter traffic. "When Tray arrived last night, I freaked out. I talked with him. He was hungry. He wanted sex. Finally this morning I slipped out while he was taking a shower. Then I waited on the street in my car."

"Waited for what?"

"For you."

His eyebrows shot up.

"Last night you told me you were coming," she explained. "Then I saw you entering through the front gate."

"Why didn't you stop me?"

"You're one of the reasons I got out of the house. I had no idea if I could trust you. And judging from what Tray had to say about you, I still don't. Then a short while later, another man followed you up the slope of my garden."

172

"Okay. I'll fill in the rest. I saw Tray leaving by the back door. Bonnie, he was wearing a Coast Guard uniform."

She furrowed her light brown eyebrows, her deep blue eyes trying to peer into Tray's murky intentions. Finally, she glanced at him, but her look didn't soften.

"First things first," she said, and cut northward, straight up a hill. Soon they were traveling against traffic into a residential section of the city.

"Did you find out what Tray means to do?" he asked.

She shook her head.

"You were with him all night," he reminded her.

"We weren't exactly talking about nuclear bombs."

She drove in silence for several more minutes, and Ferrar recognized where they were headed. She was taking him into a wooded, public-access military reservation known as the Presidio.

"Gonna turn me in?" he asked.

"Maybe."

She drove up to a spot with a view of the Pacific. The gray horizon was sharp in the lifting fog. Waves crashed against a beach far below. She pressed the emergency brake on the sandy shoulder.

He took a deep breath and opened the door. "Is this the point where I get to escape?"

"If you need to."

He climbed out of the car and straightened his back.

Red brick barracks with porches and buff-colored officers' quarters spread out along the road.

"Aren't you being a little ballsy driving terrorists onto a military reservation?" he asked.

"This is the last place they'd expect you," she said with a wink.

He circled the car and approached her, taking her hand. "I get this strange impression that you've done all this before," he said.

"I've known Tray long enough to understand the way you undercover creeps think."

He nodded. He should have known.

She tugged his hand and began to lead him through the grove of tall trees. They passed parade grounds where a color guard was raising an enormous American flag that immediately tried to break free in the breeze. Suddenly rifle fire filled the air.

Ferrar ducked and pulled Bonnie down with him. Then a bugle rang out a flawless reveille. Crouching beside him, Bonnie broke into laughter.

"Do you always do this when they raise the flag?" she asked.

He picked himself up and helped her dust off her sweats.

"Yeah, it's not easy being a traitor," he said. "It screws up one's loyalties."

Then he nudged her in the same direction as before. They passed a colorful schoolyard, where the swing set and monkey bars sat mutely behind an iron fence.

"I always wanted to be surrounded by kids," Bonnie said wistfully. "I came from a big family, and I always wanted one of my own."

"I can help in that department," he offered.

She caught his eye. "You're supposed to be working undercover. Not screwing."

He stared at her levelly.

"If I didn't know any better," she said, "I'd think you were serious."

He smiled to himself, and resumed the walk, studying the slender twisted trees and lofty mass of branches.

"Actually, I've never stood still long enough to consider a family," she went on. "Always climbing the job ladder. Always some important fire to put out."

Ferrar raised his eyebrows. Those could have been his very own words. But surely she had had opportunities to settle down. "Any handsome young man ever come your way and ask for your hand in marriage?"

She averted her eyes. "Nobody of consequence. Of course, there once was a good-looking young knight…"

He observed her closely. "Do you remember Sir Lancelot?"

"Child's play," she said, her eyes humorless, the momentary dreaminess having passed.

"I haven't thought of Camelot in years," he admitted.

"I don't seem to have time for knights in shining armor and woeful Greek tragedy any longer. Those concepts are dangerous and deceptive. They set you up for a big fall."

"I guess life seems more black-and-white overseas," Ferrar said.

"Well it isn't that way the closer you get to home. Real life's full of mundane battles."

Just then several Humvees rumbled past them, the troops inside pulling on full combat gear.

"Mundane?" he asked.

The forest cover broke to the north and west, and he could see a turbulent harbor where the Pacific's current met head-on with the warm flow out of the bay. Light fingers of a cloud extracted themselves from the struts of the Golden Gate Bridge.

They skirted around the barracks for enlisted men, and Ferrar heard an officer barking a command. Several soldiers emerged from the buildings and jumped into canvas-covered troop carrier.

Ferrar watched the truck disappear into the forest to the south.

"Let's go down to the beach," Bonnie suggested. She led him along the road that wound down a sandy slope through scrubby pines and purple flowers.

"Maybe it's time to stop playing GI Jane," she mused.

They reached the soft beach, and he stood beside her watching the rising sun cast a pink glow against the west. On the distant horizon, he made out the conning tower of a huge military vessel, perhaps a battleship.

"Are you holding maneuvers today?" he asked.

"What, dressed like this?" she pointed to her sweat suit.

He indicated the horizon, where two smaller ships were just appearing, their color as gray as the water.

"I would know of any scheduled exercises," she said.

He pulled her down to sit on a half-buried log, a giant dune looming behind them. Ahead lay the graceful burnt-orange bridge and spilling waves where several fishermen cast long lines into the surf.

A handful of private sailboats peeked out from under the bridge, then headed back into the bay. Gray seagulls swarmed over a school of fish, competing for their first meal of the day.

"Does it seem somewhat quiet to you this morning?" he inquired.

"Are you talking business, or are you trying to be romantic?"

He turned to take his first good look at her. Just inches from her face, he noticed that the salt air had turned her complexion a perpetual pink. She kept her fair hair nicely shaped, like the wave of a mermaid's locks.

Then he finally settled on her eyes in a look that was as intimate as a kiss. They were a penetrating blue, deep as the sea. They were the same eyes that he had adored throughout college and contemplated for years thereafter. Perhaps they were wiser, perhaps more cautious. But there was something else, more disturbing, about them.

They were no longer soaking up the present. They had the slightly harrowed look of someone who was afraid of what the future held.

"Time has been good to you," he said.

"Bullshit."

"Only, something seems to be worrying you," he continued. "You don't have that *carpe diem* attitude that I remember."

"Yeah, well maybe the world has finally gotten the better of me."

He looked around. People seemed to be gathering along the road above them. Traffic had stopped on the Golden Gate Bridge, and police lights were flashing behind the guardrails.

"You've taken on huge responsibilities," he said.

"So have you."

"Hey, you joined the military before either Tray or me. In fact, I doubt if I ever would have considered enlisting if it hadn't been for you." She closed her eyes and nodded. "I guess I've finally proven something to myself."

He understood. "Do you want out?"

Her shoes off, she ran her toes through the fine white sand.

"Maybe," she admitted at last, holding back her hair and throwing him a challenging look.

Something flashed from above. Ferrar tensed. He looked up and caught sunlight glinting off a metal tube. He took a closer look. It didn't look like a gun. Rather, it was a television camera.

He stood and turned around. A helicopter was circling over the bay, the whirring sound of its blades riding the breeze.

Out at sea, the battleship and several destroyers were progressing steadily toward the narrow inlet to the bay.

"Do you think you've got one more operation left in you?" he asked.

She stood up, alerted to the increasing activity around them.

Cold mist sprayed evenly in her face. Across the Presidio, a line of camouflaged tanks was taking up position, the exertions of their engines echoing back and forth across the bay.

"Sure," she said, grabbing his hand. "I think I'm good for one more round."

Twenty-seven

DARK-HAIRED, boyishly handsome, and stylishly foreign-looking, Milos Guerve had established himself, in his own eyes, as the Bay Area's pre-eminent investigative tele-journalist.

As his two cameramen took up positions around him, he worked to keep his hair from blowing in his face. One establishing shot would capture the looming Golden Gate Bridge over one shoulder. Below that lay the long golden strand of Baker Beach.

But the close-up from another angle was the killer shot. It would capture his face bathed in early morning rays of sunlight. Slightly out of focus yet menacing would be a line of American naval vessels advancing on the city.

The timing was perfect. Morning news hour, stand back. This story would eclipse 9/11.

He nodded to his producer, focused on his cue cards, and took one last swipe at his long black hair.

He lifted the microphone with its puffy wind muffler to his lips and waited for the signal.

The producer pointed to him.

"Good morning, Andrea. I'm standing in north San Francisco near the foot of the Golden Gate Bridge. Behind me, you might be able to make out preparations underway by the military to secure the city. It's an operation the likes of which San Francisco has not seen since the Great Earthquake and Fire of 1906."

The producer cued the second camera.

He shifted his stance so that the close-up could catch the approaching vessels.

"San Francisco city government has received word from relevant military authorities that there might be a massive terrorist strike against the city's physical infrastructure. That might include airports, roadways, bridges, tunnels, power plants, and various other high profile targets."

177

He paused while his assistant unveiled the next card.

"From the looks of it, Andrea, nearly every agency on the West Coast has converged on the city. We've heard reports that fifty military airplanes, helicopters, and unmanned drones will soon be circling the sky above me. As you can see, a Navy battleship, four Navy destroyers, and twenty-five patrol boats have moved in to protect the waters around the bay. But they're not the only folks interested in these unfolding events."

He pointed to the hillside behind him.

"An estimated half million bystanders have lined the hills overlooking the Golden Gate Bridge, perhaps expecting this great national symbol to be the next al-Qaeda target."

Just then another camera crew, jockeying for a better position, bumped into him from behind. He lowered his microphone. "Hey, watch it, buddy."

He took a moment to resume his pose and collect his thoughts.

"As you can see, this has become a media feeding frenzy, and people are jostling each other to get a better view. Andrea."

Andrea's voice came over his earpiece. "Can you tell us anything about the origins of this threat?"

"Well," he continued to read. "Word filtered in to the city's news bureaus in the early hours of this morning that federal agencies had identified a credible threat today to unspecified Bay Area infrastructure. FBI, military, and state, county, and local law enforcement are working together to ascertain the nature of this threat, and with hope foil any terrorist strike. Needless to say, the specter of 9/11 is foremost on everyone's mind today."

As Milos spoke, the whine of fighter jets began to drown out his words.

"As you can hear, military aircraft are beginning to patrol the airspace above the city. Andrea."

Andrea was trying to ask him another question.

"I can't exactly make out the question you are asking, but I will attempt to answer it anyway," he said, waiting for his next cue card. "I can report that units of the Army, Navy, Marines, and Coast Guard are all on red alert...and in fact carrying out combat missions with live ammunition as we speak...searching for just who might be behind this latest threat."

The cacophony rose to such a volume, that he had to cover his ears. In his entire eight years of covering the news, he had never seen any story so terrifying.

Tray Bolton pulled up to the Coast Guard station in his shiny new Testarosa, lifted the car door, and stepped out, briefcase in hand.

In addition to feeling quite confident, he felt a mischievous smile creep across his face. Planting Ferrar's identification cards on a television news crew at the Presidio as a diversion was a touch of genius, a crowning achievement on what he knew would be the last day of his life.

Before him stood a small, square building made out of white-painted iron. It might survive a conventional war, but it would never withstand a nuclear blast.

To his satisfaction, he noticed a truck several hundred feet down the wharf. On the trailer rested a shipping container wrapped like a gift in red ribbon.

He would deliver the present.

Stepping inside the station, he found a complete communications center with phones, radios, and nautical maps.

A female officer jumped to her feet when she saw his insignia. "Commander," she said, saluting.

He pulled a Glock with a silencer from his gun belt, and drilled a bullet through her head. She fell back without a cry, smashing into a row of maps that rolled one by one on top of her.

The building had one large, open room much like a small bus terminal, and several smaller rooms, such as an armory, sleeping quarters, weight room, and a small mess hall. He caught a whiff of coffee brewing behind the dead communications officer's desk, and just outside the window, he could see and hear Bonnie's cutter undergoing make-ready.

The *USS Vigilant* was a beautiful Reliance Class cutter, its prow sharp and proud, its thirty-four foot beam solid even in the roughest seas.

Two hundred and ten feet long with a displacement of one thousand tons, it would serve his purposes well.

Two petty officers had finished inspecting her and were approaching the office. Tray waited just inside the door as it swung open.

"There's a security lockdown on the entire port," the first was saying as he stepped into the room. "We should be the only ship out there."

"I've got her topped off and ready."

Tray stepped forward and shot the first officer in the side of his head. The second had little time to react.

Tray dropped to one knee and plugged him with a silenced bullet to the heart. The man twisted away, struggling to make it back out the door. But he was dead before he hit the ground.

"Where do you think you're going?" Tray said, and pulled the body back into the building, a trail of blood smearing the pavement just beyond the door and across the threshold.

Looking out through the large window, he couldn't see anyone still onboard. There had to be several servicemen below deck.

Stepping over the bodies, he opened the bayside door and signaled the truck to approach. Within a minute, his four men surrounded him, each dressed in civilian clothes appropriate for the cool weather.

He motioned them inside the room. There, one man peeled off the white uniform of the first dead officer and quickly dressed. The other man's uniform was far too soiled with blood to be of any use.

Then the four waited for his next instruction.

"Now we take the ship," he said, steeling himself and holding the Glock upright by his shoulder.

The others drew guns and, with well-timed precision, rushed out the door and stormed the *Vigilant*. They started by working their way upward into the bridge, scaling the steps up from the ship's large quarterdeck. It was empty.

Then they began to methodically make their way forward on the upper deck along both rails, their bodies crouched low. On the large foredeck they found only a mound of neatly coiled ropes and a covered winch.

"And look at this," Tray said, running a hand along the full length of a mounted twenty-five millimeter gun. "The Coast Guard plays with toy guns."

Then he motioned for his men to head inside.

In the main cabin, they made their way from room to room. There was an office with a radio and maps, but no Coast Guard servicemen. In the galley, they found pots and pans and food carefully stowed away. The tiny mess and bunkrooms were similarly empty.

In the furthest forward compartment, they found a small arsenal stocked with rifles, flares, even a rocket-propelled grenade launcher.

It was hardly a warship.

Among the equipment in the room opposite, he found several cold-water diving suits and SCUBA gear.

"No soldiers in here," his main man reported in clipped English.

The only area remaining was a set of steps leading below.

Tray approached the opening, from which a twisting and wrenching metallic sound could be heard.

He put a finger to his lips and signaled for his men to climb down. He followed them, looking back to make sure that nobody was returning to the ship from shore.

Assured that they were alone, he hustled down the companionway and found himself in a dark set of compartments used for storage, rescue equipment, bilges, and furthest aft two beautiful diesel engines.

There he spotted a couple of enginemen in their working blues laboring over the ship's power plant. Oblivious to their unwanted company, they dutifully greased the valves.

"Hold it right there, boys," Tray said, cautiously entering the engine room.

The two men froze at the sound of his voice, and then snapped about to face him. Their eyes widened upon sight of the gun.

One gripped his lug wrench hard. The other held a can of oil.

Tray's men poked their heads out from between the various machines and stepped into the dim light.

"Are you authorized to—" the engineman with the wrench began.

"No permission required," Tray said, and shot the man, the wrench clattering on the metal deck as he fell.

The other man dodged behind an engine, the oil can dropping from his hand.

Chasing him, Tray slid across the oil slick. The engineman made it halfway up a ladder. His head was poking out of a trapdoor on the quarterdeck when the Glock caught up with him. How could Tray find a lethal target when all he saw was the seat of the man's pants? He lodged a bullet in the lower part of the guy's spine.

The man hauled himself by hand onto the deck, slamming the trapdoor behind him. A moment later, the lock scraped shut.

"Damn it," Tray cried. He turned to his men standing at the base of the ladder, and ordered in Arabic, "Start the engines. We're leaving at once."

He dropped down off the ladder and swept past them, running the full length of the ship back to the foredeck stairs.

By the time he reached the back of the boat, the engineman had hauled himself halfway over the side of the ship and onto the wharf.

Tray glanced around to check if anybody was in the vicinity, then sent two silenced rounds into the man's heart, stopping him cold.

He jumped over the man, and reached the tailgate of the truck. There, he unlocked the padlock to the container and swung it open on two rusty hinges.

"Help me," he called, and three men appeared by his side. Together, they pulled out a wooden pallet. Strapped on top was a rectangular metal box, the size and shape of a large coffee table.

"Careful now," Tray said as the men lowered the pallet to the ground.

They removed the straps around the metal box and lifted it by its four handles.

Kicking the body off the wharf and back onto the cutter, Tray helped his men lift the bomb down onto the quarterdeck.

"Prepare to cast off," he ordered.

Setting his leather briefcase beside the box, he worked the box's two latches open. Behind him, the al-Qaeda crew untied the cutter.

Up above, another member had scaled the steps to the bridge and started the twin engines.

As the cutter churned out of its slip and onto the bay, the body rolled toward him, and Tray had to kick it back out of the way.

"Take the bomb inside the cabin," he ordered in Arabic, and stood up to take a breath.

Ahead, under lifting clouds, lay the Bay Bridge, its long spans bearing twin levels of traffic between Oakland and San Francisco.

But that would not be enough.

He wanted something bigger. More costly than Pearl Harbor, and more memorable than the collapse of the Twin Towers in New York City.

Back in Bonnie's car, Ferrar tuned in to the local radio station. Within a minute, he had a complete summary of the scale of the authorities' response to the perceived threat.

They closed schools across Northern California. Stores and companies were on skeleton crew shifts, or shut down entirely. Hospitals pleaded for blood donations. Major highways, bridges, and other commuter conduits were closed to traffic with highway patrolmen standing guard. BART trains had stopped running as of six that morning. Even if people wanted to, they couldn't leave the city due to the closures and massive traffic jams.

Ferrar sat in the driver's seat and headed into the city with Bonnie beside him. They drove past a grocery store, its front windows bashed in and people passing food out to friends on the street.

Two F-15 Eagles shot by overhead, and people ran for cover.

Bonnie directed him to drive to her Coast Guard station along the bay in southeastern San Francisco. But all main traffic arteries were clogged. A ramp up to the highway was blocked off, and a traffic cop directed him away.

"Great," he said. "Now what?"

They were near the waterfront, an industrial area with piers jutting out from warehouses that sat side-by-side for as far as he could see.

He began to edge southward along the waterfront road in the bumper-to-bumper traffic. "We're getting nowhere."

"Look there," Bonnie shouted. "That's my ship."

He glanced out at the bay. A gleaming white cutter with the distinctive slanting orange Coast Guard stripe on its hull was steaming northward into what looked like a battle zone.

"That's the *Vigilant*," she cried. "He must have taken it."

Ferrar grabbed his cell phone and tossed it in her lap. "Here. Call someone."

"Who?" she asked. She composed herself for a moment, then dialed some numbers. "My communications officer isn't answering."

"Line dead?"

"It's ringing. Someone should be on duty."

"That doesn't' sound good," Ferrar said, and clenched his teeth. "Hold on."

Their Toyota was mere inches from the car in front of them. Ferrar leaned on the horn and began to blare away. The car blocking their path didn't budge an inch.

He turned the front wheels hard left and hit the accelerator. The Toyota munched the left rear bumper of the car, nudging it out of the way.

Traffic cones crumpled under his wheels as he blazed a hole through the thin stream of oncoming cars. Crossing the three lanes safely, he rammed into a hurricane fence. The metal links didn't break, but the poles uprooted, and the car broke free into a warehouse parking lot.

He found a narrow road leading between two buildings, and took it. Soon he was passing under huge cranes built for loading ships.

On the pier, containers and other wrapped goods were piled up in neat stacks. Sunlight glanced off the bay, nearly blinding him. Dockworkers jumped aside as he swerved through the obstacle course toward the water.

"You can't stop the *Vigilant*," Bonnie shouted. "We've got a crew of five armed soldiers onboard."

"Not if Tray's in command."

She held her head and watched as Ferrar maneuvered out to the end of the pier.

There, thankfully, he found a small pilot boat.

"You wait here," he shouted, and jumped out of the car.

"Hey," she cried, grabbing his sleeve and hauling him back into the car. "I know my ship better than you do. I should go."

"You have to alert the authorities."

"With what, your cell phone?"

"If that's all you've got. And remember, you have one thing that I don't have—credibility. Mine isn't worth a hell of a lot these days."

She hesitated, their eyes locked. "No hero stuff, you hear?" she said, her voice firm.

"Just doing my job, ma'am."

At last she whispered, "Stay safe."

"I'll be back for supper." And he gave her a wink.

Then the next moment he was out in the bracing breeze, unwinding the pilot boat's mooring lines. He jumped up to unwrap the last line, but Bonnie was already there, heaving the rope onto the boat.

"Honey, you got the keys?" he shouted.

She whirled about and collared a dockworker. "I'm with the Coast Guard. We need the keys."

The man took a moment to size her up—a tall blonde in a gray sweat suit. What he saw didn't register as Coast Guard.

Ferrar jogged over and hoisted the man off his feet by his collar. "Do we look like terrorists to you? Now give us the keys."

"They're already on the boat," the man finally said.

Ferrar set him down and patted him on the cheek. Then he turned to go.

Twenty-eight

PERRY O'DONNELL didn't know exactly what he was looking for at Baker Beach in north San Francisco. All his men were deployed around the city, so he made himself the "rover," moving wherever his instincts took him.

Eddie Lucas' lead had seemed particularly promising. But Eddie had lost the suspect on Twin Peaks. However, a quick check with Motor Vehicles netted another lead. Bonnie Taylor owned a brown 1999 Toyota sedan.

And word was that the vehicle was sighted here.

Armed with a photo of Ferrar and a description of the vehicle, he floated among the crowd that had gathered on the road above Baker Beach. A patrolman was trying to keep a hang-glider from launching himself off the dune toward the fleet of warships steaming between them and the Marin County Headlands.

"Officer," Perry shouted above the excited voices. "I'm with the FBI. Are you the one who reported the brown Toyota?"

"Yes, sir. That's me. Whoops."

Having turned away from the hang glider, the patrolman lost his grip on the delta wing, and the young man pulled free digging up sand under his heels. The man threw his body over the cliff and soared out above the blue water.

"Damn it," the patrolman shouted.

"Let him go," Perry said. "He's not the suspect."

The crowd around them "ooh-ed" and "ah-ed" as the young man swung in graceful circles over the ships, a steady breeze lifting him higher and higher.

"Where's the Toyota?" Perry asked.

"Not here anymore. It was parked up by the Presidio base, but now it's gone."

"See who was driving it?" Perry asked, holding up the photo of Ferrar.

185

The patrolman shook his head. "I didn't see anybody."

"Which direction did it go?"

Again, a shrug.

Another dead end. But if Ferrar were there earlier, he would have had a purpose, perhaps leaving a trail of witnesses.

"Look," Perry said to the patrolman. "I want you to check out this crowd. In addition to Ferrar, look for anybody who looks like a foreigner, check his IDs, and detain him under any pretext necessary. Ferrar is working with illegal aliens, and he's a master of disguise, so keep on your toes."

The patrolman waded into the crowd, checking IDs.

Perry swept the crowd of mainly young people free from school who had been herded away from the beach by park authorities. Two retirees stood along the side of the road with fishing poles. They would have been on the beach long before the youngsters.

He showed them the photograph.

One man grabbed the picture and studied it closely.

"Yup. I seen that man this morning. Came down here to make out with a young woman." He pointed to a log at the bottom of the dune. "After that, I minded my own business."

"What did the woman look like?"

"Tall, blonde, good-looking."

That matched the photographs found in Bonnie Taylor's home.

"What were they doing?" Perry asked.

"Like I said, I don't know. I respect other people's privacy."

"Did they have weapons?" Perry asked.

This got the man's attention, then a snort. "Yup, they were rubbing their gun barrels together to stay warm."

Suddenly mayhem broke out near a television crew up the road where the patrolman had wandered off. People's attention turned from the swooping hang glider to the ruckus.

Perry pushed through the crowd to investigate.

"It's Ferrar! It's Ferrar!" a voice was shouting.

"Get your hands off me," an infuriated, accented voice cried.

Camera lights and sun reflectors turned toward several men circling each other.

"I am Milos Guerve of Channel 6 News," the man was shouting.

Cameras continued rolling. A producer had hopped up on a chair and was directing their angles.

When Perry arrived, he had to pry some young women aside. He was just in time to see the patrolman wrestling a nicely dressed fellow to the ground.

Perry knocked aside a cameraman and plunged onto the fray, clawing at the man to try and get a better view of his face.

The suspect remained pinned to the sand on his belly, his face averted, his voice shouting out epithets in a foreign language, and generally resisting arrest.

"It's Ferrar, I tell you. I saw his driver's license," the patrolman insisted.

But the producer had jumped into the action and was swinging away at the two officers of the law.

Overhead, Perry was vaguely aware of several helicopters swinging low and darting toward them.

"Oh my God, the ships are aiming their guns at us," a young woman screamed.

"Duck! They're gonna lob missiles at us!"

Congressman Ralph W. Connors marched triumphantly through the Pentagon's Ops Center waving the fax he had received from Ferrar that morning.

Amidst a chaotic hubbub of activity—officers swirling around, shouting commands, listening to several telephones at once, with Leo Pollo riding herd over the entire bunch—Lester Friedman sat calmly sipping coffee out of a Styrofoam cup.

Connors shoved the pictures under Lester's nose. "Here's your son."

Lester shot to his feet, his composure instantly gone, and grabbed the fax. His jaw dropped. The two pictures clearly showed Tray dressed in a Coast Guard officer's uniform leaving a quaint house in the dark. It was dated December 11.

"If Ferrar took these pictures today…" Lester spluttered, seemingly unable to grasp the implications.

"Then your son's been on the lam since Tora Bora," Connors finished his thought.

Just then Connors heard a shout from several officers standing before a television screen.

It was a San Francisco affiliate feed into CBS. At first Connors was confused.

It looked like several men wrestling in the sand.

The network anchor in New York was trying to explain. "It appears that officials in San Francisco are in the process of apprehending a suspect who might be wanted in connection with the imminent terrorist attack. It looks like American officials have taken one step closer to averting a potentially devastating strike."

"Get him," Lester shouted in the suddenly quiet room.

A cutaway shot showed the turrets of various destroyers and a battleship turning toward shore, and the fracas.

"Let's try to listen in on the audio feed," the CBS anchorman said.

The crowd around the wrestling men was hitting the ground and covering their heads with their hands, leaving a lone, bloodied producer shouting to his cameramen from atop a folding chair. In the eerie silence, the producer's voice carried in the wind: "Get off him. Get off my man."

The CBS anchor was handed a sheet of paper. "Apparently," he read, "the culprit is a male Caucasian named George Ferrar, a rogue CIA operations officer-turned-terrorist."

"That's him," Lester shouted. "Blow him away."

Leo and the officers around him stood frozen around the television monitors.

Connors suddenly felt faint, as if the entire world was crumbling away beneath him.

"A call from the Commander in Chief, Pacific Command, sir," a communications officer said, holding a phone to his uniformed chest.

"I'll take that," Leo said grimly.

He listened for a moment, then said, "Just hold your fire for a moment while we identify the suspect."

Sand was still billowing from the hand-to-hand combat high on a hillside overlooking the Golden Gate Bridge.

At last the plainclothesman and patrolman gained the upper hand amid cheers from the Ops Center. Briefly, the suspect's head appeared above the tussle, an expression of confusion written on his young face.

"That's not Ferrar," Connors shouted at once. "That's somebody else."

"Commander, hold your fire," Leo said sharply into the phone. "Get your finger off that trigger."

Lester sank back into his seat and looked sick.

"This guy is a decoy," Connors said. "Tray Bolton must be behind this."

Lester stirred. "No. It has all the earmarks of George Ferrar. He's diverting our attention away from whatever else he has in mind."

Bonnie tried calling her office several more times without luck.

She wheeled the Toyota around and headed back into oncoming traffic, aiming south toward where the *Vigilant* was normally berthed. Most of the patrol ships, crew quarters, and maintenance facilities were on the opposite side of the bay in Oakland. Hers was a solitary Coast Guard station.

She was going to have to report the stolen cutter to her boss, Rear

Admiral Vince Gerard, who was theater commander stationed on the Naval frigate *Tribute.*

Gerard sounded distracted when he took her call. "Speak fast," he said. "We've got our guns trained on Ferrar up in the cliffs overlooking the bay. It looks like he's gonna commit some kind of terrorist act."

"He's not there. He's on the bay, heading out to my cutter. The *Vigilant* may have been hijacked. Turn your guns on her, if anything."

"Hold on," he said, and his voice grew muffled as he talked with someone else. She listened in. "What's that, Commander? Of course you should take your guns off the shoreline," he said to somebody who had to be the Commander in Chief of Pacific Command himself. "Ferrar's already on the bay."

"Don't aim for Ferrar," Bonnie said desperately when Gerard came back on the phone. "He's not the culprit. It's another CIA operative named Tray Bolton who's hijacked my cutter."

"Does the Pentagon know about this?" he asked suspiciously, as if all truth had to originate from Washington.

"You have to call the Pentagon and let them know."

"Where are you, Taylor?"

"Here in Bayview, dodging cars. But I'm near a police port facility."

"Well, I've got a Marine chopper down there right now. I want you to get your ass up here to my ship on the double. I want you to tell the Commander in person what's going on here."

"You've got it, sir," she said.

The police port facility was an outcropping of buildings just a block away, and she noticed a chopper's blades start to whirl above the rooftops.

But there was no access road to the facility.

She jumped out of her car and began to sprint.

Ferrar watched Tray Bolton and the *Vigilant* pass under the Bay Bridge without incident. Within minutes it would join a flotilla of curiosity seekers in pleasure boats congregated just short of the Golden Gate Bridge.

Gunning his engine to the max, he pulled up in the wake of the *Vigilant* as it threaded itself through the bank of sailboats, motorboats, and cabin cruisers.

He cut back the power, broke through the huge wall of water, and sidled up to the Coast Guard cutter. A bloody, motionless arm reached over the stern of the cutter, its fingers swinging back and forth in the spray. Curiously, Ferrar spotted nobody else on deck.

He took a running leap from his pilot boat onto the transom of the

Vigilant. He caught it with both hands, his feet dangling just above the waterline.

Slowly, he pulled himself up on deck. Then he scrambled across the open area to a dark patch of shade on the port side.

From that position, he could see the world-famous, orange suspension bridge growing larger as they approached. Beyond that, a row of gunships sat poised out at sea, their turrets swiveling in his direction.

A man was shouting in Arabic above him. He translated quickly in his mind, "They're aiming at us. What should I do?"

"I'll get the chief," a man replied, and ran down the steps from the bridge.

Through a porthole, Ferrar watched the man enter the cabin, where another kneeled hunched over a large metal box.

"Hurry up," the voice shouted from above.

"I am hurrying," the kneeling man called back. Ferrar recognized the voice at once. It was Tray Bolton speaking Arabic. "Atom bombs aren't toys, you know," he added in English.

Ferrar took one last look at the metal box. Two small lids were open on the device, both of which normally covered control buttons the likes of which he had never seen before.

He didn't want to see the device blowing up in the middle of the densely populated metropolitan area. But he also had to stop the terrorists before the military did. If the gunships opened fire on them, the resulting radiation leak might poison the environment for generations.

He needed to send out a message.

Prowling aft, he peered around the corner of the bridge. Directly below the bridge was some sort of office, perhaps the radio room.

He slipped through the main hatchway past the busy men and crossed into the room, closing the metal door behind him. Unfortunately, there was no lock.

In the dim light of a single porthole, he found a narrow-band direct-printing telegraph machine, the modern name for what was formerly called a wireless telegraph.

He put on a set of earphones and turned a dial until he picked up a frequency that was chattering with electronic traffic. That would have to do.

Then he tapped out a message in Morse code, just as footsteps approached. He was tapping in the final dash-dot and dash when the door creaked open.

Since September 11th, half the Seventh Fleet had steamed from ports in

Hawaii, San Diego, and Japan to defend California's West Coast. Among the activated ships was an electronics marvel, a signals ship bristling with satellite dishes, radars, and antennae of every sort.

That morning, the *USS Endorse* had gotten a call to head two hundred nautical miles north toward San Francisco.

Not a fast ship, the *Endorse* lagged behind the battleship group. Military and police radio signals were crisscrossing the airwaves a mile a minute, mixing with communications among ships and between ships and shore.

Seaman First Class Anthony Carlson sat in the radio room, handling electronic transmissions, essentially faxes and electronic messages destined for other ships. His job was to ignore the official messages and eavesdrop on any possible terrorist transmission. His signal processor looked for key phrases such as "terror," "bomb," and "Allah."

A hand-entered message that he was picking up at that moment seemed to fit the bill.

He printed directly to a sheet-fed printer and hurried to the officer in charge of the radio room.

"Got a hit, sir," Anthony reported, handing over the sheet of paper.

It read, "TERRORIST NUCLEAR WARHEAD ON USS VIGILANT."

Lieutenant Terry Whitcomb took one look at it and asked, "Source of transmission?"

Anthony returned to his workstation and checked the screen. "Signal triangulated to a source on the Oakland Bay side of the Golden Gate Bridge. From a ship, it seems."

"Try to contact back on the same frequency."

Anthony bent over his telegraph arm. "Please identify yourself," he said aloud as he tapped.

They waited for a full minute. No response.

"I'm taking this to the Captain," Lieutenant Whitcomb said, and bounded out of the room.

Anthony turned back to his computer screen that was divided in four parts to monitor several active frequencies at the same time.

There were no more signals from the mystery ship on the bay.

Twenty-nine

FERRAR ALLOWED the metal door to swing open into the radio room. A breathless Middle Eastern men shivering in a football jacket stepped through.

The man bore a mystified look, as if he were trying to figure out how the door had shut in the first place.

Ferrar didn't give him time to work it out. A blunt blow with two interlocked fists to the back of the man's neck sent him stumbling into the room.

Ferrar caught the muscular body before it knocked over the radio table and attracted more attention.

"That was for Gopher O'Brien," Ferrar said, recalling the first victim tumbling down the slope outside the Tora Bora Cave in an ambush that had set off the entire downward spiral of events.

One down. How many more to go?

Overhead, a helicopter was shooting past.

Through the side window of the U.S. Marine Corps UH-1N Huey helicopter, Bonnie looked down at her Coast Guard cutter, the *Vigilant*. It was heading for the center of the Golden Gate Bridge.

Suddenly something clicked in her mind. The bridge! Tray had looked so earnest and stalwart that spring evening as they stood on the Golden Gate Bridge. Out of nowhere, he had produced a diamond ring for her, and proposed marriage.

She didn't want him or need him. But she feared him, so she had let him down gently. Then she had hightailed it out of California. And so had he, straight into the Navy.

The situation had felt awkward at the time, but in the end Tray seemed adequately placated. He was a big man, and he could take a hit. Or could he?

Was he seeking some sort of revenge?

"What's happening down there?" the Marine pilot asked his crew.

His copilot shook his head. "No crew on deck. They must be below."

How could she alert George? The Golden Gate Bridge was a likely site for Tray's revenge. But how did he intend to carry out his act? She couldn't imagine.

Beyond the Golden Gate Bridge, a line of warships blockaded the bay. They faced the bridge broadside in a threatening posture.

Looking down at the *Vigilant* again, Bonnie flinched. Two men were scrambling on deck.

"Watch out, sir," she cried. "They've manning the twenty-five millimeter gun, and they've brought up the rocket launcher."

The pilot performed an evasive maneuver, sending Bonnie hard against the window. A rocket-propelled missile shrieked past the fuselage to one side. On the other, tracer bullets arced past.

Then there was a terrific boom below. Just after a cloud of smoke billowed off the gun deck of the ship, an explosive projectile whistled past.

"They've got missiles and anti-aircraft guns," the co-pilot reported.

"Go to decoying countermeasures," the pilot ordered.

"Deploying chaff and flares," the co-pilot said.

Bonnie watched out her port window as chaff glittered away in a silvery cloud. Then a red flare burst out of the helicopter on the starboard side.

A heat-seeking missile flew up in that direction and exploded with a twang, followed by an ear-shattering blast that rocked the helicopter onto its side.

The pilot struggled to correct the pitch and roll.

The co-pilot fingered the trigger of the 2.75-inch rocket pods. "Request permission to return fire," he said over the radio to the Chief of Pacific Command.

"Hold fire. Repeat, hold fire," the Commander's voice thundered back in Bonnie's earphone. "We just received word from SIGINT that there's a nuclear weapon onboard."

With a sudden thrust of its twin turboshaft engines, the Huey zoomed away from the ship.

Not a nuclear bomb. It couldn't be.

The last image she caught of her *Vigilant* was of a deck crawling with men.

Then the orange struts of the Golden Gate Bridge obscured the ship from view.

As terrorists spilled out on deck to fend off the Marine Huey helicopter, Ferrar stepped over the fallen attacker, jumped out of the radio room, and headed to the front of the cabin.

He peered into compartment after compartment. Nobody was left inside.

The ship steamed on.

Tray had abandoned the metal bomb momentarily to fire off some weapons at the chopper.

From the cursing on deck, he gathered that they weren't successful, but the mechanical chattering of two submachine guns and the explosion of a rocket launcher continued, followed by a second boom that sounded like a deck gun.

Then he heard a chorus of cheers on deck just outside the portholes as the helicopter turned tail and retreated.

Ferrar looked around for cover, and decided to head for the lower deck. He scrambled the rest of the way through the cabin as men entered from the sun-drenched quarterdeck.

His first goal was to disable the engine. In the unlit belly of the ship, he followed the drone of the engine to the engine room at the very back of the cutter.

The ship was Bonnie's domain. He wished he had her knowledge of its layout.

He found a light switch and turned it on. Dim rays fell on the twin engines running side by side. Below that lay a bloody sight. An engineman lay on the deck with a bullet through his head.

Above the body, a button labeled "Power Cut-off" caught his attention.

Why not? He pressed it, and instantly both engines wound down to a dead halt.

Shouts erupted above him as men yelled to the terrorist at the helm. Cries of frustration passed back and forth, before a pair of footsteps pounded for the stairway down to the lower deck.

Ferrar grabbed the engineman's lug wrench and switched off the light. Then he moved forward to take up a position in a darkened compartment between the engine room and the stairway.

He caught the man full in the face with a swing of the heavy wrench. The would-be terrorist crumpled to the deck, and Ferrar fell on him, pulling back on his close-cropped hair. The man had deeply bronzed skin and wore a wool sweater that reeked of perspiration. A tug and twist of the head cracked the man's neck.

"That's for Pug Wilson," Ferrar said fiercely, recalling the deadly booby trap in the Tora Bora cave.

A voice shouted down the stairway in Arabic. "Find anything?"

"Yes. Take a look," Ferrar called back in Arabic.

More footsteps, this time two pairs. The second man wore a Coast Guard uniform. Ferrar couldn't tell for certain, but it could be Tray Bolton.

This would be for Al Moxley and Colt Sealock, his two other compatriots killed at Tora Bora.

Ferrar combed the dead man's clothing for a weapon. Nothing there.

The two men paused momentarily to adjust their eyes to the gloom.

Ferrar's heel banged against a canister. He reached down. It was an air tank.

"What did you find?" one of the men called, hesitant to advance into the dark.

"Come look," Ferrar called, again in Arabic.

Both men advanced, one silhouette drawing a pistol from inside his warm-up jacket.

"Where are you?" the man called.

"Come quick," Ferrar said.

The first man to arrive stumbled over his fallen comrade, his pistol clattering to the metal deck. Ferrar swung the air tank down on the man's head, connecting with a sickening thud. The man fell in a lifeless heap at his feet.

Then with a roar, Ferrar came back up, swinging the heavy tank at the second man.

He was too late.

The terrorist had already crouched low. Against the brightness of the stairway, Ferrar saw him coming upward for a full body blow.

Ferrar absorbed the brunt of the blow with his abdomen and felt himself staggering backward. The man struck out again with his fist. Ferrar took it squarely on the jaw.

With a groan, he landed on top of the two fallen men.

He groped desperately in the warm, dark, bloody tangle of limbs.

Where was that goddamned gun?

Bonnie's helicopter set down squarely on the fantail of the *USS Tribute*, where the captain was waiting to escort her up to the command deck.

There, she found her theater commander Rear Admiral Vince Gerard standing beside the highly decorated Commander Admiral John D. Hanson, a former test pilot and current head of the entire Pacific Command.

She saluted, then began. "Don't open fire on the *Vigilant*," she said, out of breath. "That man on the *Vigilant* is a CIA counter-terrorism operative. He's there to prevent a nuclear catastrophe."

"I don't care if he's John Wayne," Commander Hanson said with a thick Southern drawl. "That ship contains nuclear warheads, and that's enough of a threat for me."

"He's trained to take out terrorists," she said. "With all respect sir, give him a chance."

A phone beeped in the room full of computers and communications devices.

"Commander, you'll want this. It's a call from Washington," an Executive Officer said, handing a phone to Admiral Hanson.

"Put it on the horn," Hanson ordered.

"This is CIA Director Lester Friedman," the voice said over the speakerphone. "Do not, repeat *not*, trust the operative on the *Vigilant* to take out the ship. He's a known double agent. Fire at will."

"Roger that," Hanson said, taking a deep breath. "Arm the rockets."

A second phone beeped.

"Another call from the Pentagon, Commander," the XO said apologetically. He switched on the speakerphone without being told.

"This is U.S. Congressman Ralph W. Connors speaking. If you harm so much as one hair on the head of that man on the *Vigilant*, I'm going to single-handedly ax the entire Coast Guard and Navy budget for the next ten decades. Do you read me?'

The phone clicked off.

"What is this, a screwball comedy?" the General wondered aloud. "Washington can't tell its asshole from a hole in the ground. How could they run a war? Can't even get their intel together."

Rear Admiral Vince Gerard spoke up for the first time. "It's clear they don't have a clue what they're doing. I think it's up to us to make a tactical operational decision."

"Look at this. You've gotta see what's happening on deck, sir," another Naval officer shouted excitedly, handing his field glasses to Commander Hanson. "They're duking it out on the *Vigilant*."

Bonnie grabbed a pair of binoculars and trained them on her cutter.

"What's going on around here?" Commander Hanson roared. "Can't anyone give me the straight dope? Hold fire."

Ferrar couldn't get a hand on the gun, and the white uniform was advancing on him. He decided his only advantage was the darkness.

Backpedaling over the rolling carpet of bodies, he retreated farther into the engine room.

Then he heard another voice calling from the far opening to the deck.

Jesus, how many of them were there?

He wracked his brains to remember the layout of the engine room. From his brief glimpse in the dim light earlier, he remembered that there were two huge engines side by side.

There was a man already down, a Coast Guard mechanic killed by a single gunshot.

Then the light rays had fallen on a power switch.

The light bulb!

He reached up toward a slight warmth just overhead, and unscrewed the bulb.

He held his breath, listening for the man in uniform to arrive. Suddenly, just a yard away, hard-soled shoes scraped across the metal rivets of the floor.

Take this, Bolton, you bastard.

He squeezed the hot metal of the light bulb with the glass exposed, and swung it with a vicious right hook into the man's face.

"Aaargh!"

Glass splintered in the man's eyes, blinding him, and stabbing deep into the veins and arteries of his face. Ferrar followed up with an elbow to the gut.

The man doubled over, screaming in Arabic.

It was not Tray Bolton.

Ferrar finished him off with a swift blow to the back of the neck, which gave way with a resounding crunch.

A voice thundered from up on deck. It was Tray!

Ferrar circled the engines and located what he had also vaguely remembered—a ladder extending up to the quarterdeck of the *USS Vigilant.*

He quickly climbed the metal rungs and pushed against the trapdoor at the top. It was locked.

Then, inches from his face, the lock screwed open, and daylight flooded in.

"Here is the little traitor," a silhouette said against a backdrop of the blue heavens.

"Tray?"

"We're both going to hell today," Tray said, pulling Ferrar up the final few steps. "The whole city's going sky high."

Ferrar looked around. They were circled by the gleaming edifices of civilization and a row of warships facing off with them just on the other side of the Golden Gate Bridge. Above him, sunlight glinted off the spider web strands of the bridge with its rows of captive onlookers.

Who had brought all of these people together? Tray certainly hadn't advertised the event. Were they there because of him? Had Tray used him to lure all the people?

Then he spotted the leather briefcase lying open on deck, several vials of heroin scattered beside it. A used needle and rubber tube were casually tossed aside.

"Trying to go out in a blaze of glory?" Ferrar asked.

"Something like that," Bolton said. "I sure hope Bonnie's watching this, so she can see what happens to traitors."

"You can rest assured that the entire country and international community is watching to see what I do to you," Ferrar said.

Bolton shook his head sadly. "You still don't get it, do you."

Ferrar tried to clear the fatigue-induced cobwebs from his brain. Oh sure, Bolton had painted him as a traitor to his country. It was some show he had put on.

He nodded at Tray's briefcase. "Can't look death straight in the eye?"

Bolton shrugged it off. Then his shoulders knotted, and Ferrar found a fist flying in his direction.

He caught it with the side of his head. He expected a kick, and it came next. He fielded it with an upward movement of his arm, and it glanced harmlessly off his body.

"Martial Arts 101," Ferrar said. "Can't you come up with something more original than that?"

Unexpectedly Bolton faltered backward as if dizzy.

Ferrar's instincts told him something else was wrong. Bolton was coming unglued.

"What is it?" Ferrar asked, looking around the deck. "What's going on here?"

"It could have been a very good friendship," Tray said, staggering back several more steps.

"Oh, come off it," Ferrar said. "We've competed for everything ever since the day we met."

"...and now you'll blow up San Francisco," Tray said, shaking his head sadly, then suddenly clutched his temples in a spasm of pain.

"What are you talking about?" Ferrar said. He looked upward at several noisy television helicopters trying to corner him as they circled for a closer view. "It's *your* bomb. I didn't set it."

Tray stumbled and fell on his rear. Then, with an ironic twist of his lips, he said in a husky voice, "You lose."

His jaw fell slack and he dropped prone on the deck. He stared upward unblinkingly. A look of satisfaction was fixed on his face as if justice had finally been served.

"Holy shit," Ferrar seethed through gritted teeth. He launched himself into the cabin after the bomb.

In her home, Rebecca Friedman watched the television dumbfounded as she saw her supposedly dead son still alive and fighting Ferrar on the deck of a Coast Guard cutter.

"That's my son," she whispered proudly to herself. She picked up the phone and dialed the number of her husband's cell phone.

After half a dozen rings, he picked up. "Friedman here," he said soberly.

"He's come back to save San Francisco," she cried excitedly.

"Hold on, dear. We're not so sure."

Ferrar plunged into the interior of the *Vigilant*. The metal box stood as before just under the gun deck.

The two latched covers stood open on top of the bomb. Beneath each cover were rows of buttons and illuminated characters.

The first mechanism was a clock ticking the seconds downward from "20." He realized what that meant.

The second display read "TRA_" with a blinking cursor under the missing last letter.

What the hell? It looked like a secret code to deactivate the bomb. Tray must have used his own name as the deactivation key.

Fifteen seconds.

Ferrar stared below the TRA_ at the alphanumeric keypad. Images of his life passed rapidly through his mind, not the thoughts of a dying man, but of someone trying to unscramble the unrelated tidbits of his life in search of a clue.

Ten seconds.

Then an image of Bonnie floated to the fore. She was young again, college-aged. She was leaning toward him, offering a mug of foaming beer.

Five seconds.

In his mind, he glanced up at the wooden walls behind her. Several lobster pots and traps hung from hooks. It was her summer job in Maine. And the restaurant was named—

He typed a "P."

The clock stopped with one second left.

He let out his breath and closed his eyes.

Suddenly completely exhausted, he collapsed to the floorboards and sat propped up against the bomb.

Law enforcement could capture him if they still wanted. He'd broken more than a few rules, and saved as many lives.

At last, he stood up and wandered back through the ship. It had been Bonnie's ship all along. He was just along for the ride. He could imagine her commanding it. He would turn the helm back over to her.

Tray's body lay heaped on the large quarterdeck, the victim of a final overdose.

Ferrar stripped his own bloody shirt off his back and pulled his T-shirt over his head.

Waving the white T-shirt in the stiff breeze, he signaled to whomever might be watching.

The ship was secure. All was well.

Only a moment had passed before Ferrar heard the whirr of a helicopter approaching from behind. From long experience in special operations, he knew the sound of a Huey. He felt his body give an involuntarily flinch.

But he was too tired to hit the deck for cover. He was too tired to react with the trained instincts of a commando.

He had turned that part of him off.

The chopper hovered overhead, the cold gust tearing the T-shirt from his grasp. He lowered his empty hands and closed his eyes.

Let the bullets slice through his bare chest.

But the bullets never came. Instead, from the belly of the beast a hoist lowered a rope with a figure in a military jumpsuit and combat helmet.

Ferrar turned to face the soldier, his arms down by his sides. Landing on deck, the soldier turned and pulled off his helmet.

It was Bonnie Taylor!

Her layered blonde hair blew around her face, and she lifted a hand in salute.

Ferrar raised a weary arm and returned the gesture.

Then she dropped her helmet and ran across the deck toward him.

"George," she cried, her voice exuberant. "You really did slay the dragon."

"St. George to the rescue," he said with a relieved smile.

He reached out and scooped her off her feet. Spinning around and around, they formed their own whirlwind on the quarterdeck of the cutter. He noticed other ships circling closer: yachts, motorboats, and Naval patrol coastal ships. Suddenly he was back in Bar Harbor, skimming over the sea with his true love.

"Incoming!" a bullhorn announced from a rapidly approaching naval amphibious assault vessel.

Ferrar glanced over Bonnie's shoulder. How handsome the bridge looked—intact and strong as ever in the morning light.

Then he noticed a rectangular object spiraling down from the Golden Gate Bridge. The huge pink sail descended rapidly toward them.

"Look," he said, letting out a laugh. "I think we've got company."

He turned Bonnie around to watch as the parasailer, a naked young man with a happy grin on his face, dropped down beside her and embraced both of them as a television news helicopter swirled closer.

"Welcome home," she told Ferrar. "For better or for worse, welcome home."

About the Author

FRITZ GALT is an American novelist with unprecedented access to diplomatic life and international affairs. He has lived abroad in Cuba, Switzerland, Yugoslavia, Taiwan, India, and China. He is a world traveler and essayist, and his work has appeared in numerous publications. He lives with his family in China. For an in-depth look at his work, visit his personal website at *spythrillers.com*.

Printed in the United States
64040LVS00002B/128